Nicholas Griffin was brought up in England and currently lives in New York. He won a Betty Trask and Author's Club award for his first book, *The Requiem Shark*, and received widespread acclaim for *The House of Sight and Shadow*.

Praise for *The Masquerade*

'All three [of Griffin's novels] are well conceived, researched and executed ... Griffin is a novelist of rare gifts ... *The Masquerade* sounds a note that is so elegant and elegiac that, amid the plethora of what is published, it deserves to endure' Ross Leckie, *The Times*

'Griffin writes beautifully and his formal style ensures that not one detail of this sophisticated world jars with the reader ... A substantial, satisfying read' *Good Book Guide*

'A highly intelligent novel, with both keen observation and an absorbing plot, full of surprises and mystery' *Historical Novels Review*

Praise for *The Requiem Shark*

'A marvellously exciting and breathless book ... Nicholas Griffin has taken an old-fashioned subject and breathed into it modernity and considerable wit' *Spectator*

'Remarkable ... a vivid and authentic picture of life at sea that is second to none. What Griffin does not know about pirates is not worth a ship's biscuit ... There is more than enough action and adventure, blood and guts, disease and death, love and cruelty, acts of loyalty and deeds of deceit to keep all but the most squeamish turning the pages' *Daily Mail*

'Battles, storms and doomed love will appeal to fans of Robert Louis Stevenson and Errol Flynn ... Faultlessly rendered' *Independent on Sunday*

Praise for *The House of Sight and Shadow*

'Refreshingly different ... A confident and beautifully plotted excursion into eighteenth-century London and love' *Independent on Sunday*

'Excellent ... Intelligent writing, original plot and a remarkable grasp of historical details and language' *Daily Mail*

Also by Nicholas Griffin

The Requiem Shark

The House of Sight and Shadow

Caucasus

THE
MASQUERADE

N ICHOLAS G RIFFIN

An *Abacus* Book

First published in Great Britain in 2002 by Little, Brown
This edition published in 2003 by Abacus

A CIP catalogue record for this book
is available from the British Library.

ISBN 0 349 11648 2

Typeset in Cochin by M Rules
Printed and bound in Great Britain by
Clays Ltd, St Ives plc

Abacus
An imprint of
Time Warner Books UK
Brettenham House
Lancaster Place
London WC2E 7EN

www.TimeWarnerBooks.co.uk

To SMC

A traveller, struck with the glorious and magnificent prospect of the country, exclaimed before one of the monks, *Here happiness must dwell. Yes*, replied the recluse, *for the strangers who visit us.*

Dupaty, *Lettres sur l'Italie*, volume II, 1789

There are a thousand reasons to recommend her, but Italy remains a mistress. I like her well enough, but have no design to marry her.

Lucius Jelborne, *Impressions of Italy*, 1713

CHAPTER ONE

Off the Coast of Liguria – July 1714

It was an odd shadow that Jelborne cast: the spherical shape of a bumble bee. As bees are not supposed to fly, neither should Jelborne have walked, and yet he did, and did so nimbly. After a minute of pacing, he took a seat behind the desk, his naked form hunched over pen and paper, pale and aglow from the lantern's cast. He wrote quickly. As he signed each letter, he waved it in front of his face, momentarily cooled by the ripples of air as it dried. When all five letters had been completed, he hid them beneath the layers of canvas that passed for a mattress. Finally, he dressed in his black tutor's suit and headed onto deck.

Noon dived towards the ocean's bed, pushed himself with a sweep of arms and legs, defying buoyancy, driving deeper against the water. The pressure made him pause and he turned upwards, squinting at the dark silhouette of the ship, then kicked to break the surface. He swapped a brief wave and smile with Stilwell and Jelborne, then swam away, pausing ten minutes later to float on his back. He had never expected ocean water to be so sharp. Salt stung his eyes and stuck to his skin.

Stilwell stood in his tutor's shadow and watched his servant, half a mile away, bobbing in the gentle swell.

'Should a wind arise, they *will* leave him,' said Jelborne. They had stepped from beneath the awning of sailcloth the Genoese had slung across the deck, where the languid crew lay untroubled by their captain. It was His Lordship, the Viscount Stilwell, who had insisted that they sail. The captain had predicted storms, but instead they had settled into a calm made worse by a sun that seemed to start its journey in the middle of the sky and burn there until it dropped suddenly each night.

'Is it always this hot?' asked His Lordship, addressing his tutor's bulbous and sweaty head.

'No,' said Jelborne, and dragged a wet handkerchief across his brow. 'Sometimes hotter. An Italian sun can melt stones.'

Stilwell turned to watch Noon disappear under the water again. He felt a vicarious appreciation in Noon's movement, as if his servant's immersion cooled them both. *He is half fish*, mused Stilwell. *Always in water on a Sunday. Every week of his life. What routine; what strange routines men keep*. He turned to look at Jelborne again: a distinct comparison. Jelborne as garrulous as Noon could be silent, a moody, amusing man, responsible for the next year of His Lordship's education. Stilwell had observed how Jelborne was fond of displaying a full range of emotions. One moment he was avuncular, extravagant with affection, then cold and wise and filled with intent. Stilwell preferred to judge men by their eyes, but he couldn't quite see Jelborne's: the eyelids were too fleshy. Fat cheeks and a flat nose gave him a merry appearance that might or might not have been indicative of his character.

'We'll have wind,' said Jelborne, casting his voice to the skies.

'Three days,' said Stilwell, 'and not one breath. How long might a man drift? Can currents carry us? Where should we drift to?'

Jelborne shrugged. 'South, I suppose.'

'Then we might reverse our tour. Start in Naples, end in Genoa.'

'You forget the seasons, milord,' said Jelborne. 'You would no sooner want to spend winter in the north than summer in the south. You would think of this day as freshness herself were you to know the August oven of Naples.'

'Money runs north in this country?' asked Stilwell.

'For the most part.'

Both men watched as Noon turned and swam for the ship, steady strokes that beat against the surface, head down as if he had learned to suck air from water. The last hundred yards he increased his pace, imagined himself chased by gills and fast fins that pushed his thoughts away. He beat the water with urgency. Blood racing, water crashing in his ears, heart beginning to thrill at the certainty of escape. He grinned hard beneath the surface, alive in the water.

'Does it feel fresh?' asked Stilwell, as his servant pulled himself up the rope ladder.

Noon nodded and used the cupped palms of his hands to scrape water from his forearms, chest, legs, chest again. A broad-shouldered man of twenty-two, Noon was designed for labour yet work had not eroded his youth. His hair was held behind him in a louse bag and it had chased him to the ship, slapping in the water. He was not nearly as handsome a man as his master. They shared blue eyes, but the angles of Stilwell's beauty were replaced by an open honesty in his servant.

Stilwell's beauty was unnerving if only because it was too obvious. There was no joy for the viewer to find their own way, to appreciate some feature that another might have missed. Blond-haired, sharp-jawed and full-lipped, he might as well have been a sculpture breathed to life. There he stood ablaze. None could help but look on him, if only to begrudge the stars that had also granted him wealth. Worse, on talking to him, they would find him modest, deferential and eager to listen. Gossip concentrated on his lack of intelligence, and though he may not have been born to debate philosophies, he was not foolish.

That night, the wind finally came, drying sweat, raising the stink of the ship, carrying the scent of shore. The three Englishmen gathered on deck and watched the crew race skyward, their dark shapes moving quickly against the stars. They heard the low, deep snap of the mainsail caught by a gust of wind. The ship groaned, as if she had been woken too quickly, then she lurched forward. For the first time in days, Stilwell's hand dropped to his stomach. Jelborne and Noon swapped an amused look.

Coming out of Dover they had been smacked by heavy weather and, while tutor and servant seemed inured to seasickness, His Lordship was racked by it. Towards the end of the fifth day, the seas had levelled enough for Stilwell to take his first turn on deck. Still queasy, he had asked Jelborne how long seasickness lasted.

'For some, an entire voyage. I heard tell of a man who suffered the first day from Portsmouth almost until he reached Virginia. Three months.'

'And did it ever stop for him?' His Lordship had asked.

'Yes,' Jelborne had continued. 'They say his suffering ended off the coast of Jamestown. God bless his soul.' Noon had turned away to laugh.

Travel, to Noon, was proving to be an antidote to memories, if only because the newness of things left little room for the past. His mind was constantly engaged, even in this soporific calm. Seawater was different from that of ponds, or even rivers; not just the salt, but the way light fell on it and flickered and ran this way and that. Rivers pushed light downstream, ponds absorbed it, but seas created and released it.

By morning, a grey rocky coast stood off the larboard side, still many miles away, but cheering in its promise of solidity. The English passengers had barely moved from their positions. The captain stood by them and they talked in a confusion of English, French and Genoese. Jelborne had learned his Italian in Siena, thought to be the purest in the land, but his English accent was as easy to spot as bone on black cloth. Stilwell had little aptitude for language and was content in the knowledge that he could rely on Jelborne. It was Noon who had absorbed the most. The sailors would ignore him, or throw him a question or two. Slowly they registered amusement at his ability to learn and then imitate their language and fed him the worst of their words.

Stilwell looked aghast at the sight of Genoa. It was a busy harbour, much like that they had left in England and those they had paused at in their journey south. He hadn't known what to expect when first sighting Italy, but knew that it had not been sameness. There was much to admire – the high rocks before them, the city's perfect position, a row of grand houses looking with disdain upon the coast, the breakwaters to protect her from the dominant winds of the south-west – but Stilwell could see none of this.

He had been promised a land of myth and was disappointed to see it populated with mortals. Even the double fortification which enveloped the city, with its suggestion of intruders to defend oneself from, could not raise his spirits. Even worse, there were other ships in the harbour, and not just fishing smacks, which he could have tolerated, but great three-masted merchantmen, so much larger than their own humble sloop. This meant trade and trade meant foreigners. Stilwell had hoped that there would be no strangers in the land other than their own small party. Jelborne offered a sympathetic shrug.

Stilwell gave his tutor a damning look and quoted Jelborne at Jelborne. '"Ten miles from shore the fragrance of orange and lemon lends an aromatic promise of assured delights."'

'Hyperbole,' smiled Jelborne. 'So many have gone before. The promises must be stretched tauter, new steps cut in old stone, but we have greater concerns.'

It wasn't the depth of stevedores, merchants and porters gathered in the harbour which surprised Thomas Noon, but the mystery of the cacophonous swirl of foreign tongues. He could see the houses and trees and people and even dogs scampering about the harbour and the evidence of sameness was a relief. But the city was unlike anything he had seen before. It seemed built upon itself, one house above another, all attempting to reach the top of the hill. What an inconvenient position Genoa sat on, thought Noon, worrying that he would be constantly engaged in sweating his way up and down the promontory in such unbearable heat. The chatter was too fast for him to decipher, but it sounded so enticing and preternatural that he could not believe these were words that had English translations. It was as if the secrets of the world were being poured forth and he was helpless to understand.

Slowly the ship was unladed. Out came the crated carriage, its wheels wrapped in oilcloth. Out came the trunk of shirts, handkerchiefs and broad-brimmed hats, taffeta-lined doublets, linen overalls to be worn over clothes at inns. Boxes of medicine and spices and condiments. Stilwell's necessities of mustards, pepper, ginger, tea, sugar, oatmeal and sago. And a large bag of bay salt, now half empty, for use against seasickness. Prayer books and hymnals, notebooks and inks, swords and pistols. Noon had packed it all before their departure and made sure that everything had its place upon the carriage, with room enough for the passengers. For their horses, they would have no option but to rely upon Italian posting stations.

A man had been sent through the streets to greet them, carrying with him the city's licence for a visit exceeding four days. He wore a deep purple livery, and nailed boots to deal with the greasy cobbles of the harbour. All the stevedores were ordered and assigned trunks or wheels, Stilwell and Jelborne were escorted to sedan chairs and Noon, blessedly free of all baggage, was left to follow on his feet. Genoa's streets were, it seemed, too steep and narrow for horse and carriage. Speed was constrained by the sweated and unsteady movement of the sedan chairmen. It was ever upward, the steps always coming in twos or threes as if they were embarrassed of their number and would not affront a man's legs by appearing all at once.

Opened shutters slapped against buildings across the street. Some alleys through which they walked were so dark that Noon thought they might never have seen the sun. Everywhere was pervaded by a dampness and the stale smell of mildew. Between the stones of the lower streets ran a dark putrescence, grease and salt and the stench of all that could not breathe out of water.

At the pinnacle of the first sizeable hill stood a wide avenue. The houses on the street were built next to one another, facing an identical row of excellence. It looked as if every palazzo were made entirely from marble. Noon paused in appreciation. At Dengby Hall in Shropshire they had a single marble staircase, and he had overheard a constant admiration directed at its richness. Noon tripped on a cobble behind the sedan chair, and stumbled after his master between a vast pair of brass doors, studded with spikes. They entered a large stone courtyard at the end of which a small fountain spat forth an inconstant stream of water from a fish's mouth. The far wall was laced in ivy. Above it ran a balcony held upright not by columns but by a marble merman and his mermaid, both straining against the weight. Noon looked up at the three stories, the first low as if pressure had flattened the upper ceilings, the rooms it harboured permanently obscured by darkness. The higher floors had vaulted ceilings, a cross-colouring of pastel pink and blues. They looked fresh to Noon, younger than Dengby.

Noon was led to his master's chamber and slowly began to unpack the largest of the trunks. He was amazed at the plainness of the room, presuming it the finest reserved for guests. A high-backed bed, a fireplace. No furniture to speak of. Yet the walls were all painted, as was the ceiling: florid depictions of golden youths clad in armour. They struck poses but none was engaged in fighting. It was as if they were poised to clash, but had decided to compete only in posture.

Noon helped his master dress for dinner and then he was left alone again. He encouraged the fire he had lit for Stilwell, pushing the kindling under the logs and urging them to life with his breath. For many servitude meant hardship, but for Noon patience had been the prevalent consequence. His hands were almost as soft as his master's, his manners not remarkably different, his tones neither the clipped accent of the gentry nor the broad lapses of his fellow countrymen.

Often, while waiting, he contemplated their differences, waiting for his master to wake, to finish bathing, to dress, undress, sleep and wake again. The gentry, he noticed, believed servants to be shadows, having no ears to hear, no eyes to see, no tongues to tell. When doors closed and only Stilwell remained, Noon existed again as surely as he did among his peers. He wandered down to the kitchens, following his nose to a bowl of odd wheaten strips of wetness. Some spices had been run through them, and though Noon was disappointed at the lack of meat, he ate quickly and returned to Stilwell's apartment to await his master. He dozed before the fire until the clack of boots against the stone floor awakened him. Noon stood and smiled sleepily at Stilwell's entrance.

'There was a woman downstairs, Thomas,' began the red-faced lord. 'Signora Elmi, and there was no Signore Elmi, but she was accompanied by a younger man who paid her an extravagant amount of attention.' Stilwell laughed to himself. 'Her breasts, they heaved, Thomas.'

Noon moved behind his master and removed his coat. 'So close to the ocean,' continued Stilwell, 'I almost thought them subject to the tides. I've watched them all night and feel quite queasy.'

'Did the young man who accompanied her not mind?' asked Noon, folding the coat.

'She caught me looking and she smiled at me,' said Stilwell, and dropped onto the edge of the bed so that Noon might work on his boots. 'Encouragement, I think. We might call on her tomorrow, for a *conversazione*. Do you know what that is, Thomas?'

'A conversation, milord?'

'Exactly, and exactly not. It is gambling. It is card games and the finest of the town and Mr Jelborne says my father did not speak against it. You shall attend me tomorrow, Thomas, and see.' The young lord lay back on the bed and stared at the ceiling. 'Can we take a year of this?' asked Stilwell, as much to the beams that ran above his head as to his servant. But when no answer came, he sat up and looked hard at Noon. 'Does travel really change a man, Thomas? I think I am of firm character, do you think anything could change me?'

'I don't know.'

'Could anything change you?'

'If two pence and a pint of gin can change a man,' said Noon, 'I don't see why a country can't.'

Stilwell stood up and padded across the cold stone floor to the window. It was covered with grease paper. One of the finest palazzi in Genoa and wrapped in windows no better than an English inn, thought Stilwell. He prised the pane away so that the fresh air rushed in to disturb the room, fuelling the fire. 'This is what I like. The sea air, but without the sea.'

Noon retired to a pallet of straw that had been placed for him in the crook of the doorway before the hall. The servant's world is always incomplete. The educated, such as Noon, may play any number of games in their heads to make time pass, but still are not granted enough knowledge to satisfy, only to thirst. At Dengby Hall the marquis had let him be tutored alongside his son, with the eventual intention of elevating him into managing the farms as his factor. It had kindled jealousy among the other servants and the muttered accusation that Noon was born of bastard blood.

He laid his own coat between himself and the straw, trying to set himself away from the stone, which would cool through the night. Now that he was outside the loose bind of Dengby, Noon found himself frustrated by his apparent position. To others, he was a servant, not neatly balanced between the rooms as he was in England. He deciphered much from scraps, from inflections and inferences, echoes of importance. Yet, he did not know which family had greeted them at the dock, did not know if they were of equivalent station to His Lordship, if they were Catholic, Jesuit or Papist. Noon did not know if his party was to stay a week or a month. Perhaps shadows did know more than servants, for they were not separated by station.

In the morning, Noon awoke and shook the stiffness from his limbs. He had risen before all but the kitchen workers. From the balcony, Noon overlooked the court-yard, supported by the mermaids, accompanied by the uneven splatter of the fountain. The dark sky held that English promise of greyness to Noon. Perhaps inclement England was not the centre of the earth, as he had previously supposed, but actually a dark corner. Maybe the south of Italy, where Jelborne said the sun always shone, was the pith of God's intention. Wandering back inside, he was intrigued by the thought. Perhaps the world in which he lived was one of no importance where they spoke the wrong language and obeyed the dicta of a false church. Whispers from the top of the stairs distracted him. Curiosity drew him upwards.

Outside of Jelborne's quarters, five men stood in a line. They were all runners, dressed in the livery of dif-ferent houses. Noon waited quietly at the end of the corridor. Jelborne should not even have been awake, but his door opened and a parcel of letters and a coin was handed out to each of the men. The men turned and came towards Noon, each one moving with a hushed importance. The servant retreated as one of their number, glancing over his shoulder. In the three months he had attended the tutor, never had ordinary life intruded on his sleep. Perhaps then, guessed Noon, this was extra-ordinary.

Chapter Two

Stilwell was particularly fond of the colour blue. His mother had always told him he had 'ocean eyes'. It was one of the few things he remembered of her. As a child he had thought only of her beauty, but now he understood that it had been a vanity, and he had been an accessory to her perfection. His blue eyes were sapphires in her crown. Still, as his mother's first and only child he was dressed and doted upon and it had left him with a hankering for female attention and an uncommon ability to flirt with those a little older.

His mother had also kept a little Negro child, brought from Saint Christopher's, and had often dressed him alongside her son. She had kissed them both as if there were no difference between them. After she had died, the marquis had sent the Negro away. Stilwell often wondered if he still lived. The metal collar the child had worn remained in Stilwell's study.

His suits were inevitably of blue, all shades from corn-flower to midnight skies. He favoured blue fabrics, blue inks, and, as Noon insisted, he owed the ocean a liking, if only for its blueness. That evening, Stilwell dressed in a silk suit the colour of dark water. Noon knelt before him and gave a final polish to his buckles.

Stilwell could never tell Noon exactly how grateful he was for his existence. Life would have been friendless without Noon. He was a deep comfort, and the fact that he was his servant was most comforting of all. It guaranteed a patience, for Stilwell was genuinely scared of losing Noon. He knew that in their lessons, their lives, the servant had proved himself an equal. Blood, however, was a powerful thing when paired with riches and Stilwell could see the measure in Noon's eyes and believed him satisfied with his position.

'Why,' asked Noon, 'would Mr Jelborne be sending letters through Genoa?'

'To elicit entertainment?' guessed Stilwell.

'Why would the messengers not leave through the front gates?'

'Custom,' muttered an irritated Stilwell. 'I do not know.'

'Why send them before dawn?' asked Noon. He waited for an answer but it did not come.

Stilwell would not look at Noon. His face was framed by his curls, a blue silk bow and cream lace tie, but his eyes would not meet his servant's.

'We are late,' said Stilwell and stood.

✻

While Stilwell felt he could be entirely open with his servant, Noon did not reciprocate. Noon kept secrets. He did not consider himself resentful, but he was imaginative enough to consider what life might be like if their positions had been reversed. It was a servant's role to know his master through and through without giving anything away. Noon did not mistake power for rights or deserts; he did not confuse superior status with superiority. And while he would never deny his liking for Stilwell, neither could he separate it from duty, and duty was, he knew, the absence of choice.

Jelborne was waiting for them in the courtyard below, dressed as ever in his black tutor's suit, clipped with white cuffs. The duke had gone ahead with his retinue, leaving behind a group of sullen chairmen to escort his guests, one of whom was busy carving callouses from his hands with a well-honed razor.

'The trick of a *conversazione*,' said Jelborne, settling down inside his sedan, 'is in your performance. Play if you must. Losing a little money will be considered in the best of grace, but do not let them tease you on. Withdraw with a few scudi in your pockets.'

The four chairmen picked up their parcels and headed towards the open brass gates. Noon followed on foot.

'If you wish a little exercise,' called Jelborne to Stilwell from inside his sedan, 'I would choose from among the older wives. You may even flatter the husband in your choice.'

❀

Signora Elmi's house hung off the skirts of the city, where they draped towards the sea. It had a long drive and was lit by a hundred torches, each teased by the wind. Every door and window of its two imposing stories was some twenty feet in height. Three men, standing on each other's shoulders, would have failed to brush the ceiling for dust. There were seven sets of long windows on the upper floor, the middle three leading out to a balcony where men and women were already poised in their finery. The Englishmen were led up a long set of stone steps, where two snarling lions were carved into the base of the balustrade, then along a gallery whose gilded ceiling was lit by torches. Noon stared upwards, imagining that they had crawled under the grate of a fire and walked beneath the burning embers.

There were perhaps thirty people present, and the first to acknowledge their presence was the duke, who made a polite attempt to rise. The room converged slowly around Jelborne and Stilwell and Noon pushed himself backwards until he touched the wall. He turned to his left and exchanged nods with the dark, proprietary eyes of a servant several years his elder. Noon wondered what a roomful of flesh would do to his master. Its effect on Jelborne was immediate, his face a vivid mixture of celebration and salivation. From his visit the previous year he remembered many of Genoa's finest and they did him the favour of greeting him amicably. *You are well known,* thought Noon. *Are these the recipients of your letters? What have you shared with them that Stilwell will not share with me?* Jelborne kissed both men and women on the cheeks.

18

Stilwell stuck his hand in front of him, a barrier that might keep temptations at bay, and was told again and again of everybody's great esteem for his father and their delight to meet his progeny.

The ladies were aglitter, each one matted in powders but then accentuated by some rich sparkle of concentrated wealth. Pearls were wrapped three strands thick around slim wrists, meeting either side of a miniature portrait of an absent husband, a stamp of ownership. Lace ruffles hung about some women's throats. They were manacled and chained by jewels and lace. Signora Elmi was easy to spy, Stilwell bowing low before her and lingering in his kiss of greeting. She was a large, heavy-chested woman in a lime-green dress whose décolletage attracted the eye as surely as the breasts of a naked mermaid on the prow of a ship.

Only one table was set in the room, a game of faro, and play seemed open to both ladies and gentlemen. The servants moved with silver trays of a brightly coloured fruit. Pink flesh and green rind, not unlike Signora Elmi, thought Noon. The rest of the servants had their backs pressed against the walls, rigid and straight-chinned. *Cover us with flour*, thought Noon, *and we are marble columns*.

The servant surveyed the room. What was money but the invitation to commit pleasure, and what was servitude but the order to witness it? Noon rested his mind, would not allow himself to think. To observe those blessed in their birth, those who wallowed in their wealth, would have rankled with Noon, had he not learned how to disregard in silence. *At least*, he thought, *my master holds a secret*. He knew that as human as it was to keep a secret, so it was to reveal it. Noon was confident that when Stilwell spoke, it could only be to him. At the faro table, Jelborne sat to Stilwell's right, intent upon the cards, but easing conversation between the players, offering pithy news of England and compliments to all he had known. Noon listened and was puzzled by such fawning tones, but flattery seemed a language in itself and such amity was paraded back and forth, spiced occasionally by an angled word.

'And what,' asked a strong German voice, 'do you think of the passing of your Queen Anne?'

Noon started and stared at Stilwell. *How could he not have shared such news?*

'The throne, as expected, has passed to Hanover's King George,' said Jelborne.

'You have a king,' smiled the German, and pinched his arrow nose between his fingers, 'who speaks not a word of English. Why would King James in Paris not convert? Is it too much for an Englishman to bow before one god or another for his throne? Or even for his people?'

'I have a father who talks of these things,' smiled Stilwell, 'and is of such a fixed opinion that the dining room is not a place of debate.'

'What,' asked the German, 'do you think outside of your father's dining room?'

'I wish a stable nation,' said Stilwell with great diplomacy.

'And you, sir?' asked the German of the tutor.

'We are Protestants in Catholic lands,' smiled Jelborne, 'with a German on an English throne. I would say our position is at least as uncomfortable as King George's.'

Noon listened intently. Stilwell and Jelborne had excluded him from whatever lay in those letters, but their secret was theirs alone and not shared with these inquisitors.

The bank was made by the German, who carried too much powder in his hair. He had a Bolognese lady who hung as close as an amulet to him, and every time she put her hand on his shoulder it seemed to Stilwell that a little cloud rose from the top of his head. Stilwell was the only man who seemed to be winning even the odd hand, but all continued despite the calls of debt that interrupted the giggles and moans of disappointment.

The men would pause in their gambling if one of the younger women passed before them. They studied a pair of sisters who walked arm in arm towards the balcony.

'Which girl has the better legs?' the German had asked.

'It is hard to tell,' smiled Stilwell, watching the sway of their skirts.

'One does not see the whole leg,' said Jelborne. 'Though I agree that while measuring a woman's beauty the first thing I would put apart is her legs.'

Signora Elmi shook with laughter and Stilwell looked up when her eyes were closed in glee and watched the happy storm of flesh swell and subside in her breasts.

Between hands, Jelborne and Stilwell had described their intended route throughout Italy and been promised letters of introduction from Rome to Venice and Naples. The German, well mannered but always conveying superiority through inflection, was more interested in the movements of people and constantly attempted to engage the tutor in conversation. Jelborne looked at him with some dislike but patiently explained how travel was an education in itself, how their countries had much to share but how the age of Italy made her a more perfect tutor than he could ever hope to be.

'That is your hope,' said the German. 'Perhaps it is the marquis's hope, but what is the hope of the son?'

'Does it matter where a man is from?' asked Stilwell. 'For instance, a man *dresses* not for where he is from, but for where he is going. Does it matter, then, how a man thinks before he leaves compared to what he thinks when he returns?'

'The man who leaves,' said the German, 'what exactly does he return with?'

'A full mind,' said Stilwell.

'Or pockets,' said Jelborne, but the German did not rise to such obvious bait.

'Paintings or portraits, books or busts,' murmured Stilwell. 'Those things that remind a man where he has been, what he has seen, that will help him remember the things that have passed before him.'

An hour later, the German closed his bank for the evening, to a few hollow protests. Noon shifted from one leg to the other and hoped that the evening was at an end, and though the crowd had thinned and it was closer to morning than the midnight bells, a circle had gathered about the duke, who held a small court with his guests and the Signora Elmi.

'Come, children,' said the duke and invited his hostess to sit beside him. Stilwell watched his host pat the signora upon the knee, watched the hand rest there, those fingers with their half-moon nails and fatted knuckles. 'Has the baron stripped you of your father's money?'

'No, no,' said Stilwell. 'I remain ahead for the evening.'

'A man of cards,' exclaimed the duke. 'A better man than his father. If only he could see. We shall write and tell him that his money shall be safe.' The duke took his hand from the signora's knee and Stilwell allowed himself to smile again.

'And what have you been talking of?'

'The passage of men,' said Jelborne.

'And the passage of crowns,' smiled the German.

'You have reached conclusions?' asked the duke.

'That it is unfortunate for the Tories,' said the German, 'that their queen should have died so soon after they had gained such position. Within two months they might have had King James on English soil, had Anne lived. One party wagers all its money upon one horse and it falls at the first hurdle. The Tories shan't see power for a hundred years now. German George will not approve of their attempts to keep the crown from him.'

'You say that as a German?' asked Jelborne.

'A mere observation, my friend,' smiled the man. 'You are happy with Hanover?'

'I am happy with peace,' said Jelborne. 'Let us not forget how rare it is for our countries.'

The duke raised his glass, but the German was not to be put off so easily.

'I have friends in the French court,' said the German, 'and they say that King James was sure his sister would pass him the throne. Shall he still try? If there is no course to power for the Tories, save through a revolution and King James, would they not support him?'

'The friends you mention are your friends,' said Jelborne. 'You should ask them.'

'They say he will land in England within the year.'

Jelborne shrugged. 'We are not men of politics, sir. I would think it a foolish thing. England has become the paymaster of Europe, half the continent is in thrall to her. Now with German George you shall find a parliament in harmony with its king. Who would raise their hand against that?'

The German nodded as if he had heard sense for the first time that evening.

'But wherever there is money,' said the duke, 'there will be conflict.'

The evening had been both typical and exceptional. Stilwell carped about the lack of food, but Jelborne convinced him there were few left in all of Italy who could afford entertainment such as he enjoyed at Dengby. Signora Elmi's *conversazione* had been the best evening Genoa had offered in months, insisted the duke, begging that they had not timed their visit as his father had to coincide with one of their feasts. Stilwell apologised to Noon for not relaying news of the Queen's death, explaining that the sight of Signora Elmi had pushed the information from his mind. Outwardly, Noon nodded graciously at the excuse.

All the men slept late the next day, even Thomas Noon, who had fallen into his straw pallet and been woken by a dog's tongue in his ear. He had slept long past sunrise, until close to midday, but the house had not yet stirred. There was a great feeling of lethargy, such a lack of agitation that Noon felt the city itself had fallen into some fairy-tale sleep.

In their drunkenness the previous night the guests presumed they acted with a subtlety that they had not possessed. It had been obvious to the sober Noon that the German was needling both Jelborne and Stilwell, pressing and prodding for responses. It had been an uncomfortable dance to watch and Noon suspected that the tutor was filled with information, that his exterior was a dull book-binding inside of which lay precious texts, and that Stilwell was his mute accomplice. His exclusion ate at him. It was not that he wished to resent his own position, but why had Stilwell's father schooled and cosseted him only to stunt the progress of his education?

The next week was, for all the travellers, one of orientation, where the two youngest became accustomed to the differences between the lives they had left behind and this adaptation. The first few days, the newness was overpowering and Stilwell did not think he could ever adjust to the temper and fondness for different things. Men who did not ride confused him. And yet the novelty faded quickly, for the days moved together in an identical fashion, as if you might hold a mirror between one and another and see no difference. Genoa was a city marked by the tolling of church bells. They seemed mostly intended for the poorer population. Though the rich would attend church daily, the hour they spent instructing their sedan men to walk in circles about the piazza made it obvious to Stilwell that the journeys to and from the church were at least as important as the service itself.

Their journeys by sedan chair were followed by a trail of begging children who look turns receiving cuffs from the chairmen as they tried to approach either Jelborne or Stilwell. Noon observed that Genoese nobles, even those of threadbare pockets, still comforted themselves in a mass of footmen and runners. Every time they entered the doors of a palazzo, his master was besieged by men who wished to be tipped for the opening of a door, for the offer of a helping hand, for their mere presence. Noon was forced to carry half a stone of small coins on any lengthy wanderings. He would wait outside closed doors, recognising the liveries of those runners who had collected Jelborne's letters, knowing that yards from him secrets were passed between sips of coffee.

CHAPTER THREE

Each night they attended a *conversazione*, interrupted, or enhanced, by music, finely played to all their ears, yet discordant and unapproachable once joined by voices. And, of course, the endless parade of sedan chairs, that Stilwell had seen as amusement, then as ennui.

Noon could not restrain his curiosity. Knowing full well that he could hold a secret, he felt there was little harm in pursuing one. On a Tuesday night he disturbed Jelborne, begging for some calomel for his master's riled stomach. His entrance, he noted, caused embarrassment to the tutor. Jelborne made no effort to push aside the papers that sat between tutor and duke, but looked at them and then at the servant. It was always a sure sign to Noon that he was to return to invisibility. Jelborne excused himself and left for his apartment. Noon was made to wait outside, but he could not resist peeking through the crack in the door and was amazed to find that it was a larger room than his master's. There was a carpet on the floor, and the unmistakable shape of a woman in his bed. Jelborne slapped this bundle on the rump as he passed. Taking the calomel, Noon thanked the tutor and retired, not bitter, but confused.

'Why,' Noon asked Stilwell on returning, 'would Mr Jelborne's room be grander than your own?'

Stilwell looked steadily at his servant. 'What would you be doing in his room?'

'He was kind enough to give me calomel.'

'You are not well?'

'I am better now,' shrugged Noon.

'I know you know me,' said Stilwell. 'I read your eyes as you read mine.'

'Who is Jelborne?' asked Noon. 'Why does he weigh more heavily than the son of a marquis?'

Stilwell shook his head. 'The Genoese have great respect for age.'

Noon dipped his eyes and apologised. Such a shoddy lie signalled the bolting of the doors to the cabal. Patience, smiled Noon to himself, I must swallow another dose of patience.

At the end of ten days, Stilwell began to feel bridled by politeness. When he and Noon were alone, he no longer sat to discuss the effects of travel and learning on his mind, but instead wrote in his diary. Every night they attended the duke as he paraded with all of the city's gentry in their useless circumnavigation of the piazzas.

Four nights they were forced into theatres, which both men found hot and uncomfortable, besides utterly untranslatable. Harlequins and serving maids, outrages and petty scenes of jealousy and retribution. But Stilwell was looking for the heroic, and found it neither in the city, its theatre, nor its people. His greatest fear was that his Italy could be found only in her history.

Stilwell often complained when alone with Noon. *You say you are bored*, thought Noon. *Take your pleasure and dilute it tenfold and you have mine. Take your action and then consider that I am limited to observation and I may show you boredom.* One evening, as they were carried over the hot stones of the city, Stilwell turned to his tutor and admitted, 'I do not feel as if I have learned much.'

'Of course not,' said Jelborne and placed his hands in the small of his back and turned his head. 'But you are absorbing custom. It is very important before we move. On Monday we shall see some paintings your father appreciated.'

'Where are they kept?'

'In churches,' said Jelborne.

'Dare we enter?' smiled Stilwell.

'Will the Pope turn our hearts and make us kiss the bones of some brittle saint?' laughed Jelborne. 'What do you say, Thomas?'

'I dare say a painting or two will not lead to our conversion,' said the servant quietly, walking in step with the chairman.

'My grandfather was a Catholic,' said Stilwell, beginning

to laugh at his own doubts. 'Perhaps my blood shall be stirred. Shall I be able to resist my papist urges?'

'Of course, milord,' encouraged Noon politely.

'Mr Jelborne, our Thomas is not a godly man. We would shovel him into church on a Sunday and sit him with family so he'd have no excuses. My father would keep a careful eye on him.'

Noon laughed and remembered his fondness for the marquis and the comforting timbre of his voice, his amused befuddlement over Noon's pagan nature. But it had never made sense to the servant, how the vicar had opined that God was everywhere at all times and then insisted that at twelve on a Sunday he was most apt to listen. If all the world were praying upwards at the height of day on Sunday, why not talk at midnight on a Tuesday, when he was less bothered by such a wave of chattering prayer?

'His soul is well protected,' smiled Jelborne.

'And tomorrow, what shall we do?' asked Stilwell.

'Sunday?' asked Jelborne.

'If it is Sunday,' said Stilwell, 'then Thomas must have his swim.'

Noon knew that it was said to assuage and include him, but appreciated it nonetheless.

It was Stilwell who insisted on leaving the chairmen and their sedans behind. Everyone lay still on Sundays, recovering from their evenings or attending a slew of family services. Noon felt they wandered together as men of different faith, happy to have no church in which to kneel. Following the western path from the city, they made their way down the steep outcrops, where fingers of rock rose unevenly, forcing a man to leap like a mountain goat from pinnacle to pinnacle. The two younger men were patient with Jelborne, who seemed always at the point of falling, his belly making him sway like a drunk. It made Noon happy to watch them move together as a group. Soon they came to large rock, smoothed by angry waves but now, in gentle weather, a platform above the sea. There was a slim reef beneath them, which might be cleared by a long leap.

Every man needs moments of peace to prepare himself for the lows to come. Noon sometimes thought that even looking at water improved his mood. Stars did much the same thing, but they were too far and couldn't be touched. Water encased a man. Noon hurled himself in silence, twenty feet in the sea. Under the water he opened his eyes and watched the bed of shifting sands. He could hear them shiver, these tiny monuments reduced by time. And a school of fish, each no bigger than his finger. He blinked and tried to clear his eyes, but they hurt him and he pushed towards the surface.

Stilwell was making his way down the rock face carefully, still fully dressed, shoes protecting him from the sharper outcrops. 'What do you see?' he called.

'Fish,' called Noon.

'Catch them with your hands,' shouted Jelborne from above.

Stilwell turned his head up to smile at the tutor and laughed.

Noon forgot the vague sense of jealousy that their pairing had caused him, and grinned, diving back under the water. His Lordship scrambled back up the rocks to his tutor, carefully choosing his footholds and pleased with his progress.

'What does he think of?' said Jelborne. 'Why does he love the water so?'

'His daughter, I suppose,' said Stilwell.

'I didn't know he had one.'

'She's dead,' answered Stilwell. 'Two years ago.'

'How?' asked Jelborne.

'Drowned,' said Stilwell.

'Then how may he still love water?'

'I think he talks to her out there, not aloud, but within.'

'Drowned in Shropshire,' considered Jelborne. 'I imagine that would be difficult. Though I once heard tell of a man who drowned in a bucket. Drunk as a Teague, head in, never woke up.' He paused to remember if he had ever been so drunk. 'How old was she?'

'Three,' said Stilwell. 'Pretty little thing. A bastard child.'

'He's not very maudlin then,' answered Jelborne.

'He was,' said Stilwell.

Noon was swimming towards them as fast as possible, once more chased in his mind by the beasts of the deep. Pulling himself on to a low reef, a foothold to the rocks above, he saw a small fish floating belly up, washed back and forth by the swell. He plucked it from the sea and threw it up at Jelborne.

It came shooting back down, slapping Noon mid-chest. Stilwell was scuttling down the rocks again towards his servant.

'A live fish, Thomas,' shouted Jelborne, 'rather than one a beggar'd not chew.'

The rocks beneath Noon's feet were sharp. They made him walk like a tiptoeing trespasser.

Jelborne looked down upon the two men from his perch, standing side by side, one almost naked, the other fully clothed, and thought they might be brothers. Not so different in age, nor their hair, nor even the timbre of their voices. He liked the quiet servant, efficient and faithful as a dog, but more uncommonly of intelligence and learning, never stretching them for show. *Now you are a man I could use beside me*, thought Jelborne. How difficult to be born to such a life, to understand but to withhold, to be given the gifts of growth, but not the room to grow. He knew that Stilwell and Noon must talk without him, knew well that their friendship was too old to adjust, but he wanted something from them. It wasn't youth, because he had not been fond of his own. Not money, for one had all, and the other none. It was, perhaps, their trust.

At their first meeting three months ago, Jelborne had been most uncomfortable. Noon's strange position within the household at Dengby was difficult to interpret. He seemed to dwell alone between the served and the servants, a position not dissimilar to that of tutor, the role in which Stilwell's father the marquis had hired him. Jelborne had, as requested, read aloud from his book after lunch that day, looking up at Stilwell every three or four words: 'The purpose of the Grand Tour is to wean a young man from his mother, from his home, from all that he is used to, to fill his mind with appropriate erudition and let him learn the finest of what this world may offer.' He had known very well that the young man's mother was long since dead and watched closely for a reaction. A dip of the eyes, that was all, but Jelborne did not think it weakness and agreed with the marquis that his son might be trusted.

Perhaps, he thought, there was danger in Noon – a suspicion that was directed at Jelborne, though he did not think the servant would stoop to gossip. Jelborne was a stopped secret. It had always been his belief that information shared was always thrown to the wind. Better to let Noon grope in darkness than burn his hand on the truth. In his ignorance Noon was an added cloak of disguise. Jelborne did not see how it would help them if the servant was corrupted by the knowledge of their true purpose in Italy.

CHAPTER FOUR

'Art,' Jelborne announced over chocolate on Monday morning, 'is the soul of man, his expression, and the Italians are the greatest artists of this world.'

'Shall we meet one?' asked Stilwell.

'All dead,' shrugged Jelborne.

The cathedral, the Duomo, stood before them, cut in layered stones of black and white. It looked like a gaming board the marquis kept at Dengby. It went up and up, twice as high as a ship's mast, cut black and white against the sharp blue sky. It resembled a confectioner's creation, and should there be a drop of rain, thought Noon, it might dissolve, running syrup through the gutters.

They were guided by a dealer of paintings. Cragnotti was not a large man and had to stand on his toes to embrace Stilwell. He had been blessed with a formidable nose, a blunt instrument of good sense, and a tiny pair of feet that made Noon think he might tip forward and wedge his beak between cobbles on the piazza. He was dressed with the affectation of a man with taste, no powders for his hair, no colour to his black clothes. He might have been a simple priest had it not been for gold buckles that gleamed on his shoes, and a gold pin he wore against his breast.

They were escorted about chapels, the baptistery and two Crucifixions, one carved in stone and the other in wood. It was a world of symbols, and Noon did not grasp their meaning, but he suspected he was supposed to feel contrition before the martyred Son of God, and sensed an intimidation that Cragnotti would have thought limited to Catholics. They paused before a statue to the side of the altar, John the Baptist dressed in camel skins, touching his own breast, eyes peering from above his thick beard.

'"Repent ye, for the kingdom of heaven is at hand,"' quoted Jelborne, still staring at the figure of Saint John.

'Exactly,' said Cragnotti. 'We believe that once you are baptised you must confess your sins. If you do not confess, your sins weigh upon you, they get heavier and heavier, and soon they corrupt the soul.'

'And when the soul is corrupted?' asked Stilwell.

'The trees that do not bring forth good fruit are hewn and cast into the fire,' explained Cragnotti.

Candles and echoes, thought Noon, bleeding Christs and mournful chants. What a strange, archaic religion was this Catholicism. Full of reliquaries and rosaries, popes and endless prayer. And confession: what was the point of confessing, thought Noon, if you were then cleansed? Did that not give a man a reason to sin again? He knew responsibility and he knew guilt and he did not wish to be forgiven. These things *should* affect a man and not be brushed from his back.

Noon stood beneath the cupola and felt that the sky had been lowered upon them. Saints seemed to peer from everywhere, some were hidden like children playing, peeking behind columns, others stared down from frescos, some from paintings hung against the walls, others from stained glass. Noon felt there were hands on his shoulders, pressing him. He turned and walked out of the cathedral. Even passing out under the door there was a depiction; a semi-circular table of Christ and his disciples at supper and they looked to Noon like a pack of bandits readying themselves to leap on the unfaithful from above.

Jelborne watched the servant retreat, ducking low despite the great height of the door. He linked arms with Stilwell as His Lordship turned to follow Noon and escorted him among the paintings of saints martyred and risen. Cragnotti explained the difference between good and bad painting. He held a lantern to the paint and tried to show the lord how a man moved his brush to convey an effect, how a painting was designed to capture then lead an eye, how great men had posed to play the parts of saints.

The studio proved to be filled with sunlight, and though the pictures were all turned to face the wall, those that stood on easels in the centre of the room were much more to Stilwell's liking than any of the sombre paintings in the cathedral. Stilwell moved slowly towards a depiction of the Rape of the Sabine Women and stared intently at the muscular arms of the men wrapped around the milky flesh of desperate women. One had her hands raised to the sky, pleading for mercy from unseen gods. Stilwell noted how all the men's heads were turned away. They may have felt lust and anger, but also some degree of shame. The women were all staring outwards. Oddly, he felt the need to rescue them, but didn't know how.

'I must have this one,' he said pointing at the painting.

'Should you not also choose something for your father?' asked Jelborne.

Cragnotti bowed and began to turn the stacks of pictures. Out came Christ and a plethora of Last Suppers, Davids carrying Goliaths' heads, numerous saints in poses of ecstasy, Nativities, a compendium of still lifes. Every time a painting with a putto would arise, Jelborne would make Cragnotti pause. They decided on a picture of the Virgin Mary turning a rosary before a small host of angels: naked, sexless children who clasped each other in delight, looking down upon the child Jesus. The young lord left the studio with his servant, leaving the low matter of negotiation with his tutor.

'What did you make of our purchases?'

Noon shrugged. They resembled nothing at Dengby. The marquis exhibited no love of painting and had barely brought a canvas back from his own travels the previous year. Noon sensed a twist in the truth and felt excluded from their purpose, but could not voice his doubt.

'I think I prefer pictures of land or sea,' said Noon. 'Those paintings you'll buy, they're all from a man's imagination. What good is that?'

Stilwell smiled. 'Without imagination, there can be no adventure.'

'Is that what this is?' smiled Noon.

'Of course,' laughed Stilwell. 'We have had our high seas, we are now ending the period of readjustment, and then our travels recommence.'

Jelborne emerged, huffing slightly from the walk down the two flights of stairs. ''Tis done,' he said. 'Thomas, you are to carry the pictures tomorrow. Make certain of them then take them to the dock and give them to a captain called Brigson. He'll sail for Portsmouth with the evening tide and the marquis shall have his first paintings.'

The following day, Noon wound his way back to Cragnotti's studio. Yesterday's guide was busy wrapping the Rape of the Sabines in thick canvas cloth, waterproofed for the voyage. Neither painting was large, both had been removed from their frames and rolled, but Cragnotti had bound them in such thick cloth and rope that Noon had barely walked quarter of a mile when he was forced to pause against a porter's rest. Since the paintings were heading to the marquis, Noon did not see why the cylinder of the smaller Cupid could not travel inside the larger Rape. He walked to a butcher's, with its table of stringy meats covered by cloth against the sticky feet of summer flies, and borrowed a knife. He took the knife, slit the smaller package open and then cut a neat hole in the larger roll, inserted one within the other and returned the knife. He thanked the owner, waved the flies from a corner of the meat and then continued his walk towards the water.

It was strange to see another Englishman. Brigson, a small, stout-chested man, sun-burned, thin-haired and short with words. He took the paintings from Noon and turned his back. The paintings were two weeks from England, and Thomas Noon a year. Noon stood, empty-handed, by the dockside and looked at Brigson's ship, the *Henry*, with its bare masts, sitting pregnant with goods, low in the water. Her crew were balanced on the yards, looking up at Genoa, and yet above it, considering them-selves a superior species. Part of Noon longed to go with them. If they had been travelling far, perhaps he would have, but he had confidence that England would not change without him and was in no rush to resume life at Dengby.

He did not know if it had been the sight of the sea or perhaps that array of painted children that made him cast his mind back to two years before. It was not fresh water, not like a running river or this lolling ocean that gently rocked the *Henry*. A black pond on the marquis's estate, but large, long enough to take him five full minutes to swim across. She had left him and he had not minded. It was as if half the shame had departed, even though the child remained as the echo of their sin. For the first six months, Noon had pretended his bastard did not exist. He paid for the wet nurse and for another to mind it through the night and endured the barracking that his brief labour had brought upon him. They called it the bastard's bastard. One day, when he was visiting to see if his child still breathed or perhaps had passed away, the nursemaid was called for just a moment, and Noon was left to hold her. The girl had looked up at him with unblinking eyes. He pushed his finger into the tiny palm of her hand and she gripped it so hard he laughed. She laughed too as if she understood and in a moment Thomas Noon was overcome with his neglect.

It was his child, his recreation of the world, and now it must be loved and shielded. That Sunday he had carried her down to the pond and holding her tight in his arms, lowered them both into the water. She kicked out and screamed but Noon knew it was a love they must share and so he was patient and bore the wails that day and the following Sunday, until on the third attempt the child submitted to the water without a murmur. The wet nurse called her Sarah.

Noon did not care about the wake of scorn that parted behind him as he carried her through the grounds into church on a Sunday. His own father never mentioned the girl but both Stilwell and the marquis would grant Sarah a smile, which was blessing enough to blast the ill will of the estate. Two years of this behaviour had won most hearts and it had helped that Sarah was granted an open face of innocence and a string of giggles that showed a delight with all before her. The peak of her happiness remained the Sunday ritual with her father, when after church they would change from their bests into rough cloth and Noon would carry her to the pond. He would hold her by her stomach with one hand and call for her to kick and wave her arms. In truth, she had no urgency to swim. She knew it would take her from her father's grasp.

How could a father forget? Forget being called from the kitchens on a Monday morning, running with a footman towards the pond, not knowing why and yet knowing all the time. Seeing a farmhand, red-faced and grave, wading back towards the shore, Sarah's body in his hands. Poor child, thought Noon, she has done this for me. It was a numb world, yes it was, one with muted sounds and it seemed to have nothing to do with Noon from that moment. Sarah had ceded it on his behalf. Noon learned that a man could turn the corners of his mouth upwards but not smile, could talk without saying a thing, and sleep without being able to tell one day from the next.

Two years had passed by and Noon would not forget how bright the world had been. Few, save Stilwell, had seen the dourness that had consumed the man since his daughter's death. It was Jelborne's appearance that had given Noon his rebirth, the knowledge that he could leave Dengby, leave it with a purpose and not be seen to be running from his sins.

He paused in a small piazza shadowed on all sides by smoke-blackened buildings and dipped his hand in the fountain to bring water to his mouth. Noon was startled to find his hands were stained red. At first he thought that it might be blood from the butcher's shop but it was paint, and though he had smelled tar on the docks, he could not recall a trace of red. The only alternative was that it had come from the smaller canvas, that of the Cupids, and yet he remembered Cragnotti insisting that they were both over a hundred years old. Jelborne had asked him to ensure that they were the correct paintings, and perhaps would not have asked had he trusted Cragnotti. Noon hurried to the promontory and could see, two miles above the docks, the crew loosening the halyards of the *Henry*.

CHAPTER FIVE

Noon held up his hand to Stilwell.

'You are cut?' asked His Lordship.

'Is paint,' said Noon. 'Your paintings were no more a hundred years old than I am.'

'Do not worry,' smiled Stilwell. 'We have not been cheated.'

'Was meant to be?'

'Yes,' said Stilwell.

'I am not supposed to enquire?'

'No, though I am sure you will again.'

'Am I not part of this too?' asked Noon. 'Am I not?'

Stilwell ran his thumbnail against the palm of his other hand. 'My wager is your gamble.'

'So tell me.'

'I will ask Jelborne,' said Stilwell, 'and if he is in agreement so be it. Now that he knows you I am sure he trusts you. I will ask him before Venice.'

'Why to Venice?' asked Noon. 'Why not Florence first?'

'It is not my itinerary but my father's. If we wish funds we must follow it. The notes of introduction to the bank.'

Ask Mr Jelborne, thought Noon. *What strange inversions when viscounts are subject to the authority of tutors.*

Noon's first task in preparation for their departure was to hire a second servant, a man who might double as their *vetturino*, or coachman. Noon was guided along cobbled streets by one of the footmen, out to the walls of the city, where coaches stopped and the post horses were corralled in a stubbled field, flecked with gnawed patches of grass. The coachmen made their home about a small piazza, pressed just inside the thick wall of the city. Noon's entrance was noticed. He pretended to look at the sole of his shoe while the duke's footman shouted their desire to hire a coachman. He would be needed, explained the footman, for the better part of a year, to carry a group of English all about the country. After Noon sat on the soot-streaked steps of a dilapidated church, he glanced sideways at the prospect of his travelling companion. They made a poor group of men. Noon would have thought them beggars were it not for their considerable heft. Little money had been invested in their appearance as if all anticipated both job and livery.

When Noon returned with their *vetturino* in tow, Jelborne looked the newcomer up and down as if he were a carthorse. The man brushed his shock of black hair from his face so that the tutor might study him uninterrupted. Low twenties, thought Jelborne, decent enough shape, but a mocking man, not a good trait in those who served.

'You chose this?' said Jelborne, slightly amused but keeping a pleasant tone, mellow in its falseness, so that the *vetturino* might have no idea he was the subject of the following words. 'But look at the man, Thomas. He has the countenance of a thief, the ears of an ass, the eyes of a ram in heat. He might rob us, stab us, bind us and sell us. Why should we hire such a flea-bitten scoundrel?'

'He speaks good English,' smiled Noon.

'I speak good English,' said the Genoan.

'How?' asked Stilwell laughing.

'Two years since now, I taken gentlemen like you. I taken them from Venice, to Florence and Genoa and Leghorn and—'

'For how long?'

'Six month, more, seven.'

Stilwell saw that Jelborne had not been entirely wrong in his accusations. The man's eyes were dark, the lines from smiling so deeply etched about his face that it made him look as if he found amusement in all he saw. As for the countenance of a thief, Stilwell was not sure what thieves looked like, never having met one. They had been warned by his father not to change coachman, for they would all overcharge a man, and it was more economical to be over-charged by one scoundrel than a dozen. Why not employ one that they all might talk to?

'You are a little short,' said Stilwell.

'So short,' said the man, 'that I cannot steal your clothes to wear.'

'What is your name?'

'It does not matter,' said the man. 'You may call me what you wish. Every master call me what he wants.'

'I do not give you clothing,' said Stilwell, 'and you will be at orders at seven every morning.'

'I rise with the sun.'

'Good,' said Stilwell. 'Well, what shall we call you? Mr Jelborne, Thomas?'

'Caesar,' smiled Noon.

'Why not?' said Jelborne.

'Welcome, Cesare,' said Stilwell.

'Ave,' laughed the tutor.

They instructed him to return the following day with the minimum of luggage. He smiled as if to imply that luggage was for lesser men, then walked between the duke's disapproving footmen through the front gates.

Jelborne was amused. 'He will still prove a vagabond.'

'Why?' asked Stilwell.

'Because he is a *vetturino* and they are all thieves and vagabonds.'

'Every rule has an exception,' replied His Lordship.

'And if every rule has an exception,' said Jelborne, 'then you must also conclude that there is also an exception to the rule that every rule has an exception. He remains a vagabond.'

It was Stilwell who raised the subject of their departure to their host and the duke protested that his father had stayed another entire week more than the son. Eventually they compromised on three days added. This not only gave Noon time to prepare for their travels, but also alerted the finer citizens of Genoa to a goodbye party at the duke's palazzo. Out came banners and drapes until the courtyard looked like the waist of a ship shadowed by silken sails. Slight breezes sent tactile ripples up and down these vast swathes, caresses that made the watching men think they deserved to be touched as tenderly. Most impressively, the duke had promised to feed his guests meat, rather than the familiar ices and melons. For the two days before the party, the city's elite restrained themselves in anticipation of dining at the duke's expense.

A hundred and fifty came, and those who received no invitation cursed the duke by name for all of Genoa had been smelling the roasting flesh of pig, cow, chicken and duck for a night and a day. That evening, Signora Elmi professed that her heart would break without catching her daily glimpse of the young lord, but Stilwell had learned enough in his three weeks to know that words and meaning had nothing in common. He responded nobly, begged her for some remembrance and was rewarded not only with a bow that had been tied about her neck the night they first met, but a hurried kiss.

As the duke had promised, it was an evening that did not end. It did not end when the flesh had been gnawed from the last chicken leg, nor when the final meringue had crumbled against lips, nor even when the sun arrived early and without invitation. People seemed to melt away, and all the time Noon had stood and Noon had watched, stiff-backed and made of patience.

He had seen his master drawn and teased, seen him reconsider and reach for his kiss. He had seen Jelborne drink and stand upon his chair to raise a toast to Genoa. And when he had fallen, Noon had rushed to his side and suffered his drunken embrace. Perhaps a little shine was taken from the English party, but not from Noon, who would not be remembered, which for a servant was the highest accolade of all.

That Sunday was not a day for churches, whether you were a Catholic duke or a Protestant lord. The great slept and the humble cleaned and ordered, washed and folded those vast banners and scrubbed the stains of wine from the flagstones and the scent of piss from the columns. No one stirred that evening either, but Noon brought his master jugs of hot chocolate and cool water, which this September night helped him to sweat and eased him back to who he remembered being. And on Monday everybody rose together after their empty day of recuperation and came to say their goodbyes.

Noon and Cesare had risen at dawn and, with the help of some of the duke's chairmen, had been assembling Stilwell's carriage outside the walls of the city. The carriage, which had been unrecognisable in its pieces, was soon transformed into a large caleche which held two men inside, three if necessary, and their trunks. It was strong, low-strung, double-perched on corded springs and iron axle trees, with two drag chains with iron shoes. It would need a pair of large horses to give it its speed. Cesare climbed up and down it like a child, but assumed a very professional air as if to convince Noon that he had made the right choice in *vetturino*.

'She is good,' said Cesare. 'She will come back from Naples.'

On returning to the palazzo, Noon took the precaution of ferreting out from their luggage both swords and pistols and with the help of Cesare was oiling and polishing them.

'These good people?' asked Cesare in English.

'Yes,' replied Noon in Italian, 'you'll not be treated better by an Englishman.'

Cesare grinned and joined Noon in his native tongue. 'I'll teach you the best words. The fat man, the teacher, he likes to drink a lot, yes?'

'We all like to drink,' said Noon, 'because we are English.'

'Me too,' said Cesare. 'We shall have a competition. With *burzino*, the special drink of where I am from. It will make your head fall off. Like this sword.' He swished it to cut the air. 'On the ground, your head will be on the ground, and mine on my shoulders.'

'I see, Thomas,' said Jelborne, descending the steps with Stilwell, 'that you are preparing us for battle.'

'*Banditi*?' asked Stilwell.

'We should be robbed of little more than our gold,' said Jelborne, 'though I believe we are allowed to keep our skins.'

Noon ran his finger against the sword. 'Feel that, milord.'

Stilwell brushed the sword on the heel of his hand. 'Mr Noon, I believe the sword is now too sharp for its sheath.'

Noon had thought it strange from the start. His master was not the wealthiest man in England but they were rich nonetheless. Noon had seen accounts of the estates and knew they might travel as lavishly as they wished. The decision to limit their expenditure to a single coach and servant was deliberate. He had begun to suspect that the intention was for them to slide softly about the country, noticeable in the cities but silent in-between. *Come Venice*, thought Noon, *I shall know*.

They trotted over one of the two stone bridges that spanned the slow rivers seeping into the sea. In the middle of the afternoon there was nobody about but young boys fishing in the low tidal waters. They heard the horses, sharp shod, clacking their hooves against the stone and turned to watch Cesare and Noon perched atop the caleche, both men smiling to be on the road.

The excitement of uncertainty appealed to Stilwell: not knowing whether they would travel five miles in rain or twenty-five under sun, whether they would meet a soul in a day, whether the landlord would welcome or spurn them. For Jelborne travel was an ache and a bore, but for Stilwell it would always be better than drawing rooms and measured stares and gamblers. This country was comprised of men more skilled at cards than him. Let him go where money had no meaning, where life rushed high and low and not flat as a marble floor. He hoped it was a long road to Venice before the resumption of their business.

Since Cesare knew their surroundings well, they did not hesitate but drove their horses into the night. It was the first time in months that Noon had seen a countryside bathed in moonlight, and everything was new again. In England, the country meant the scent of earth, often mud, but always a dampness, either in the sky or underfoot. And English night was hedgerows, curled ferns, clouds and the sound of your own footsteps causing rustling in the undergrowth.

The dryness of the Italian summer had brought a surfeit of smells to the air. Noon didn't know them all, could sniff more sweetness, a floral confection, for the dead flowers of spring still perfumed the night. The horses continued their gentle gait and Noon could hear their breath and the beat of hooves thudding like spades levelling the earth of a new grave. And behind that, like the noise of a crowd above a conversation, was the summer requiem of cicadas. He had asked Cesare what the sound was. Lady insects, he had been told, who rub their legs together, rub them faster and faster to make such a noise. Noon pictured a vast *conversazione*, and well-dressed women and the rustling silks pressed between their thighs.

Any romantic notion of Italy's inns were kindly disposed of at their first stop. The inn, twenty miles from Genoa and recommended by the duke, was soured by the stench of skinned animals, all of which were spread about an outhouse in the yard. They slept in beds that stank of other men. Stilwell fussed about fleas and turned all night in his clothes. His tutor, a more experienced traveller, made a bed of four chairs and laid his head on his leather portmanteau. In his prone position, he drank two bottles of weak wine and collapsed into sleep.

The following day, after paying a large and unreasonable bill, they passed meadows, cornfields and acres of olive trees and even Stilwell was tempted to forget his miserable night. Noon was astonished to see vines stretching across the gentle slopes from tree to tree, all fruit suspended between them. Maples and elms acted as supports for the produce, the ground beneath still available for the planting of corn. How simple and ingenious, thought Noon, and he immediately began to wonder if the same thing might be possible in the estates of Dengby.

At midday, they passed through a long and shaded copse of oak trees. Their trunks stood close together, like frozen men about a fire, and combined to block all but the greenest light falling from the sky. Cesare looked between him and Noon for their pistols. Once they passed back into the bright sunlight he laughed at his own fears, but an impression had been made on Noon. Nervousness is most infectious, and doubly so when conveyed by the experienced.

The carriage may have originated at Dengby but the horses, like their *vetturino*, were local. They were to be changed at posts arranged by ostlers, so that the same horses were always running back and forth along familiar trails. Dealing with their first ostler the day before, Stilwell had shown little surprise with the lack of speed, the complaints about the construction of their English carriage, the arms stretched for ill-deserved rewards. By the time they were dealing with their third ostler on the second day, even Jelborne's patient temperament had been aroused at the charge of four shillings sterling for just one stage. This was the sort of figure expected if you hired the carriage as well as horses, and a screaming match resulted in a grudging compromise. Jelborne was mopping his brow from excitement when the ostler finally emerged with a pair of horses. The tutor knew little about horses, but even to his eye these were young and un-broken. Noon objected but Cesare shrugged their worries away and off went the caleche at a fast trot.

The spine never adjusts to carriages, thought Jelborne. Riding a horse, it was all flesh between a man and the earth, and once he accepted the motion of a well-trained mare it was better than his own feet. But carriages had their own peculiarities, their rusting springs, uneven axles – an endless equation of metal and wood that con-spired to discomfort the occupants. Carriages were good for conversation but poor for thought. Minds couldn't lie still but were constantly jogged from those internal wan-derings that helped lessen the boredom of travel.

Now, now for instance, his mind had been visiting Paris a dozen years before, and before that was with the mar-quis in his study, and before that in a country churchyard resting beneath a yew with a wheel of cheese too large to carry. Mostly, though, Jelborne thought of women. Womanhood was large and soft and welcoming to the tutor, teeth that pulled on his ear and whispers of desire.

Jelborne entertained himself by allowing enough ideas to harden, then dismissing such thought as sin until he subsided, where he would promptly return to dreams of Venetian thighs to see if he might stiffen again. He kept his erection hidden under his leather portmanteau.

The others couldn't imagine, thought Jelborne, perhaps no man can. Cities are easy to conjure once you have seen one, but then how to conjure a city on water? A child might do it, fresh but full of fairy tales, but grown men know better. Noon's brain will melt, thought Jelborne. He will want to swim in the canals. He will do nothing but wish to swim until he sees that a canal is a sewer, a grave, a dumping ground for everything discarded. Floating excrement, apple cores, splinters of wood, dead dogs.

Jelborne's thoughts were interrupted when he found his hands suddenly braced against the roof of the caleche and his rear well removed from the seat. When it touched down again, Stilwell's dirty boots were in his tutor's face and the carriage was lying on its side. He could hear a great whinnying and the panicked cries of Thomas Noon calling to see if either of the passengers had been harmed.

Stilwell was hoisted from the upturned carriage by the two servants, then the procedure was repeated, less gracefully, with the larger Jelborne. The buttons of his waistcoat caught against the door and with one strong heave, all five burst in a row like ducks scared from water. Stilwell busied himself finding the buttons along the road and repressed a smile at the utter bewilderment etched on his tutor's face.

Cesare had managed to resurrect the fallen horses, but they had kicked up so much dust in their fright that the four men looked as if they had emerged from an attic after a year of neglect. Remarkably, their cases had suffered no damage though the caleche had splintered one of her axle trees. The single rolling wheel had come to rest a hundred yards down the road. Jelborne was spitting bile at the murderous ostler some ten miles behind them.

There was no damage at all to the occupants, both Noon and Cesare leaping from the carriage as the horses had driven a wheel against a protruding rock.

'There is no difference,' Jelborne was insisting, somewhat composed, 'between plunging a dagger into a man's back and supplying him with unbroken horses.'

Two men good with their hands working before their betters feel a sudden brotherhood of ability, a certainty that their skills were measurable and not those inherited shrouds that draped other men. Noon and Cesare took satisfaction from repairing the caleche. They congratulated each other on their foresight of bringing a bladder of grease, a hammer, a spare iron pin, nails and a large knife, and sweated together bare-chested under the sun.

Soon all blood cooled, and even the bruised horses were nonchalantly grazing at the wisps of grass within their tethered reach. They ended their unplanned stop with a brief meal. Noon had laid in a provision of Bologna sausages in Genoa, as well as neat's tongues, chocolate and tea, only counting on the inns to provide the basics of bread, butter and milk. Having overcome their ill humour and filled their stomachs, they advanced, albeit carefully, along the road towards Casserta. In the small village that had grown out of the post house, they happily exchanged their horses for a team only a year from a stewpot, while Jelborne sought out the local magistrate to complain of the ostler's villainy.

The inn that evening was little better than the previous nights. While Jelborne was arguing with the innkeeper about the populated cobwebs in their rooms and Cesare saw to the horses, Stilwell helped his servant find the linen coveralls that he would wear over his clothes to bed. The previous night he had thought it too hot but had suffered so many bites that he now chose to endure sweat in quest of sleep.

'It's better, isn't it, Thomas,' said Stilwell, hunting within the largest of their trunks, 'to be travelling. Genoa was too dull.'

'And Signora Elmi?' asked Noon. All notions of resentment or frustration had melted now that they were busy on the road, on their way to the lagoons and to revelation. Jelborne's presence in their personal equation seemed to have been removed.

'An ancient dream,' laughed the young man. 'Marvellous shape, but there were too many internal obstacles to overcome the outer barricades. Venice, now there is a city. Jelborne says that you can sit in your boat and they row you beneath windows where women stand quite naked. They are bare-chested, Thomas, and you simply ask your boatman to pause where you wish to admire. They ask, when? You tell them. You agree on a price. So much simpler, I feel. There is no real sin in it.'

It wasn't a question, but Stilwell's words curled at the end as if he expected an answer.

'I think it more of a satisfaction than a sin,' said Noon.

Stilwell nodded. 'And Cesare?'

'A good choice,' said Noon adamantly.

'A fine company we have then.' He pulled his coveralls over his head. 'Now, if we are spared bites tonight, I feel as if we might sleep on a while come the morning.'

'As you wish,' said Noon, and they retired to separate rooms.

CHAPTER SIX

At dawn, Noon found himself wakened by his master, freshly emerged from his linen cocoon. The first of the sun was spilling through the grease-paper windows. To Noon's bleary eyes, Stilwell looked even younger in the morning light. The sun had turned his skin the colour of betel nut, erasing the dark patches of exhaustion, mementoes of their last evenings in the city. Even his eyebrows had turned blonde in their days out of Genoa.

'Now, Thomas,' smiled Stilwell.

'What time is it?' groaned the servant.

'Just past daybreak,' said Stilwell.

'I thought we rested this morning.'

'I thought so too,' said Stilwell, 'but I feel I've slept a hundred years. And then Cesare was about as well. Then Jelborne woke himself with a snore and I thought, why not Thomas too?'

Noon rolled to his feet and stretched.

'Shall I get you water?' asked Stilwell.

'You wish to serve me today?'

'I wish to leave,' replied Stilwell. He walked to the window and peeled back the paper. 'Look at the light. We'll do well to ride in this.'

They drank only water for breakfast and ate a little of the Bologna sausage, Cesare carving slim rounds from the tip. Jelborne looked weary, but dipped his whole head into a bucket of water and emerged with a leonine roar that brought laughter. The whole morning, Jelborne remained in the highest mood, pouring wine down their throats and entertaining all with a lewd song about a Welsh whore who had slept with a regiment in one night and then retired wealthy to Virginia.

> *'My arse was worth two acres,*
> *my mouth was worth a barn.*
> *Now my cunt has been forsaken*
> *and needs a soldier's horn.'*

Once they had exhausted their songs, they wound their way in happy silence, interrupted only by their tutor's loud humming of tuneful fragments.

Rounding a corner in the afternoon, Noon was surprised to find their path blocked by a dead horse lying in the middle of the road. No, it wasn't quite dead. One leg was moving. A large pool of blood was still seeping from its neck. The dusty ground was thirsty and Noon could see the patch oozing through the dirt like a cloth dropped to mop spilt wine. From where he sat, balanced on top of the caleche, Noon couldn't see a broken bone that might have caused the four men standing in the road to put their beast out of its misery. Further down the road, he noticed that they had tied their other horses on short tethers, and pointed them away from the scene of butchery.

Cesare slowed the caleche to a stop before them.

'Friend,' cried the man closest to him. He was a thin figure with arms so long that Noon wondered if he might leave finger trails in the dust when he walked. 'Will you help drag our horse from the road?'

Noon stared at Cesare, not knowing whether this was commonplace or unusual. Cesare looked at the men, seemed content and leapt from his seat. Noon followed. Jelborne was leaning out of the window, but the inquisitive Stilwell emerged, not with the intention of dragging an animal's carcass even a foot, but to watch this strange event from a closer position.

The thin man took the position of a foreman and ordered the others, including Noon and Cesare, into position around the dead beast. The skinny figure waved the punctured sole of his boot over a blanket of flies that had settled on the horse and they hummed away a dozen feet and returned. Noon took his position about a leg. He had his hands on one fetlock and Cesare on another and they pulled together and the horse moved not one inch.

Noon looked up to see a smile and a pistol levelled at

him. Cesare and he dropped the horse's legs and stood there dumbly. Jelborne had emerged from the carriage and was also frozen, hands on hips as if he had been about to give a great yawn to relieve the discomfort of the carriage. Stilwell had perched himself in the driver's seat and had one of his notebooks and an ink pen sitting across his lap. His eyebrows had moved up towards his hairline, a caricature of surprise.

Noon and Cesare were ordered to lie flat against the ground, just a yard from the dead horse. Noon tilted his head so that he could keep his master and Jelborne in sight. He could feel the dust stick to the side of his sweat-covered face. An army of ants scurried past him on their way to the mountain of horseflesh. The thin man, his pistol levelled at Stilwell, had begun to raise his voice.

'They are asking you to get down,' translated Cesare for his master, still atop the caleche.

One of the two men with the pistols pressed his boot against Noon's throat and whispered something to the servant. For the first time, Noon felt panicked. The boot weighed against his windpipe and he squirmed in the dirt, trying to breathe. It made the anxiety spread through his body and he inhaled a desperate mixture of air and dust and began to cough. The boot lightened for a second and Noon spat into the dust. His eyes were streaming and he could barely see, but he could still make out Stilwell's figure on top of the caleche, Jelborne standing beside it, their horses still.

Noon was horrified by his helplessness. He knew his

heart beat faster than a bird's and was ashamed of it. The man above him knelt down so that it was the hard bone of his knee now lying across Noon's neck. He could smell the man, strong and unwashed, a dirty musk. Noon was amazed at himself. His hands were shaking and he could not stop them, not with the deepest breath. He clenched his fists so that the trembling stems of his fingers would not be seen.

I am a coward, he thought. *All these years inside my own skin, and here I am a damned coward. A worthless man*, and his eyes were leaping face to face to see if he might share his fear, *a worthless man*, and he wanted to confess his terror to his companions, to stagger to his knees and press his head against the soil and find comfort, to weep in front of these strangers. *Who are you?*

Stilwell had not even looked at the pair of pistols that sat to his right. He could see Noon and Cesare pressed against the ground. There were only four of these men, with two pistols between them. Perhaps they were primed, perhaps not. Stilwell concentrated on the one man, this puny ghoul speaking to him. *Are they bandits, or does this run deeper?* Even a fool could understand the rapid gesticulations of the man's empty hand. He wanted Stilwell off the caleche immediately. In a moment, thought Stilwell, you are going to look at Cesare and ask him to translate your words to force me from my perch. *And then I will have you*, thought His Lordship. *I will have you first and the rest shall scatter. I will have you like a rabbit. I shall move my right hand and draw it fast and level it and breathe*

63

out and I will have you. I am here to see, to collect and to return.
You are tomorrow's tale.

Jelborne's hands were still sitting on his hips. Despite his
racing heart, he was at least pretending a familiar nonchalance. He had, after all, been robbed before, been
beaten, been nicked by knives and had bottles broken
over his skull. Being robbed was by far the least painful
instance. One stood by, surrendered, went on one's way
poorer and soon recovered. In Venice they would find the
marquis's banker and sit with gold again. Unless this brig-
andage was premeditated. What could the thieves hope to
achieve with such bluntness? The acquisition of letters,
notes of introduction?

Jelborne looked at the carriage to his portmanteau,
then turned his head upwards to His Lordship, intending
to nod in a comforting, avuncular fashion when he noticed
the young man's hand move quickly to his left and raise a
pistol. The single report was deafening. Back fell His
Lordship, unfired pistol in his hand, held impotent before
him, the right eye gone, the entire side of his face muti-
lated by the blast. Long dead before he dropped to the dirt
from the caleche.

Noon pushed suddenly upwards against the knee and
catching the man off balance toppled him backwards. The
servant brought his boot down firmly on the wrist that
had held the pistol and kicking the weapon from the road
he ran. Not towards Stilwell, but at the thin man who had
fired the shot. He threw himself, his shoulder levelled into

the man's ribcage. They fell together, Noon astride him, heart still rattling like a regimental drum and thinking of childhood play, falling together with Stilwell amid mock cries of horror. His right arm reached out and grabbed the pistol by its barrel. He had time to bring it down twice. The first blow shattered the nose, the second seemed to flatten the side of the man's skull. Brittle bone showed its ivory shine. Then Noon, in turn, received a blow, so unexpected to him as if it came from the stars. He had forgotten there were others alive, and his last sight, as he fell backwards, was of the horrified figure of Jelborne, his hands raised in an attempt to distance himself from the proceedings.

CHAPTER SEVEN

Jelborne was cleaning the wound on Noon's head. The servant's brain felt loose like a bone die shaken inside a cup. He opened his eyes and watched Jelborne tending to him. Noon could remember everything.

'I shall have to sew you up,' said the tutor.

He could not find the will to answer and so let Jelborne go about his business. Perhaps a moment later, perhaps hours, Noon again felt the sensation of a man kneeling on his neck. Cesare pressed him into the grass as Jelborne threaded the needle and ran thick stitches through the skin covering Noon's skull.

'I've made a mess of it,' confessed Jelborne, whispering as much to himself as to Noon. 'Skin is stretched too taut on a man's head. Best I am able to do. Isn't so bad, just a bloody business. Not bad at all.'

They propped the servant against a tree and shared a few slices of sausage. Noon stared straight ahead, refusing the proffered food. He was thirsty, but could not admit it, thinking only of Stilwell.

'Have you buried him?' asked Noon quietly.

'With what?' queried Jelborne, looking up. 'Our nails?' He chewed upon a piece of sausage and wagged a finger at Noon. 'You're a fool. If Stilwell wished to get himself killed that was his concern. But you, sir, you could have done away with the lot of us. They don't just murder a man about here, we might have been nailed to trees. We might have had our sides slit open, and dirt pushed inside us. We should be tied to trees and begging for death.'

'They why aren't we?' asked Noon.

'They think you dead,' said Cesare. 'They kill us, we kill them, they kill us again. It was enough, I think. They take everything and move.'

'He died?' asked Noon.

'You knocked in the side of his head,' said Jelborne.

'Where is Stilwell?' asked Noon.

'Over there,' said Jelborne, jabbing his finger behind them. 'About a hundred yards. We've covered him and the other in branches and stones. There's nothing for us to do.'

'We must take him with us,' said Noon.

'And how do you suppose we do that?' asked Jelborne. 'Carry him along?'

'We'll return for him,' said Noon.

'Yes,' said Jelborne. 'We'll return.'

'How did you keep that?' interrupted Noon, pointing at Jelborne's dusty portmanteau.

'A traveller's trick,' said Jelborne. 'I loosened the ties on the top piece of luggage. They leave with everything. Inevitably they are in a hurry, the horses forced to gallop, and there it was lying in the middle of the road not a quarter mile west.'

'What is in it?' asked Noon.

'Papers and letters,' said Jelborne. 'Half a sausage I was hoarding. Not a single coin.'

'And the needle?' asked Noon, running a hand over the back of his head.

'Was Cesare,' answered the tutor. 'Has a pair of them, one each side of his coat.'

Noon nodded but did not wish to talk more. His mind was slowly forming questions, all regarding Jelborne's response to his master's death. Noon would have waited upon the road for the next carriage. Then he would have reported the murder immediately to the closest town and called for the magistrates to raise a party to hunt down the highwaymen, and yet here they were, under trees and off the road, Jelborne peculiarly quiet. For the first time Noon wondered if their secrets had brought about Stilwell's demise.

Lucius Jelborne watched an exhausted Noon fall into a deep sleep. Cesare built a fire. When, at about midnight, the two men heard the approach of horses, Jelborne refused to allow Cesare to wave them down. It seemed peculiar to the coachman, unless, of course, the tutor guessed it was their assailants returning for the dead. The thought was enough to make Cesare cover the fire, but the moon was so bright and their flames far enough from the road that the coach didn't even slow.

The tutor did not rest at all. There was far too much to consider, a great responsibility of action that Jelborne had not thought would ever be pressed upon him in this way. There was no restoration of life, no resurrection he might perform in the morning to make a tomorrow out of today. He was sorry for Stilwell's death, most sorry, but death only caused trouble for the living. Sorrow was the most useless of man's emotions. He had said a prayer over the dead men's bodies and blessed both their souls, and left their judgement to God above.

Everything must be very carefully considered. He thought out the possibilities as if each were a separate ripple sent out from a stone dropped in water. He traced their paths and followed their reasons, calculated the effects that Noon and Cesare might have on the arc of his intentions, and finally at about six was sure enough in his knowledge to allow himself two hours of sleep.

Noon's bleeding had already stopped in the morning. Cesare, up at dawn, had found a rill not more than a mile to the east and returned with water slowly dripping from the bottom of his hat. He washed the back of the servant's head and then walked again for water, this time letting Noon drink deeply from the brim. On his third trip to the rill, he was accompanied by the tutor, who undressed on the bank and washed the dust from his flanks. When he signalled that Cesare should join him, the *vetturino* pointed upstream, where a dozen sheep were busy soiling the water. Jelborne shrugged and threw a rock in their direction, then waited a few minutes before drinking from the stream.

Left alone for a half hour, Noon had decided to climb a tree. He paused in mid-ascent but didn't know what he was waiting for or why he was climbing. *Fear*, he thought. *Where has the fear gone?* He remembered climbing as a child and being frozen in fright, petrified and white-knuckled. He could look neither up nor down, was old enough to know better but could not move. No one could convince him otherwise and they had to carry a ladder to fetch him. Stilwell had watched from beneath, a worried expression on his young face. And now? There was nothing felt, no joy just an efficiency. Even fear would have been better than such numbness. *Where have they buried you? Can you forgive me?*

When Jelborne and Cesare returned from their walk to the rill they found Noon missing. Jelborne let out an exasperated sigh before Cesare noticed the servant sitting astride the limb of a tree twenty feet above them.

'What are you looking for?' called Jelborne, and when Noon did not answer began to plead with him. 'Come down now, we think we saw a place some miles off, will be a walk for you in your condition.'

Noon didn't speak, but descended in three quick movements.

'They had names for days like this in Rome,' said Jelborne with sympathy. 'They were called *dies nefasti*, the bad days, in memory of terrible losses. Nothing could be done on them. They were the opposite of holidays, forty of them a year. Forty days a man should do nothing but think of the disasters of those who came before him.' Jelborne patted him on the back. 'Now I shall carry my bag,' said the tutor, 'and you shall walk unaided.'

Not a quarter of an hour had passed since they had begun their walk when they spotted a figure, dressed all in black, sitting against a tree in their path. Noon stood still, but Cesare walked merrily onwards to greet him. Amidst the confusion of their state, it was as if the *vetturino* was unaffected. And why shouldn't he be, thought Jelborne. Who mourns for a master you have known for a week? Noon remained very still, looking at the seated figure, convinced that it was an emissary of death.

'An *abate*,' said Jelborne, reading the confusion in Noon's eyes. 'A priest who wanders to carry God's message.'

By the time Jelborne had slipped his arm under Noon's and propelled them level with the *abate*, Cesare had evidently explained their woeful position. The *abate* insisted they walk with him, at least as far as a neighbouring farmhouse. Noon watched the way his black robes stuck to the *abate*'s skeletal body, not an ounce of flesh upon him. Did they not feed these priests? There was no fat on his face. His smile was contained in his lips and did not stretch across the face because there was no flesh to lift upwards. The eyes were glassy, reflections but not indicators of any thought.

If the *abate* did know of a farmhouse, his faith in God had not been rewarded with any sense of direction. Nearing nightfall, they found themselves standing outside a poor hovel, a weak stand of mud and stone. At the back of the structure in a rough enclosure sat one cow and a dozen hens. A grizzled dog raised his head but did not deem the visitors worth a bark. The *abate* called, 'In the name of St Francis, you must feed us.'

Out came a young girl, no more than twelve, broad-shouldered and bare-footed, who looked upon the *abate* as if he were a saint rather than a visitor intent on extracting free food. She bowed and said, 'He is almost dead.' Inside the hut, in the last light of the day, they found an old man lying on a pallet of straw on the dirt floor. He was as pallid as ash and in his first weak breath ordered his daughter to kill one of the hens for their guests. The *abate* sat by his side and held his hand. No dying man could reject the servant of God, or even those who travelled with him.

The girl served them first one chicken and then upon the dying man's instructions a second. There was nothing to drink but water. After the meal, the girl laid down straw about the hovel and Cesare and the *abate* settled down to sleep. How either could rest next to the disquieting rasps from their host's throat, Noon could not guess. The girl removed herself and sat outside. Soon she was joined by the servant who wandered past her through the discarded feathers of the dead birds until he found a slight rise in the ground that he might lie his head against. It was a cloudy night, no stars shone down, no moon gave light or comfort to him, and everywhere it seemed death was scratching its way about the land.

Jelborne emerged from the cottage, looked left to the girl then right at the murky figure of Noon, and walked slowly towards the servant. He carried his portmanteau, laying it on the ground next to Noon then leaning back to rest his head. Noon knew enough about nature to know Jelborne had come to talk. It had not escaped his notice that Jelborne was also affected by Stilwell's death. But Jelborne, thought Noon, was immersed not in grief but in anxiety. He was a man torn, guessed Noon, but by what? His payment, his employment, the letters in his portmanteau?

'You have papers,' said Noon, pointing at the portmanteau. 'We must write to the marquis and tell him.'

Jelborne rolled on to his side to face Noon and managed to nod and shake his head at once, an odd circular motion of uncertainty. He was relieved to hear Noon talk.

'There is no immediate need,' said Jelborne.

'What are you thinking?' asked Noon. 'You are about something, aren't you? You have both been about something, and see what it has brought.'

'Do not confuse fate and action,' said Jelborne. 'They were thieves.'

'That is all?'

'If they had been on orders,' said Jelborne, 'they would not have treated my letters so lightly, and had they realised they had lost them, they would have returned in search of us.'

Noon nodded, partially convinced, wanting to know more.

'Stilwell chose to waste his own life. Be sad for him.' Jelborne smiled sweetly. He seemed to be touched with affection for the wounded man. 'Until the marquis reads the letter,' continued Jelborne, 'he shall believe his son alive, though he is long dead. Every thought he has of Stilwell between this moment and the arrival of the news is an illusion. He will not want to believe the death, but he will have to trust us. So our responsibility is great, Thomas, for we must decide what we tell, what we make him feel. It matters not whether we send news today or in a year, the man is dead.'

'So what do we do?'

'We continue to Venice, draw on the funds established by the marquis there.'

'Is it money you're after?' asked Noon. 'Is it the marquis's money you want?'

'In truth,' said Jelborne, 'you are exactly wrong. It *is* the marquis's money we were after, but not to spend it, to gather it.'

'They are notes of promise,' said Noon. 'If no man should collect them, then the marquis's funds will not be drawn on.'

'Not the notes of promise,' said Jelborne. 'This lies far deeper than that.'

Noon removed Jelborne's bandage from his head, then ran his hand about the wound. Jelborne's stitching had held, scabs were forming up and down, slowly beginning to merge together.

'How is it?' asked Jelborne.

'Healing,' said Noon.

'We are on tour,' continued Jelborne, 'and we are directed by the marquis's itinerary. It is not a tour of education. *We* are at work, *we* are raising money for the marquis.'

Noon sat up and wrapped his arms around his knees, hugging them to his chest, then nodding for Jelborne to carry on.

'I am no more of a tutor than you are a coachman. I work for the marquis and the marquis for the king.'

'The marquis would have little to do with a Hanover king,' said Noon, shaking his head.

'Not King George,' said Jelborne, 'but King James in exile. A year from now, he shall be placed back upon his throne. The Stuarts will return. Not German blood but English.'

'The marquis is a convert,' chafed Noon. 'His father converted, there is none of Rome in the family.'

'A paper convert,' said Jelborne, 'but his heart has never changed. He is as grand a Catholic as the pope himself. Armies need money, this is what we raise.'

Noon pushed himself to his feet and stared through the gloom at the ungainly tutor, his stomach resting like a sack of goods between them. That this man might be an agent was so preposterous, so very unlikely, that it was almost obvious in the sudden revelation. His head hurt again. It was as if a man walked back into a room a moment after leaving it, only to find it painted red instead of white.

'If you are a Catholic,' said Noon slowly, 'and are travelling in a Catholic land, then why act the tutor?'

'There are many agents, Thomas. My face is familiar in the Low Lands, in Paris and the north, in Scotland. Even here, travelling alone, I might raise eyes, but as a tutor, with charge and servant, I am noticeable but familiar. When we return, we will gather our funds with us. Such sums cannot be drawn in England without suspicion. We are essential, both to raise and then to carry funds.'

'And now you have no charge,' said Noon plainly, 'you'll be exposed for what you are.'

Jelborne shrugged and pushed himself upright. 'If you have ever believed in a king, then you must believe in God. It is a divine right to rule and it is carried in blood. I am hardly the most fervent of churchmen but I will not stand for this bartering of blood, such dilution, while the king sits waiting on French soil. There is still much work to be done for King James, we cannot leave yet. We must return *together*, with our money.'

'It is treason,' said Noon.

'Treason,' said Jelborne, 'is to let your country pass to another land's king. Catholic or not, James is England's king.'

'And I am supposed to care?' said Noon. 'Care about kings? What good am I? And what good are you now?'

'We might continue together in search of funds,' said Jelborne.

'To do what?' asked Noon. 'Recruit another master? A young man, an English boy lost on his way? Stilwell is dead, is that not enough?'

'No,' said Jelborne, shaking his head.

'Or perhaps,' said Noon, 'we should dress Cesare in fineness and bow before him.'

'Or perhaps,' replied Jelborne, 'we should do the same to you.'

Despite his fragile state, Noon managed a laugh. 'Now that is a fine idea. And I am pleased to know that we were both hit about the head.'

'Would you not want to please the marquis?' asked Jelborne. 'He has left all matters in my hand. We will go to Venice, receive our funds, dress you and introduce you as Stilwell.'

'I'll not do it,' said Noon. 'I'll not play his ghost.'

'Come now, Thomas, is this so bad a thing to ask of a man?'

Noon flashed angry eyes at Jelborne.

'Has it *never* occurred to you?' asked the tutor. 'Have you never wondered how it might feel to play such a part, to spend an hour in silks? To have dreams larger than playing factor for His Lordship? To *be* His Lordship?'

Of course it had occurred to Noon, and of course he would not admit to it.

'It is an opportunity,' insisted Jelborne. 'You are not so unlike me, we both serve without truly being servants, we are both now in danger of being cast off.'

'No,' said Noon.

'Besides which,' smiled Jelborne, 'we have a common attraction to gold.'

It was not true, a little misstep on Jelborne's part, but one that Noon's fracturing morality could seize on. He pulled Jelborne to his feet by the lapels of his coat and shook him, made his belly shiver, and as Jelborne tried to push the servant away they both fell to the ground. Noon was astride the tutor and lifted his body again and thrust him back down. The servant paused. He could feel the wound on his head leaking blood down his back.

'Calm yourself,' choked Jelborne.

Noon spat in his face and left, leaving the tutor prostrate.

The servant walked and breathed and stared into the darkness above him. He knew that many wish to run from the lives they were given and that none did because they were already defined and set in their actions. Here was the opportunity to stride forward as another. What fool would deny himself? Who would choose constant regret over risk? But to do this, in these circumstances, felt both incestuous and treasonous. Noon could not sleep but he knew that his inability to rest signalled that he was still considering what he had meant vehemently to decline.

At dawn, it was Noon who poked Jelborne awake.

'Forgive me,' said the servant. 'For last night.'

Jelborne shook his head. 'There is nothing to forgive. He was your friend, my acquaintance, please forgive *me*.' He yawned and signalled for Noon to wait for him outside the hovel.

'I have not been honest with you,' said Jelborne in the dawn. He fished for his cock within his breeches and sighed as his piss splattered into the soil. 'I have not been instructed to reveal this, but I do not know what else to do. A man should know these things. Stilwell was like a brother to you?' asked Jelborne turning his head to Noon.

'Aye.'

'And should your father ask something of you, he who brought you into this world and guided you, would you do it without question?'

'I would.'

'You do not know the name of your own father.' It wasn't a question, but a statement.

Noon looked at him in silence in the morning mists. Jelborne finished pissing and pushed his cock back within his breeches.

'Have you not always been treated different, Thomas?' asked Jelborne, placing a hand on Noon's shoulder. 'You've not been a servant, nor have you been family. Your position has been mixed, because so was your blood.'

Noon shifted uncomfortably.

'He you thought your brother *was* your brother. Behave as he did. Because of what you are, behave as he did. If not for yourself, for God. If not for God, for your father.'

'Who told you that?'

'The marquis.'

'What proof?'

'He said that if I were to tell you, you would know well enough that it was true.'

Noon's blood was up, high and fast, confirming memories within his head. How he was given learning when all others were not, the rumours that followed from kitchens through gardens. It had not been a similarity in age or temperament that had made him and Stilwell close, but a shared blood. And the Marquis's smiles at his daughter, his acceptance of her when all sought to spurn her. It was a recognition of the bastard of a bastard, and how shame could survive and blossom.

Jelborne placed his hand gently on Noon's head.

'I know there is much to think about,' said Jelborne, 'and am sorry that news should fall on you so quick.'

The tutor walked back into the hovel. Noon had never seen him so sober. *What am I now*, thought Noon, *and what was I then?* Then a servant, now, neither servant nor master. And to play at lordship, what sin was that? A great one, and yet, was it not just as great to have played at servant while richer blood beat in his veins? If anything, this might be a restoration, or at least a balancing of the accounts of merit.

And treason, where does a man stand? Where should he stand? Behind God, king, or family? If he chose family then it was a sign of his belief in blood, and to believe in the importance of blood would mean to stand by King James, despite his reek of Catholicism. *Where are you, my friend? You wished me to know and now I do, but how must I act? Did you know that we were brothers?*

I must remember, thought Noon, *that my blood is still tainted. It has brought me a strange position within Dengby.* But why not, if he was his father's son, why not take up his purpose? Why do something for a god when it can be done for a father and brother? There were rewards on this earth, and rewards beyond it. Noon was in the odd position of suddenly being within reach of both. Stilwell's death, he was numb enough to death, his daughter had ensured him of that. But this was a dizziness rather than a pain, and he knew what Stilwell had been, a friend and a master, but also an anchor, an inanimate weight that had limited his ability to drift and to discover.

CHAPTER EIGHT

After all had risen, Jelborne constrained himself to gentle enquiries after Noon's health. The servant found that he felt much the same as normal, and was surprised at the speed of his recovery.

'A thick head, after all,' smiled Jelborne and clapped him on the back.

They left their dying host with prayers for his recovery and walked back to the road for Fornovo, accompanied by the *abate* at his own insistence. With the priest's help, they stopped a horseman running an eastern canter and asked him to plead with the next ostler to send them a carriage in the service of God. Nothing came back from the west all day. The priest was an adherent to the economy of movement and ordered Cesare to fetch more water from their familiar stream. He sat in shade, waving flies from his face and smiling every now and then to Jelborne and Noon, who sat across from him with their single portmanteau.

Everything that Jelborne had confessed hung heavy above them and yet, with the tutor whistling through his teeth, Noon knew that Jelborne had no intention of raising the subject again. It began to annoy him. To push so much upon a man when all about was sorrow and disappointment, when they could find nothing but the closeness of death either upon the roads or away from them, it was unjust.

Noon could not help himself. He wandered alone down the road and there was the dried patch of horse's blood bisected by the mark of a wheel. A yard from the road lay the bloated carcass of the horse, already ripe and rotting in the August heat. Noon walked off the road and after a brief search disturbed a trio of crows that broke into the air. He knew what lay under the crossed branches and stood there for a moment in consideration.

It was a stronger smell, sweeter than the horse, and Noon's mouth turned down. He thought he might weep. *Was this what happened to men? Did they mean nothing, this distant pair, lying side by side and brought together by no reason, no reason at all? Could you receive a blessing from a body or merely grant one?* Noon walked slowly over and with the toe of his boot moved the branch to the side to reveal a corner of Stilwell's face. It was intact, the open eye undiscovered by crows, and it was empty and there was no trace of God there, no reason for belief and no reason not to believe. Noon shifted the branch back over his master's face, then tore some more low-hanging limbs from the surrounding trees. He chased the watching crows away, running after their throaty caws, and once he had started he could not stop himself. They would fly thirty yards and settle and Noon kept running at them, shouting, determined to drive them into the air or to kill them. He was crying and running, pausing to gasp for air. Eventually, they flew up and arced over a field and Noon lay panting on the ground, his eyes stung with sweat. *How can the world continue in its ways? Does it not notice pain?*

The sun was directly overhead when a composed Noon returned to where his companions sat in silence. He realised that he had not eaten in a day. He deliberately set his mind on Stilwell, using him to dispel his hunger, but even the thought of the dead lord would not remove his appetite or the remainder of his confusion. Instead, he grew more and more peeved at Jelborne. There sat the tutor, whistling quietly. He did not seem touched by sadness. And worse, thought Noon, the tutor let the silence grow between them, knowing that the servant would battle best with his own thoughts.

After an hour of mulling and considering the correct extent of resentment, Noon asked, 'Do you not wish to know what I think?'

'Not unless you are certain of your answer,' said Jelborne, smiling at Noon.

'Does my decision affect nothing?'

'It affects everything,' said Jelborne most seriously, 'except for the course of our travel. Our passports take us only as far as Venice, our empty pockets will not carry us a mile further. Your father's friends expect us, whether you come as Noon or otherwise. Should you wish passage back to England, it shall be so.'

'And you,' asked Noon, 'what shall you do should I decide to return?' The reference to his 'father' had not escaped Noon and he thought it both sly and soft.

'I shall stay,' said Jelborne. 'Will be like a game of faro against a strong bank, but I shall stay.'

'We will really leave him, will we?' asked Noon, pointing back towards the body.

'You saw it?'

Noon nodded.

'And you've seen others before,' said Jelborne. 'There is nothing to flesh once the life is gone. Just a touch of sentiment within him that looks, not him that lies breathless.'

Noon agreed, and for a moment felt strangely in unison with the tutor, as if only age divided them. Perhaps Jelborne was more accustomed to grief. Noon thought of his daughter in his arms. He had laid her on the grass beside the water and yet he had raised his head to look out across the pond. Why had he looked for her? He had been certain that she was no longer within the flesh at his feet. She was whispering that the body was nothing.

'When must I decide by?' asked Noon.

'I suppose,' said Jelborne, 'that what we decide must be done before we talk to another soul. We shall tell them of Stilwell's death or Noon's.'

'And Cesare?' asked Noon.

'I have explained some,' said Jelborne, 'that you might play a part. He thinks we do this for money and has asked for a doubling of his wages. It is fair enough. It does not matter what he thinks. He knows his good fortune is tied to our performance, he will keep his part.'

Jelborne resumed his sharp whistles through his teeth. There were no clouds to shade the August sun. They sat two more hours until their shadows stretched before them. And still Jelborne did not press him, as though he felt that Noon in silence would decide more quickly then Noon in open debate. A coach came by and the four gleaming horses were grateful to be reined to a stop before the black-robed priest, who stood in the middle of the road with one arm raised in entreaty of man through God. He explained the plight of the travellers, how one of their number had been killed and how their coach had been stolen and reminded this coach's occupant of the story of the Good Samaritan. The *vetturino* looked down upon them, his horses creating small pools of sweat on the dust of the road. There was no pity in his eyes, only suspicion, and Noon saw it and did not blame him. Yet the ill-humour outside the coach did not reflect the ease within. Thanking the *abate* for allowing him to perform a service to God's good name, a high voice invited the two Englishmen into the carriage. Cesare took a seat beside the scowling postilion.

The occupant, a Venetian merchant, had fled his city for the summer and was now returning in expectation of the cooler autumn weather. He insisted that the simple fact of their shared destination was an indication that their meeting was directed by God. He kissed the two men and introduced himself as Giuseppe Capretta. He was very small, not much larger than a child, and could stand inside the carriage while his two guests would have been bent almost double. His voice was pitched high. Indeed Jelborne had thought their saviour a woman until he had shaken the man's hand.

Jelborne bowed and introduced himself, then turned and bowed once more before Noon. 'And may I have the pleasure of introducing . . .' he began, and let his words drift away to place the onus firmly on the servant's shoulders.

'The Viscount Stilwell,' said Noon.

'Of Dengby Hall,' added the tutor, with a smile that showed only humility for a tutor to find himself with two such distinguished travelling companions. Capretta understood the look and made his own position very clear. A *cittadino*, not a noble, not a member of Venice's Golden Book, but in charge of supplying the Venetian State with cattle, importing them from Styria and Hungary. It amounted, he confessed, to over 10,000 ducati a year.

Noon's heart was savage in its attempt to betray him, beating so loudly in its nervousness that he was convinced its echoes carried to Dengby. He need not have worried, for Capretta had seen but never talked to an Englishman before and considered it his greatest good fortune to host the remainder of their journey. He learned of the marquis, and of their letters of introduction to the Dorias and the Fezzis, and nodded and spoke of their ancient breeding.

Twice he offered to dress them in his clothes, and apologised both for his slight stature and that his country might prove so dangerous to their health. If a hair on either of their heads was harmed in the Venetian Republic, Capretta would hold himself personally responsible. Jelborne could not decipher all the conversation, for Capretta spoke unusually fast, always slipping helplessly between a formal Italian and the softer Venetian. Noon, gradually relaxing, began to listen.

Over the miles, they understood that Capretta was in some hurry because his daughter was pregnant, perhaps with twins, and he was most anxious to be in the city before the birth. This, he hoped, would not be too severe a breach of etiquette, for most of the nobles would not be restored to the city for a few more days. They would, he insisted, be his guests if their hosts had not returned from their summers.

They stayed the night at Borgoforte, where Capretta insisted on visiting the local tailor, saying that Noon's honour must at least be given precedence over a humble birth, and then spent an odd day while a heavily bribed tailor adjusted a suit intended for a Paduan landowner. His Lordship was not permitted to owe him a single *zecchino*, for Capretta was merely doing what any Venetian would do to welcome him after such a disturbing journey.

After a meal of roasted pork and wine and a second pleasant night, the tailor arrived and Noon emerged some hours later, his chin obscured by an extravagant amount of lace about his neck. His chocolate-coloured coat fell neatly away, arms leading to vast cuffs out of which poked his hands circled in more lace. His waistcoat fell almost to his knees, a cream silk touched with gold brocade and bright buttons. His brown breeches were met with white

silk stockings and his feet were covered by a buckled pair
of shoes. Jelborne and Capretta bowed. It was impossible
for Noon to see the smirk cross Cesare's face.

Noon held up his hand and stared at the width of the
cuff. The tailor had insisted that it was the local custom,
the higher a man was born, the wider his cuff, and an
English Lord would need great cuffs to kiss. Jelborne
walked forward and took him by the arm, directing him to
where the carriage waited.

'You look well in the part,' said Jelborne. 'How does it
sit?'

'Is Jelborne your name?' asked Noon. 'Your true
name?'

'Of course not,' said the tutor.

'What is it?'

Jelborne shrugged. 'It matters not.'

'So not one of us,' said Noon, 'now travels under his
true name?'

Jelborne smiled. 'We are all even, milord.'

Noon tugged at his cuff, looking uneasy in his new
clothes, feeling as if one hard stare or sharp question
would strip him of his disguise.

Capretta stopped the carriage at midday and allowed
them to stretch their legs about Mantua. He led them into
and out of the empty cathedral. All Noon would remember was the strange barrel of the cathedral's roof and the
sensation that he had been used like a hasty ladle, dipped
in and out so quickly that he had emerged with nothing at
all. During their brief excursion, Capretta had sent his

vetturino, accompanied by Cesare, on a quest for cold meat, fresh bread and wine, and they began their meal inside the carriage as it rolled from Mantua. Their horses were fresh and Capretta announced his intention of continuing at speed, not wishing to stop at either Castellaro or Bevilacqua and especially not Este, citing a clash of business interests and unpaid bills.

After their lunch, Capretta complimented Noon on his fine Italian and suddenly seemed to have noticed that he had spent so much of the last two days talking that he knew little about his guests. Now he assailed Noon with a series of questions. How did England fare with France? What did the English Church think of Mary, the mother of God? Did they think that the French king would really support the English exile? How did the English regulate the circulation of their coins? And land, how did His Lordship manage his land? Noon's lack of knowledge in some areas merely proved to Capretta that Noon was generally both above politics and material issues, but his vast knowledge of the marquis's land and its working was a discussion that the two could share. Hours were taken with figures and calculations familiar to the managers of estates and the tutor could see that Noon, talking now with knowledge, was beginning to grow more sure in his part.

Jelborne closed his eyes, slumbered to the tune of the chatter and silently congratulated himself on Noon's growing acceptance of his new role. As an agent, Lucius Jelborne had often been suspected but always thought too much of a drunk, a buffoon, a lecher to be of any true danger. He let the layers of ignominy fall upon him in disguise. Those whose opinion he valued knew the truth of him and the rest he cared not for. To serve a king is born of country, but to serve a king in exile is a decision made coldly, despite his protestations to Noon, and often with motive.

All of Jelborne's interests were subservient to history. He knew that history did not mind who worked for her, nor was she concerned by those who toiled and died in her shadow waiting to be noticed. She cared only for sides, for competition, and would not remember a Greece without a Sparta, or an Alexander without a Darius. History was a larger field, less presumptuous than faith. Faith, to Jelborne, was merely one of history's sides.

Jelborne considered himself a reasonable man, full of flexible opinions. Yes, he believed in the Stuart line to the throne and that a crown should pass through blood and should never have leapt to the German head of Hanover. And yes, to call oneself a Catholic was a dangerous thing in England, if not for the life, then certainly for the wallet. History decided the subject, in this case the intangible one of faith, and then men positioned themselves to compete.

Men were made in moments and from moments. And history was the transformation of these moments into public memories. The trouble with history was that she was not a god, not omnipresent and eternal. She chose her location and then her moment and a man must travel to meet her. The following year, Jelborne was sure that she would appear in England in the form of restoration.

It was his purpose, and his gamble, to ensure her presence and to do so she must now be roused from her sleep in Italy. Without Catholic funds, there would be no Stuart restoration, no returning England to her popish roots. While much money would be gathered in France, it was odd that Italy might play a role, when all the English who travelled there considered it important only for its past. How they walked through the lands of their education, quoting Martial and Livy but presuming Italy dead.

Could England ever be more delicate? A dozen years of wars might have brought fame to Marlborough but the nation was taxed and wracked though well primed for trade. Who thought further than the depth of their pockets, who cared whether they were governed by one state or another, other than that one state might lean less upon a people? Why would a nation resist its own blood, when the crown could only pass to German hands?

'And you?' asked Capretta and tapped him on the knee.

'I did not hear,' said Jelborne.

'You do not mind if we go on to Padua?' asked Capretta in his squeaky Italian. 'I know a journey in the night deprives a foreigner of land he may never see again, but this way I can assure you of a finer inn.'

'Sir,' said Jelborne, 'we are indebted to you many times over. We are most content to follow your instruction, are we not, milord?'

'As I said,' nodded Noon. Jelborne smiled and remembered his first assignment, when he had been approached and paid to travel through England and gather a list of those favourable to the Jacobite cause. There was a love of adventure in him then, as now, that he believed Noon shared. To present yourself as one man and to know yourself another was to be secure, protected from eyes and judgement because it was never *you* who was seen or judged. It was an absence of accountability that Jelborne had long thrived on. He believed it would do wonders for Noon's confidence and character.

They were allowed a short walk about Padua, enough to allow Jelborne, who confessed to having avoided it on his last visit, the opinion that he would not be back again. The university, which had brought the city such fame across the continent, was, announced Jelborne, miserable and small. Capretta showed them the steep theatre of the anatomists and Jelborne curled his lips. Cambridge, he insisted, offered a better climate, finer buildings, more spacious rooms. Capretta shrugged and admitted he had never seen another university, but thought them overrated in general.

Cesare, following in their shadows, sidled up to Noon when Capretta and Jelborne entered the College of Physics.

'Do I trust him?' asked Cesare.

'Jelborne?' replied Noon.

'He holds the money, maybe he won't want me. I know what is said of Venice. I am a *vetturino*, there are no horses, no carriages. It is a city of water.'

'We'll not stay there for ever,' said Noon. 'We'll be in Florence, Rome, Naples. You will be much needed.'

Cesare shrugged. 'Work is work. I am earning and everything is good, God bless his soul.'

Noon felt that Cesare was necessary, a buffer between tutor and servant. He desired to placate the man, to keep him close.

'You have my word,' said Noon. 'If you do not trust Jelborne, then trust me. Without me, he cannot proceed. We are together, three as one.'

'Father, son, yes, I know,' smiled Cesare.

Noon sensed an oddness that he could not dismiss and it was to do with the weight of the clothes. At the inn at Il Dolo that evening all eyes had fallen on him instead of passing over, and to play his part he performed as Stilwell had done, imitating an unconsciousness of much of what happened around him. The innkeeper existed, but the stable hands were no concern of his; the porter did not warrant a glance for he was instructed by Cesare. Three children stood by the door to the inn and all bowed like automata as Noon and Capretta passed within.

'Welcome, sirs,' said the innkeeper and led them upstairs and into a pair of rooms.

It was the tidiest, most genteel inn Noon had ever seen. His room even had glass in its windows, not necessary for warmth in these last days of summer. Noon walked over to see if he could open it, but scraped a finger against the wood and brought it to his mouth, catching his reflection. With pomade in his hair and lace sprouting from his throat and framed in fine dark cloth, he might have been

a brother of Capretta. He did not look even faintly familiar. Despite the presence of Jelborne and his knowledge
of the country, Noon had never felt so alone. Stilwell's
loss would have been hard enough among English acres
but now it was magnified. Faced with his own reflection,
it seemed there was nowhere for a man to hide from his
grief.

Inglorious memories had evaporated in death and all
that Noon was left to consider was Stilwell's posthumous
radiance in comparison to his own anxious existence.
Noon perched on the edge of the bed and pushed his coat
and waistcoat from his shoulders. The heels of his hands
were pressed against his eyes, but his loneliness was cen-
tred in his stomach. It was a malevolent air and forced up
bubbles that were trapped at the base of his throat. The
only way he could calm himself was through deep breath
and idle thoughts. He considered the path of fish, thought
of Genoa, thought of Dengby, but Stilwell was not far
from even the most remote of Noon's memories. Noon
felt he was washed in sin, unworthy, unwilling to return.
And while dressing as a noble, calling on half his blood,
still felt a lie, it was preferable to the truth that waited in
England.

Jelborne entered without knocking.

'Not so good today, are we?' said the tutor, noting the
red eyes. 'I should not disturb sorrow.'

'This,' said Noon, pointing at his clothes. 'It sits
strange.'

'Of course,' said Jelborne, 'and will do for many
months. Life has changed, Thomas.'

Noon shook his head, as if to say that was abundantly clear.

The tutor sat close beside Noon. 'Do you know I was a church boy? My mother wanted me a preacher.'

'Can't imagine that.'

'A kind intention that at least provided an education.'

'And a belief?' asked Noon.

'Is most important to find a belief,' said Jelborne. 'You can build a life around a belief whether you believe in it or not.'

'And now an agent.'

'Now there is something you might work as. Don't you think? Yourself as an agent?'

'I like to know what others don't,' confessed Noon. 'I see the attraction in it, but all those wanting to know you, who you are, where you are, now that I would not like.'

'Do not worry about being watched,' said Jelborne. 'You can stand as close as skin to skin and they may not see you. I was in Edinburgh once, at a drum, and was intent on making love to this young lady. I had not known she was the wife of the man I'd been sent to observe and he challenged me to pistols.'

Noon smiled. 'What did you do?'

'I went to see the wife again that evening but the husband was home and I bluffed I had come to apologise. He sat me down for a drink or more, and on leaving his house I slipped down a dozen steps and broke an arm. He was so ashamed of our drunkenness that I stayed for two weeks in that house. I had his trust.'

'And his wife?'

'And hers too,' smiled Jelborne. 'You do not know when you are observed, so play your part strongly and do not doubt yourself. In your case, the lie of you is the truth of you. Enjoy life, Thomas, no matter what happens to others.'

CHAPTER NINE

The next morning, they drove south. Off to his right, Noon could see a range of mountains that accentuated the dull contours about them, still dressed in snow despite the warmth of the summer months. Every small house they passed had a roof loaded with pumpkins. Jelborne said the buildings looked like Scots: all ashen-face and fire-headed. At the gentlest rise in the land, they could see how the green fields rolled slowly away from them, down towards the lagoons, dotted with the bright white stone of villas and churches.

Outside of Padua, Capretta apologised for having to submit briefly to a form of public transport, a long black barge that would pass down the Brenta canal towards the lagoons of Venice. It was pulled by a team of horses whose hooves had long since dug a deep furrow along the tow-path. The banks of the canal were punctuated by lush gardens, the soil about the river's banks wet enough to have endured the sun. Behind the gardens lurked summer houses built for those citizens of Venice who did not like to venture far in the heat.

The four men sat towards the stern of the barge rather than join their fellow passengers under the aft awning. There was a slight turn in the canal just before it emptied into the lagoon, a turn sharp enough to obscure the gondolas that waited to meet the barge. They gathered like dogs at dinner, barking their offers and slipping through the water. Noon stared at their unfamiliar shapes, black prows like swans' necks, with their glass backs and black seats, and boatmen standing with poles in their hands, looking as sure-footed as any man on firm ground.

Capretta called out to a familiar face among them, who cried and pushed, battering his craft forward until it lay against the side of their barge. Cesare handed the gondolier Capretta's single piece of luggage and then stood watching as first Noon and then their host managed to board the slim vessel. Cesare had never been on open water before. He had not hesitated on entering the barge, but now, stepping into the gondola that seemed to shiver with every gentle slap of the sea, the *vetturino* looked uncomfortable. His arms were out, seeking balance, his knees bent as if he were walking on something thinner than rope. He sat in the bottom of the gondola and refused to help Jelborne with his portmanteau. Capretta laughed and offered the tutor his hand, and in one heave of the pole they slipped away from the barge.

The last gondolier of the watery flock called after them, causing Capretta to laugh.

'What does he say?' asked Noon, not grasping the quick burst of Venetian.

'That your silver is like manure,' laughed Capretta. 'Spread it and you will reap, keep it in one place and you will only notice the smell.'

'You must get used to this, milord,' said Jelborne. 'The Venetians can be familiar, no?'

'Everybody talks,' shrugged Capretta. 'It is what we like to do. Between the low and the golden it is easy, between everyone it is good. There are problems only between men with money and no family, and those with family and no money.'

As they glided across the lagoon towards the city, Jelborne and Capretta were laughing at Cesare's white-knuckled attempt to play the seafaring man and Noon's bulging eyes of disbelief. Entering the tail of the Grand Canal, Noon was transfixed by this city built on water. Such a possibility had never entered his mind. The gondolier pushed them west, then poled them around a dozen more gondolas and called greeting to them all. A thousand islands, thought Noon, all divided by these narrow strips of water, and all leading back to the Grand Canal. A man might swim from one appointment to the next. The canals ran like arteries, populated by these skinny vessels that pushed and poled their way against the high houses. Everything was built upwards on these cherished blocks of land. And the land rose to greet these houses, covering their bases in thick moss like solid fingers reaching from the sea.

Balconies hung above their heads as Stilwell had said

they would. Staring upwards, Noon could even see people peering over their rooftops. It was the form of movement that was so novel, this gliding, no jolting carriage or uneven steps: along these canals the water was smooth, not subject to waves or swells. They glided like summer insects across a pond. There were dozens of bridges, some of wood, some stone, even small spans of marble, arching their backs to allow the passage of gondolas. They led into dark, funnelled alleys that squeezed between buildings.

'Why was it built here?' Noon suddenly asked his host.

'Because no one would follow,' said Capretta with pride. 'Who would want to be subject to the sea?'

'Milord is fond of swimming,' said Jelborne.

Capretta seemed horrified at the idea. 'Not here,' he said. 'The tides only remove so much of our dirt. Our paths are water but they are gutters too. Take a boat to the islands, swim beyond the lagoon.'

The gondolier rapped his pole against the side of the craft to indicate their arrival.

'I shall leave you here,' said Capretta. 'Pay your hosts my respects.'

The men kissed twice in farewell while Cesare gathered their meagre belongings.

There was no more than a yard of paved stone between the travellers and their destination and Jelborne rapped on the door. The palazzo seemed old and beaten, flaking paints and battered shutters, creeping mosses and a door painted red then blue in one of the corners. The building stretched five stories out of the water, supported by stout neighbouring houses.

'Don't look so horrified, milord,' said Jelborne. 'Is a family rich in knowledge and respect. Had we come a hundred years ago, we would have been greeted as kings.'

'Why do they not keep themselves better?' asked Noon.

'They are Barnabotti, they do not keep themselves,' said Jelborne. 'They are penniless, kept by the republic.'

'Why are they kept at all?'

'Because of their blood,' said Jelborne. 'They were born into the Golden Book, the list of the oldest families in Venice, more important than the Bible. The book must be respected. Only the Barnabotti cannot marry.'

'There can be no heirs?'

'Only the illegitimate,' said Jelborne, 'and they are not supported by the republic.'

Noon nodded, once again feeling the odd balance of his position.

'Do not worry about our hosts,' smiled the tutor. 'The rest of the Barnabotti counter their poverty with an extraordinary conceit. These are good men and will wish to believe in you. Let them.'

The door opened and a man, whom Noon supposed a servant only because of his silence, dipped his head and waved them in, as if they were no more surprising than a delivery of wine. The entrance hall had high ceilings and polished wooden floors, buckled near the walls. There was a musty smell of wet wood rising beneath them.

'A week early, my friends,' said a voice in perfect English.

The three men looked above to a marble landing, from where a long figure had begun his descent.

Paolo Pisani looked to be about fifty and as he marched down the stairs, and it was a march, hands swinging at his sides, Noon saw that he was unnaturally tall. He loomed over his guests, thin and somewhat wilted, a kind, flat face balanced on a thin neck, a sunflower straining without sun. He was dressed similarly to Noon, though everything about him was more modest, the edges of his cuffs frayed, and even in these September days his clothes hinted at the drabness of winter grey. His waistcoat, which must have been a vibrant red in its early life, was faded like the well-worn seats of a carriage.

As he came to the bottom of the stairs, two more men appeared on the marble landing, younger than their host but so like him in stature and deportment that they could only be brothers. Their dress was simpler, black upon black in the even style of Venice, where sartorial uniformity hoped to disguise the vast differences in wealth.

'Welcome,' said the oldest.

'We hoped we were not too early in the season,' said Jelborne, 'and are happy to find you are at home.'

'A year has changed us, Mr Jelborne,' said their host. 'We have leased our country house to an acquaintance and have suffered through a summer in this city. And this young man, the son?'

Noon made to bow, but was raised and kissed once upon each cheek. The process was repeated with the two other brothers.

'And your father, sir, how does he fare?'

'Very well, thank you,' said Noon. Again, he was uncertain. Noon worried that there was a secret language of breeding, an international tongue that he had not learned, that had, despite his years of observation, somehow eluded him. Errors, he hoped, would be attributed to the difference in their countries and not the impurities of his blood.

'He is in England?'

'Yes, sir,' said Noon. 'At Dengby.'

'I do not think,' said Pisani, 'that the difference in our age is so great that you must address me so. I am Paolo and you, I know, are George. You have tales to tell I see,' continued their host, 'for how to explain how a man might arrive dressed already as an inhabitant?'

Jelborne laughed. 'We have a long tale to tell. Have even lost a servant along the way.'

'To the waters?'

'No, no,' said Jelborne, 'to the Mantuans. Murdered, I regret.'

Their host shook his head sadly. 'There is no guarantee, except here. I will look after you myself. We shall stay well together. And how did you travel here?'

'We relied on the kindness of Capretta. We are, I would say, indebted to him.'

'The cattle merchant?' said the host. 'At least, then, the debt is digestible.'

Jelborne and Noon were shown upstairs by their concerned host, who immediately sent out a note to his tailors to gather the next day. He offered them any garments that might make them more comfortable. The house, like their host, had the benefit of being tall, but with the three brothers and their servant there was only a single room reserved for guests and Jelborne and Noon were to share it. Pisani apologised once more for the further dip in his own fortunes and blamed a poor season at the Ridotto, where all three of the brothers worked for the republic. His percentage of the bank had been reduced on the very last day of the carnival by a papal emissary.

'It is hard enough to lose money to men,' said Pisani, 'but to lose to God in a game invented by the devil, it is the sort of thing a Venetian should take to heart.'

'Has it turned you into a believer?' asked Jelborne, smiling.

'I pray only for luck,' said Pisani.

Their chatter continued pleasantly enough, their host asking them to relate the tale of their servant, which Jelborne did with such sadness and grace that Noon found himself impressed and melancholy. What faith this poor fellow had displayed, how he had resisted the robbers out of honour when perhaps prudence would have saved him, and how he would be missed at Dengby. Though, confessed Jelborne, they had not yet sent news to the marquis for milord wished to tell the man's family himself.

'You seem saddened?' Pisani asked Noon.

'I had known him from my birth,' said Noon. 'I miss him every day.'

'They say in Venice,' replied Pisani, 'about the death of the young, that they are sent ahead of us to God to sing the path and clear the ways for our own coming. We call them "family advocates". I am glad, however,' he continued, 'that you are still with us.'

Their host turned to Jelborne. 'Did you lose letters?'

'No, no,' said the tutor. 'The incident was pure misfortune. No premeditation, I assure you, simply brigands.'

'Perhaps they were merely clumsy,' considered Pisani, 'poor in their work.'

'Then we have even less to worry about.'

At these words, Pisani turned and left the two men in their sparse room: two beds and a washstand, a basin of lukewarm water, a cloth to dry themselves and a cabinet for the clothes they did not have. Beside the washstand was a small parcel of letters. They both walked towards it, the tutor raising the package in his hand and weighing it, as if he might guess at its contents.

'Perhaps I too should read it,' said Noon.

Jelborne cocked his head at his charge. 'You wish to enter deeper?'

'How can I not? Who plays the role must learn the part.'

'Very well,' said Jelborne, 'let us see.'

The first piece of paper that Jelborne pulled out was a promissory note for five hundred pounds, over ten years of Thomas Noon's wages. It might be drawn from either of two bankers in Venice. Jelborne handed it to Noon, who held it before him. While Noon studied the note Jelborne pulled a letter from the wallet. He broke the seal and began to read.

'From the marquis,' said Jelborne. 'Merely an extended list of names of those we must talk with, though this is the only city we shall ever visit where they will seek you out.'

'How can they seek us if they do not know we are here?'

Jelborne smiled. 'Tomorrow I shall take you to San Marco as a part of your education. There is a box there, inside the mouth of a stone lion. Venice employs her own web of agents within the city: all that is seen is reported, messages dropped into the lion's mouth. There will be a dozen concerning our movements by the end of the day.'

'Does it not worry you?' asked Noon. 'Perhaps they shall find things.'

'Why?' said Jelborne. 'Already, they know who I am, they think they know who you are. The council may not entirely approve of our actions, they do not like money leaving this city. You can't expect a Venetian to be moved by faith to part with money. The only thing they believe in is investment. Investment in the name of faith; perhaps it buys them a better pew in God's country. They are traders, more so even than the English.'

'Will we find enough for my father?' asked Noon and Jelborne looked him hard in the eye to hear him use the term.

'Should they think King James a likely figure, or even more preferable to German George, then they will find a way to fund us, heavily I would expect.'

That night, in his high-ceilinged room, Noon could not sleep, Jelborne disturbing him with uneven grunts and splutters. The tutor smelled of musty sleep. The dampness of the city had spread upwards from the wooden pilings and moist flakes of paint curled from the walls. Noon lay abed with the window open and fought for rest, turning on his front and then his back, one side then the other, until the sheet had wound itself about his body. Eventually, he gave in and walked to the open window, leaving the tangle of bedclothes behind him. Beneath him he could hear the lapping waters and the occasional burst of laughter that carried to him clean. No wonder, he thought, that this is a city of rumour when a whispered word might cross a stretch of water and emerge as loud again. What might a city be if everyone were acquainted with each other's sins? Were they all forgiven together, or were some sins heavy enough to sink a man?

CHAPTER TEN

The next morning they joined their host on the rooftop for breakfast. The sun was barricaded by thick cloud and the breeze so slight it would not have lifted a single sheet of paper from the table. A letter for Jelborne lay beneath a glass jar.

'Proof,' said Jelborne, sliding the letter from under the jar, 'of the infallibility of rumour.'

Noon laughed gently. 'Who is it from?'

'Perhaps our friend Capretta,' said Jelborne. 'He has already placed his hand in the lion's mouth and writes to confess. Or certainly babbled so strong that others are aware of our arrival.'

'What will the council know,' asked Pisani, 'had Capretta written of your journey?'

'The council,' said Noon, 'will now be most familiar with the soil of Dengby. They will now be as familiar as a farm hand with the marquis's hedgerows and his irrigation, they will know his crops, perhaps guess at his income.'

Pisani laughed. 'Of all your choices in conversation, you choose to wave soil under a Venetian's nose? A city of water and he tempts him with land.' He dabbed a handkerchief about his mouth and dipped his eyes at the unread letter. 'If friends know you arrived today, then foes knew yesterday.'

'You do not have to frighten the boy,' smiled Jelborne.

'He should know,' said Pisani, 'that there is danger is this business.'

'He has already proved himself resilient.'

Pisani squeezed Noon's wrist as he stood. 'Trust not at all and begin with me.'

As he left, Jelborne slit the seal with a knife.

'It is from a friend of your father's,' said Jelborne, reading, 'an Englishman called Silver, who asks us to dine with him.'

'What manner of man is he?' asked Noon.

'A trader,' said Jelborne. 'We shall meet him again in Naples, when he shall carry us home. He has a part in many ships, perhaps half a dozen by now. And tonight we shall dress well,' insisted the tutor, 'for you shall meet his daughter.'

'And of what value is that?' asked Noon.

'To you,' said Jelborne, 'perhaps none, but I may take her as my wife.'

Noon smiled for the first time in days. 'You have known her long?'

'I have met her before,' said Jelborne coyly, 'some years

ago, when she was still a child, but now her father wishes her well married.'

Noon didn't say a word, but Jelborne challenged him with a defensive look. 'My work apart,' said Jelborne, 'I am a man of surprising wealth.'

'You are a *surprising* man,' said Thomas Noon, 'rich or poor.' Jelborne smiled broadly, warmed by the compliment.

Their gondolier pushed his craft between the others, his fellow watermen allowing him the space to unload his foreign passengers. The Campanile stretched above them, the Doge's Palace to their right, a huge rectangular cake of rose-coloured marble all resting atop a two-storied arcade. It seemed to weigh too much for such slim legs and made Noon think of his tutor's physique. On the capitals sat Adam and Eve draped by their modest fig leaves. In front of them lay the piazza of San Marco which Noon at once considered a terrible waste of land and then immediately recognised as a breath of space within a city where there was no room to breathe. He knew that no matter how much he delighted in swimming under the water, he had always to return to the surface – and this was San Marco, where all Venice gathered for air.

There were many eyes in the piazza: the stone lion with its muted glance, those arrogant bronze horses and the high tower from where a man could see into a thousand rooms. Noon felt nude before all this. He thought his Italian clothes might fall from him and Jelborne abandon him and Cesare return through the air to horse and carriage. And then, who would he be? Alone on this earth, miles from familiar hills and handshakes and perhaps not even welcome should he ever return with the truth.

Jelborne put an arm around his shoulder as any tutor with a muddled student might do and walked Noon once around the piazza, returning the odd greeting and leading his charge up the tight and winding staircase of the Campanile. It was nearly midday and they looked out at the Lido, a precious strip of land that enclosed the lagoons. Beyond it lay the sea. The lagoons held sloops, frigates, galleys and other sails pushing across the horizon. North and west were the hills of Padua and Vicenza and the Tirolean Alps. It was a full world again, not one that Noon had imagined since he had stood before the docks in Genoa and watched the English sailors sit astride the yards.

'We are an effect,' whispered Jelborne to him. 'We must play our parts well now. I am proud of you. You look well in your suit.'

'I do?'

'The only eyes that follow you,' said Jelborne, 'belong to women.'

So they walked down in tight circles and entered the dark cold cathedral, then walked up to her roof and stared down in the piazza, like many visitors before them.

'There is much waiting for us here,' said Jelborne. 'You see before you a hundred men of no consequence, fifty of some wealth, and a handful powerful enough to buy men's souls. We are here for them.'

From their perch, Noon watched the array of clothes chosen by the different classes. The aristocrats, forbidden to wear bright colours, kept their golds and silvers, scarlets and roses close to the skin and draped themselves in black. And yet, from this height, it was apparent to Noon that they had all found ways to obey and defy the laws simultaneously. These black drapes, which Jelborne called *taborros*, were often carried insolently over one shoulder, like a bothersome cloud that dared to meddle with the sun.

They descended and took a brief turn inside the church of San Marco, walking under the dusky glow of the mosaics that divided vault from vault and brought such a shimmer to their surface that it reminded Noon of water. It was a church crowned with a series of domes, the greatest of which even held a picture of God himself with his apostles seated beneath. The three men walked past a pair of red marble lions, poised before helpless sheep. But still, no matter the skill of those who had worked on these strips of land, there was nothing that could compare to her waters.

With equal relief, tutor and student left the church and took seats about a small table in the Venetian Triumphant Café that spilled out into the square, so many tables and chairs that Noon could not imagine them inside the tiny shop. Perhaps, he thought, they were never moved and on the high tides that Jelborne had described merely floated around San Marco and rearranged themselves for better views. He did not know quite how to sit, but watched Jelborne make himself comfortable and then imitated the tutor's slouch.

All sorts sat about them, both labourers and gentlemen sipping at coffees, others who sucked at ices. Jelborne and Noon faced one another while Cesare wandered about the piazza looking for a countryman to listen to his tales. They had not been five minutes together when a well-dressed stranger approached their table and stared at the tutor oddly. Jelborne looked up at him, then down again at his coffee, in obvious discomfort that he should be stared at so. Without a word, the stranger fell on Jelborne with a hug of such sincerity and two such scorching kisses that other tables turned to watch. For the first time in their acquaintance, Noon could see only puzzlement on Jelborne's face. The stranger pulled a chair to their table, sat on it and laughed.

'You do not remember me?' he asked.

Jelborne looked at him intently. 'I am ashamed to say I do not.'

'No reason for shame,' said the man, 'only happiness.' He was excited, but was making an effort to whisper. If he truly had something of import to say Jelborne wished that he might have chosen a more discreet setting. But to rise and lead this man away without even knowing who he was would only send a dozen hands scribbling for the lion's mouth.

'It is my dress,' said the man. 'One year ago I could barely afford a shirt and now when I look at myself in the glass I always thank you.'

He glanced at Noon. 'I may speak openly, of course?'

Jelborne shrugged because he could not imagine what the stranger might say. 'I wish that you would.'

The stranger leaned in and Jelborne bowed his head towards him. Noon looked about them nervously.

'You saw me a year ago,' he whispered. 'You had come from Padua and you had carried some marks of Venus, down below.'

'Aahhhh,' smiled the tutor, 'and you were the skinny young doctor friend of our gondolier.'

'It is I,' said the doctor and rose to kiss the tutor one more time. 'You left Venice and I thought I would never have the chance to thank you. You passed the pox to Signora Borsatti and from her it went to Angelo Tiepolo and from him it became one a week, and then a pair, then four, then dozens. I was paid again and again. And now it is gone, but I am established and am in favour.'

'I am afraid I have nothing for you this visit,' laughed Jelborne.

'And I trust that you shall find nothing here that you have not already encountered,' smiled the doctor, 'but should there be troubles I am at your service and my service is free.'

'Too kind,' said Jelborne and the man rose to kiss him one final time. He waved and walked south towards the Campanile.

'Forever helping out the young,' smiled Jelborne to Noon.

'And your wife-to-be,' whispered Noon. 'I wonder if your fame is the only thing to have spread to her.'

The afternoon was spent back in the district of St Barnabas where a trio of tailors arrived in separate gondolas, all equally disappointed to see the shabbiness of their destination and all greatly pleased to see the well-dressed young Englishman and his tutor. They brought with them a selection of winter-weight cloths, a smattering of ideas should the visitors intend to stay for carnival and a healthy rivalry that helped keep their prices a touch below the rapacious. Jelborne ordered a pair of dark English suits, black, short-cuffed and double-tailed, while he encouraged Noon to add a further four suits to his own collection. A pair would have the wide cuffs of the Venetians and the second two were thinner, more popular in Rome, one of which would be made from a deep sea blue.

The tailors had brought dress coats with them for Noon to try and one fitted vaguely enough to cause chirps of admiration and promises of improvement. Looking upon Noon had an odd effect on Jelborne, who had always thought of the servant as workmanlike and heavy-boned. He realised now that Noon was becoming accustomed to these finer silks, and in turn was enhanced by his clothes. They had clearly changed the man's behaviour. Jelborne remembered Noon's discomfort with Capretta's Paduan tailor armed with his clothes pins, and now there he stood, with one man kneeling and measuring the cut of his leg and another stretching a cord to note the breadth of his back, showing little surprise. In fact, it was plain to the tutor that the servant's mind was entirely elsewhere.

The three Pisani brothers were most gracious in their absence. Noon had thought it awkward to bring their riches into such a humble house, but he did not yet understand the Venetians. The oldest families remembered wealth as something so distant that it was no longer trusted. To the brothers, Noon deserved his money and suits, if only because of his youth. Perhaps he would also find in time that the fortunes of even the greatest could wane. They had no objection, not even to Jelborne's recommendation that Cesare be made a simple suit of green livery.

That evening, Thomas Noon, Jelborne and Cesare stepped aboard a gondola and were poled slowly to the Grand Canal until they rocked before a small palazzo, painted blue and gilded by the setting sun. It was the sometime house of Martin Silver, rented from a fading family for half of every year. Not the six long months of the carnival, when Venice was filled with visitors from afar, but for the heat of the summer, when fine weather enabled Silver to use Venice as his base in trading along the Aegean seaboard. The palazzo was neither modest nor grandiose among its neighbours but set a little back from the canal as if it feared the water. They knocked upon the door and a pair of servants pulled it open. It was a show of wealth rather than strength, since the hinges swung so effortlessly that a breath of wind might have performed the same service.

Martin Silver was a short man, knock-kneed and fond of standing with both hands behind his back and his chest forward, holding himself at an aggressive tilted angle as if he were the captain of one of his own ships rather than just the dominant investor. Silver's head was large and his skin weather-beaten from spending months as a passenger on deck and the days in-between always exposed to coastal weather.

He shook His Lordship by the hand. He had been shy, perhaps for the first time in his life, before the marquis the previous year, but having dealt deferentially with the parent and found him direct, he saw no reason to scrape before the son.

'You're a better-built man than your father gives you credit for.'

'A year at that age,' said Jelborne, 'can turn a body.'

'It can,' said Silver. 'When I was a boy and wished to hide, I'd turn sideways and strangers would pass me by. Now look at me.' He patted himself in the stomach to show just how solid he had become.

Noon smiled appreciatively.

'Milord,' explained Jelborne, 'is now a familiar with his father and knows as much as any man as to our intentions.'

Silver looked him up and down as if he might see the truth but was interrupted by the approach of footsteps and raised a fingers to his lips that were now parted in a comfortable smile.

Noon had known she would be young, but had not presumed she would be much younger than him. At twenty-two, he was many years her senior. There was a doll-like clarity to Silver's daughter, pale-skinned and slight, brown hair tinged with redness and worn in a chignon held with silver pins. She did not dress like the women he had yet encountered, but seemed behind the fashion despite wearing the finest material, coloured like a harvest moon. She was slim and filled with fire and it was apparent from a dozen yards. Her nose was a little wide, her eyes too interested, and her neck was long and designed for jewellery though she wore none. There was an inquisitiveness to her, not simply her youth, but an avian curiosity that was half the dove and half the hawk and it fascinated Noon at once.

'This,' said Silver, 'is my daughter Natalia. She is with me for a week or two.'

'Why so short a time?' Jelborne asked the girl.

'She may join her mother in Parma or accompany me on my travels,' answered Silver. 'Either way, we shall all meet again in Naples in December.'

She had opened her mouth to speak and then closed it again, lips pursed against her father and his will to speak for her. Instead, she bowed quietly before both men and Silver stood aside as if he were presenting a gift that should, for a moment, be admired. There are many eyes called beautiful, blue serenity or mournful grey, but Natalia's were coloured with exhortations. Noon could see the hatred of boredom and an intense dislike of everything to which she had become accustomed. Her eyes passed over him, he knew he had no effect on her whatsoever, and was in some way grateful that he should escape notice. Instead she was staring at Jelborne as if she refused to judge this man on age alone, or on his bulky body, smirk or heavy brow.

'This is not your first time in Venice?' she enquired of Jelborne.

119

'No, my dear,' said the tutor. 'We have met before, though I think you are too young to remember.'

'I suppose,' she said simply and Noon smiled because her choice of words was neither polite nor impolite, but withdrawn and waited in judgement.

Having an English father and Italian mother and having been raised everywhere except England had left the girl with a peculiar accent, not the singing Italian, nor the lisp of Spain, but a unique confusion, exotic to Noon's ear. She bowed to him and he smiled, but she had greeted Jelborne with greater warmth as if he were not so distant from her world as a lord might be. He wondered what she might make of Thomas Noon. Would he have been seen as a trusted servant, or not seen at all, invisible again?

As quickly and quietly as she had been ushered in, so her father signalled for her to leave. Within the family she was apparently still a child and would not be joining the three men for their supper. Silver talked of his interests in a dozen ships. He was the source of the freshest information that flowed from the sea lanes about the globe.

As a monied man he was fond of the occasional extravagance, as if to emphasise his usual modesty, though really to remind himself of how far he had risen. He was no longer fond of Englishmen, though full-blooded himself, and had married an Italian of small wealth and great beauty whom he had succeeded first in wooing, then in ignoring for nearly twenty years. In some ways he was even embarrassed of his daughter, knowing that he had made someone much finer than himself. Though he liked to show her to his guests, he remained uncomfortable in her presence. He was happiest in business, the more complicated the better. It was not simply a question of money, but of gambling against others. He regarded his acquaintance with Jelborne as a vital addition to his store of knowledge, a card up his sleeve that in a year might double his worth should they both interpret Europe's sway correctly.

'It has happened already and is no surprise,' said Silver, 'but the throne is German. If only England were more like Venice.'

'Past caring?' asked Jelborne.

'Past action,' said Silver. 'Patient.'

'And losing land, losing respect, spectating?'

'Considerate and open,' said Silver. 'The Venetian Republic is the only Catholic country on God's earth that has yet to burn a heretic.'

'Because they would not waste their wood,' said Jelborne. 'And now we are pressed with a king who speaks not a word of English. Does that not bother you, milord?' asked Jelborne, turning to Noon.

'Seems more fit for theatre,' said Noon, happy to join the conversation. He was beginning to grow easy in Silver's company, though his eyes were turned towards the door in expectation of Natalia's return.

Martin Silver shook his head. 'We've moved too slow,' he said. 'Had the queen lived another year, then perhaps.'

'Nonsense,' said Jelborne. 'All expected George, this is what we have known and now at least it is sure. Our concern is no longer speed, but certainty. We are the old story where every pound we collect before us will swing the scales. It shall not continue as it is.' Jelborne shook his head.

'You are wanted,' said Silver, jabbing a finger towards Jelborne. 'It is fresh news. They do not know about His Lordship but they'll not wish you stirring things now.'

'They know me?' asked Jelborne. 'By name, they are sure of it?'

'No,' said Martin Silver, 'but there is rumour in the new court.'

'There is always rumour in a court,' said Jelborne. 'Without rumour there could be no court.'

'They think you in Germany beneath their noses, but there are enough about this place to find you. And in this city of all cities, nothing is safe. You will be better on road or sea.'

'And road and sea,' said Jelborne, 'are but those things that separate the promise of one bank from another. We must stay a while.'

'They are looking,' said Silver. 'The marquis is still safe at home. There is no danger in that and thus no danger in him.' He pointed at Noon. 'Keep him close to you. He is your greatest ally.'

'We work well together,' said Jelborne smiling, 'do we not, milord?'

'Well enough,' said Noon softly.

'Keep it sure,' said Silver. 'Even here. Go see a thousand churches, take your ices with these golden fools.'

'And you?' asked Jelborne.

'You are not the only busy man,' said Silver. 'I sail and bring money from along the coast. We will do well this season.'

The confirmation that he was hunted, Stilwell's death apart, came as no surprise to Jelborne. There was, in some respects, a code between agents where identity was presumed and then protected. Should a man be accused, or worse, flushed out and murdered, it was likely that his replacement would be much harder game to find. The talent came in disguising your own effectiveness and in this Jelborne was without equal. His bluffness, his lechery and apparent drunkenness combined with his new position of tutor had held him low in others' estimations. He was not worried, nor would he be until tracked by name. Jelborne satisfied himself that he was in no more danger than usual.

Martin Silver called his daughter back after dinner and asked for her to sing. She did not protest, but it was apparent to all but her father that Natalia's voice was a poor one and her performance was given grudgingly. Afterwards she bowed to the polite clap of hands and sat patiently with the three men, allowing her father to pontificate without interruption on the current constituents of Venice's Council of Ten. He described those who had been favourable to his business, who held percentages of his profits, and those he had come to fear.

Natalia stood and walked to the window while Jelborne and Silver switched their conversation to the concept that republics and monarchies were no more different than two hats sitting on the same head. Noon wandered outside to relieve himself against the outer wall of the house. He spread his feet far apart and avoided the puddle that gathered between. On returning, he walked to join Natalia by the window rather than steer straight towards the low rumbles of the two older men. *I am a lord, I am Stilwell, I will do as he would wish to do, I must play my part even as I learn it.*

'Why do you not talk to me?' asked Noon.

'I was not addressed,' she replied.

'I know you are not shy,' said Noon, 'but you are shy with me.'

'With no one,' she said, 'but I'll not speak for the sake of hearing my voice.'

'Perhaps you should,' said Noon, 'for it is a pretty voice.'

She winced on his behalf and he apologised for the crudeness of his flattery and immediately she warmed to him.

'Why did you say that?' she asked.

'I wish you to like me,' said Noon.

'Because I am pretty to you?' she asked.

'I hear there are a thousand beauties in Venice,' said Noon, his confidence returning, 'but you look to me something deeper than mere ornament.'

'Perhaps then,' replied Natalia, 'because I may be intended for your tutor.'

'I feel you are intended for no one except the man you choose.'

She smiled.

'I speak plainly,' he continued.

'And you have never told a lie?'

'I'd not say that.'

'And what manner of lies do you tell?' asked Natalia. 'Lies to your father, to your tutor, to yourself?'

'Or just to young women?'

'Well?'

'All these and more.'

'You are stranger than I thought,' said Natalia with great consideration, and turned her back on him as if he had been an exhibit, blue-veined marble, that did not have the power to follow her. She returned to sit by her father and after a moment Noon deposited himself in the chair next to his tutor. Over the next hour, they swapped no more than a few glances of mutual boredom. To Noon it was a communication. She had smiled at him once, as if to say, I know you care no more for this than I do, and he wondered what they would talk of if they were ever to find themselves alone. What would she say if she knew the truth of him?

CHAPTER ELEVEN

'What did you think of Natalia?' asked Jelborne, as they walked the following morning across a wooden footbridge to take their coffee in San Marco. Cesare followed behind them, already outfitted in a forest-green livery, proud of his new duds and a glaring symbol of their foreignness. Noon had done nothing but think of Natalia. He had stayed up all night listening to the cries of the gondoliers singing between the percussion of his tutor's snores, wondering if she might pass beneath with her father.

'I thought her a great beauty,' said Noon, staring down at his feet.

'And too young for me no doubt,' laughed Jelborne.

'She is rather, fresh,' said Noon.

'And I a prune?' laughed Jelborne.

'No, sir,' continued Thomas Noon, 'it is just that she is barely a day from childhood and you are . . .'

'. . . barely a step from the grave?'

Noon managed a laugh. 'You cannot deny that there are many years between you.'

'Many indeed,' said Jelborne, 'and it is not that which dissuades me.'

'Dissuades?'

'I see your eyes. I watched you talk with her a while. Perhaps there will be something between you and perhaps not. She's too bright a flame for me to face. I'd wear horns before my marriage bed was cold.'

'You think her unfaithful?'

'I think her aware,' said Jelborne. 'Beauty is a gift, grace is a gift, speech is a gift and sirens have all three. But she watches, Noon, and knows men already, I would wager on it.'

'She has been taken?' asked Noon incredulously.

'No, not taken perhaps, but she has watched the likes of you and I before. She knows men for the pawns that they are.'

'She is not eighteen.'

'All the worse, the only grace being that she thinks she plays a game that has never been played at before. We may not be as sharp as them,' said Jelborne, 'but men have an instinct and it works once and then any woman of power will dizzy you.'

Noon walked quietly in pace with his tutor.

'And worse,' said Jelborne, 'you will not let yourself be wrong. Once in love you will insist on your love when hers is long gone and you shall soon sprout horns of your own.'

'I have barely said a dozen words to the girl and you

speak of love.' Noon bristled. 'Besides, I am what I am. We both know this.'

'Exactly,' said Jelborne. 'You are of *mixed* blood, so please stop presuming that you are tied to a life of servitude. She is only a merchant's daughter, no matter the wealth.'

Noon considered this for a moment, then asked, 'Have you worn horns before?'

'Worn them?' cried Jelborne. 'I discovered them. I found them in Paris and Dresden and Glasgow and if any of those women still breathe, hags as they may now be, I wish them buried in a dirt grave.'

'I did not know you felt so strongly about women.'

'Not women, you fool,' said Jelborne. 'I am most fond of women. I am talking only of love.'

They divided their time over the next two days between their patient hosts and Martin Silver. It seemed that the two younger Pisani brothers were prisoners to the house, while only Paolo walked the streets in pursuit of unknown interests. Jelborne guessed it was either a mistress or meetings with his fellow aristocrats to gather the only other financial income available to a noble, the ability to sell his vote. Still, it was rare that all three brothers were not present as the contingent of foreigners came and went. With Silver the talk inevitably returned to money and to its obtainment, and together with Jelborne the merchant drew up lists of those they deemed most approachable on behalf of their exiled king. Noon said little at these meetings and felt very much like a greatcoat that was vital in the street but once indoors was laid upon a chair and ignored. It bothered him little, for he was grateful enough to be brought along and thrived at the sight of, and his small chances to talk with, Natalia.

The few walks that Noon took alone plagued his mind. He already knew how Venice encouraged noise: her street corners were filled with it, her waters amplified it and her people constantly contributed to the cacophony. But for every tongue there were two ears and two feet that seemed to follow Noon wherever he went. Despite waiting in alcoves, doubling back on himself, Noon could not confirm if these phantoms were physical or illusory. At times shadows seemed as slight as Capretta, as stretched as Pisani, as corpulent as Jelborne or as spry as Stilwell. *If I am followed*, thought Noon, *am I followed because I am Stilwell, or because they know me to be Noon?*

He knew that both the elder men observed the attention that he paid Natalia, or at least wished to pay her, and rather than discourage it they seemed content to parry by keeping the two apart. It was to his great surprise, while plotting in his head how he might forge more than a minute of the girl's time for himself, that the question was raised by Jelborne as they prepared to retire for the evening. Jelborne was not shy about his body and undressed before Noon as openly as he would have done before a dog. His heavy paunch was brushed with fair hair and his balls swung low between his thin legs, outdistancing the length of his cock. He bent his knees to rearrange himself and watched Noon undress.

'Thomas,' he asked, 'would you like to accompany Natalia to the theatre?'

Noon paused while releasing the buckle of one of his shoes. 'You do not mind?'

'We are in Italy,' said Jelborne, 'so let us behave for once as Italians. I am not green-eyed, you may pay her all the attention you can, she is young and will thrive, but keep your hide tough.'

Noon did not know what to say but hoped that his face was free from sinful intentions. He did not quite trust Jelborne, despite his knowledge of the tutor. He wondered what the motive behind such a question was, if he wished him absent so that he could keep him from the marquis's business. Noon pulled the shoe from his foot and scratched his sole through his stockings. 'But what of Martin Silver?'

'He thinks he knows you,' laughed Jelborne, 'and perhaps he does. So whatever you be, he has decided to trust you.'

'How can that be?' asked Noon.

Jelborne laughed at him. 'Perhaps he shouldn't. Why, tell me what you believe he thinks.'

'Perhaps he does not mind the title I bear, perhaps he now thinks me more suitable a suitor than yourself. Perhaps he does not wish to tell you that.'

'I think you are correct,' said Jelborne. 'So let us both take some amusement from this. You may have your evening of entertainment and I may have my smile. She may walk with her lord, and Silver will congratulate himself on his upward manoeuvring. It will merely be an act of happiness committed four times over.'

'Is he not your friend?' asked Noon.

'We work as one,' said Jelborne, 'and there are matters I trust him greatly in. Friends? Now there is a slight word for grand intention. It's better to count your friends at the end of your life when you know who has stood by and who has fallen.'

Noon must have looked puzzled by the answer, for Jelborne added, 'I did not mean your lord. He was a good man and a friend to you, across whatever lines your father drew between you. Death shouldn't destroy a friendship, but should settle it.'

He gave Noon a wide smile, as if to say he had not meant to talk of such grave matters. 'Now,' said Jelborne, 'you will need money for her entertainment.' He walked to the dresser and reached into his purse, pulling two hundred zecchini from it and handing them to Noon.

'I'll not need half of it,' said Noon, looking at the large sum before him.

'You'll not need any of it,' laughed Jelborne, 'but she might wish double that and more. Shall we attend to your education?'

After a short stroll they ended up back in San Marco, sipping at coffee and waiting for their ices. Just as they were pushed on the table in front of them, Jelborne nudged Noon with his foot and said, 'There is our man. The end of mystery.'

Noon looked up to see an unpresuming face of middle age, with a heavy stubble that probably shaded him an hour from the barber's door. He might have been Italian, or perhaps Spanish, and had a modest tilt to his black eyes as if deference were central to his trade.

'Who is he?' asked Noon.

'Look away,' said Jelborne, his tongue lapping at the ice, 'and I shall tell you.'

Noon obeyed. 'Is he Italian?'

'A very poor Catholic,' smiled Jelborne. 'A Portuguese by birth, though he will answer to the name of the Chevalier de Montpassant and pretend himself French or Milanese.'

'How do you know him?' asked Noon.

'We are suspicious of one another,' continued Jelborne. 'In Paris. I wonder what he is thinking. He will talk to you, you know. He will find you alone at one point or another. We shall be careful.'

'Is he dangerous?' Noon let the lemon ice melt in his mouth.

'Shadows don't harm a man,' said Jelborne, 'but in the sun they often betray his position.'

'What do we do?'

'Engage him, avoid him,' said Jelborne. 'Bluff him and confuse him. We will see him often, he will make sure of it. Let us walk south now.'

Noon sent Cesare to Silver's house the next morning, bidding him to wait for an answer to his invitation for Natalia's presence at theatre in San Moise that evening. Cesare arrived back an hour later. The note held no extra scent of promise other than a simple acceptance.

'Did she say anything?' asked Noon.

'No,' said Cesare.

'Did she pay you?'

Cesare smiled and let out a small laugh. 'Very well.'

'Why are you laughing?' asked Noon.

'I am enjoying myself,' said Cesare. 'All this is not such a strain as horses. Venice is easy. And to watch you play at money. While we talk of it, I believe I need more.'

'More?' asked Noon.

Cesare shrugged. 'This is good for all of us. But I have met this woman. She is more money than I have. I want her. You have yours, I want mine. You are one servant, I am another, we are not so different.'

'Are you in love?' smiled Noon.

Cesare laughed again. 'It has just been a while for me. Ten zecchini. That is all I want.'

When Noon passed this information to Jelborne, the tutor sighed as if it had been expected, but ten zecchini was a modest enough amount and Cesare seemed content with the ease of his life and so the money was handed over without hesitation. It was at least of comfort to Jelborne that all had become occupied in their own worlds.

'Life,' he sighed to Noon, 'is becoming complicated.'

'You are worried?'

'Preparing myself with a deep breath,' said Jelborne, 'for I was born to juggle.'

The first of Noon's suits had arrived in time for his evening, made of dark blue silk that he brightened with a shirt the colour of a summer sky. It took his plain blue eyes and gave them richness. Even Jelborne commented appreciatively on the finery of his dress. Noon walked alone to Martin Silver's house and, greeted at the door by a servant, was slightly bewildered to find Natalia wearing the same dress she had worn the night they had first met. Beautiful as it was, he had expected her to make an effort of innovation on his behalf. Still, it suited her so well that he could not imagine that she would look any finer, her hair well marked against the orange silk. She looked up at Noon. He had forgotten how small she was. Her skin was pale yet olive-hued, as if even a day in slight sun would darken it.

Her green eyes were noting full well the improvement and effort in his dress and they seemed amused as if enough had been revealed to confirm her suspicions. Natalia was a smirker and this he liked, because there had been a thousand times he had wanted to grin at the foolishness about him. She felt no such inhibitions. They were greeted outside the door by a linkboy, his torch already lit though the sun had not yet died. Noon paused a moment to admire her slender shadow.

After they had walked a minute or two, taking turns that already had the Englishman disorientated, he turned to comment, 'I believed that Venetian women did not walk the street.'

'I am not Venetian,' she replied. They paused and so did the linkboy who stood patiently ten yards before them. In the gutter, his flame revealed the sleeping shadow of a pig.

'Shall we speak in English or Italian?' she asked. 'Or Spanish?'

'Perhaps it is best with that which we both know well. English.'

'Did you tell your tutor of our meeting?' she asked.

'I did,' said Noon.

'You're an honest man,' she said, 'and not the liar you promised me.'

'But we have known each other so little,' smiled Noon, beginning to enjoy himself. At her age, he reckoned, she would have little knowledge of English lords. He could not be measured against memories.

'What does your tutor think of me?' she asked. 'He has no taste for me, does he? I could see it at once.'

'He thinks you fickle,' said Noon. 'That you were spoiled by coins and that you will prove too young for me.'

Natalia seemed shocked by the accusation. 'I am not sure I have ever been judged so hard.'

'He is a tutor,' assuaged Noon. 'Their trade is to judge and then impart their knowledge.'

'Why would you choose to walk with me?' asked Natalia.

'For the same reasons,' said Noon. 'Because you are young and fickle and perhaps you shall change for me.'

'You are very confident,' laughed Natalia.

'I am as strong as oak,' boasted Noon and she gripped his arm to see.

'Another truth, milord,' she smiled.

'Do not call me that,' said Noon. 'I would rather that you call me by no name than by that.'

'Very well,' said Natalia, 'then we shall pretend our-selves equals.'

'You will lower yourself?' smiled Noon.

'Yes, I will,' said Natalia and held her silence most disconcertingly.

The narrow streets were still crowded in the early evening, forcing the couple to pause occasionally to let others step by. Most were attended by their own linkboys and, always, Noon could see the flame first and then the shadows that danced behind. No noble women passed. They rode instead under the covered gondolas and Natalia's willingness to walk pleased him. It displayed an openness quite contrary to the nature that Jelborne suspected. Noon stood the lack of conversation for a minute or two, but it seemed more deliberate than awkward and he felt it best to dismiss it.

'Have you seen this play before?' he asked.

'Why do you think we attend the theatre?' she asked.

'Because it is what we had agreed upon?' smiled Noon.

'Do you gamble?' she asked.

'I do not.'

'I thought all Englishmen gambled.'

'I suppose I am a little different.'

'That is good,' said Natalia. 'You may watch me then.'

'But the Ridotto is closed,' said Noon. 'For a month more, no?'

'The official Ridotto is closed,' said Natalia, 'but there are many other *ridotti* about. Gambling is not a seasonal occupation in Venice, sir, not like duck hunting or carnival.'

'And how do you know about such things?'

'I have travelled more than you,' said Natalia, looking up at him. 'I may be younger, but I am no more naive.'

Noon laughed at her. 'You are so old. So needful to surprise.'

'So we may play at basset?'

'This evening,' said Noon opening his arms, 'is yours to decide on.' He pointed at their linkboy casting his shadows ahead. 'And will he not tell your father?'

'He is my friend,' said Natalia.

Their path carried them out to the Grand Canal, where a hundred gondolas seemed to bob about the water, their lanterns leaving trails of ever changing light about them. Crossing the Rialto with its narrow shops and gracious arch, a barge full of musicians passed beneath them playing loudly enough to halt all conversation. Apparently it was a familiar tune, for even Natalia with her poor voice joined in the air. Noon didn't understand a word of it but listened to the echoes play back and forth under the white marble. He studied the passing faces for signs of recognition as if he too was an agent and not an accessory. Their walk began to take the form of an adventure and, despite the harsh turns that had brought about his position, Noon knew that he was taking pleasure in the moment.

The house they entered lay on the south side of the Grand Canal and Noon could not believe the Council of Ten truly wished to control gambling, for the conspicuous façade had been strung with two dozen lanterns hanging from knots in a rope. It gave the building the appearance of having a bright and burning mouth, turned down in disappointment.

Natalia explained to Noon in whispers that the house

had been redecorated to resemble the Ridotto. It was, she said, like redecorating a mistress's room in the taste of one's wife to ease the sense of betrayal. The hallway was hung with stamped gold leather and led to a two-storey room where fourteen tables stood close to one another. Oddest of all to Noon was that the majority of those playing were women, while most of their escorts lounged on red-padded benches that ringed the room. Many of them sat in silence, except those who balanced tiny cups of coffee on their laps, as if conversation was forbidden unless a man's hands were occupied. Noon could feel the eyes brush and measure him and then pass to Natalia who, he admitted, deserved the longer look. Above them, painted on the ceiling, was a recreation of the Ridotto's Triumph of Virtue. It was a very high ceiling that no man could hope to reach.

As any gentleman would, Noon at once offered her a portion of the money that Jelborne had wisely given him. She protested, but not for long, and Noon followed her to a table empty of all but the dealer and the pair of lit candles that signalled he was ready to play bank. To Noon's surprise, Natalia seemed most adept at the game of basset and amid the constant cries of *uno*, *due*, *re* and *tre*, he began to admire her skill. Within an hour she had turned the fifty borrowed zecchini into six hundred and, with a promise to the bank to return in a moment, she led Noon to a small antechamber where fruit and coffee were on offer to all who gambled. Here she gave Noon back his original investment and asked him not to doubt or protest her actions once they returned to the table. Noon could only smile because, from the beginning of the evening, he had had no idea what to expect. Natalia seemed excited, breathing a little deeply in preparation for her return to the table as if it were a stage, but Noon was unsure whether he was part of the company or merely a member of the audience. *You are used to observation*, he told himself, *and are well practised for this*.

'You need only follow me,' she said as they walked together back to their expressionless banker, 'and do not protest and do not show your money. I will return in a moment.'

Natalia had not been gone from the room a breath or two when Noon felt a soft touch on his shoulder. He turned to be faced by the Chevalier de Montpassant.

'Milord,' said the Chevalier with a bow. 'We were introduced the other night.'

Noon returned the bow with great courtesy, hoping to cover his nervousness with formality. 'Only with our eyes.'

'You come from where?' asked the Chevalier.

'England,' said Noon.

The Chevalier laughed. 'I had guessed that far,' he said. 'From the north?'

'Shropshire.'

'Your accent,' said the Chevalier. 'Forgive me, I should have known. You are fond of this country?'

'Is it your own?' enquired Noon.

'I have adopted it.'

Noon nodded at the choice of words. 'It is fine,' he replied, 'though a little thick in its antiquities.'

139

'Yes,' agreed the Chevalier. 'It tires even the young. It is why we must travel in company.'

'Mr Jelborne?' said Noon. 'An educated man.'

'Employed by your father?'

'Yes,' said Noon.

The Chevalier nodded but said nothing, letting the silence hang between them. He let it lag into discomfort until Noon spoke for the sake of speaking.

'Though he would not have been my choice.'

'Too old?' asked the Chevalier.

'Too drunk,' laughed Noon and was proud of his recovery.

The Chevalier smiled. 'He sounds the youth and you the tutor.'

'Where did you learn your English?' asked Noon. 'It is so fine.'

'You are kind,' answered the Chevalier. 'I learned it from a compatriot of yours.'

'She was accommodating?' ventured Noon.

'Often and with pleasure,' laughed the Chevalier. 'It has been a delight, milord. I see your lady returns. May I leave with you luck.'

They bowed and turned away from one another.

'Come,' said Natalia and escorted Noon back to their table. She lost the first hand and then the second. Instead of levelling her wagers and riding streams of luck either upwards or downwards as she had before, she now plunged recklessly through her winnings. The banker spoke so little and faintly that Noon could not even be sure that he was Italian, let alone from Venice.

The candelabrum above their head burned brightly. Noon looked about to see the whole room stilled by light. So many candles were lit that it made a man think why. Was it to encourage the eyes to open, or to stay cheating hands? Either way, Natalia was concentrating on her cards, and now, after the tenth hand, it was apparent to Noon that she was trying to lose and to lose quickly.

She looked up at him every now and then to see that he understood and did not stop her. She gave him the most conspiratorial of smiles, curling gently in only one corner of her mouth. It made lines he had not seen before appear in her cheeks and about her eyes and he thought that she had been right. She was not naive, but playful and deliberate, and he was thrilled to have been included in her antics.

It took no more than another half an hour for her to lose the remainder of her money. She slowed her last hands down, looking ponderous and mournful. Noon noted that she had worn no jewellery that evening. She called out when another hand turned against her, and Noon saw the surrounding tables shift in discomfort to witness such loss, regular as it may have been. Natalia had begun to weep. The dealer played on, undistracted, but several of the gentlemen leaning against their cushions paused and put down their coffee cups and focused on the distressed young lady. Again she lost, and gave a small yelp that would have gone unnoticed save that it was timed to hit a blank moment so that it leapt about the room.

'Shhhhhh,' said a woman from a neighbouring table and Natalia nodded in understanding and let out a sigh that made Noon feel awkward, standing impotently behind her, unaware of the extent of her intentions. He wondered if the Chevalier was still there, watching his performance. One last hand and she placed her final ten zecchini down upon the table. Five hundred and fifty zecchini reduced to ten. The dealer turned his card and scraped her money from the table, thanking her kindly for her business. He stood and left Natalia with her head held in her hands as if she could not believe the very thing that she had witnessed.

'Brother,' she said, turning to Noon and speaking loud enough so that even a busy room might hear what it wanted. 'I have ruined us. Ruined us.' Her tears were real. They ran down her cheeks and she reached for Noon's hand and he helped her to her feet. Unsteadily, they walked between the gaming tables, amid surreptitious glances at this trail of grief. A small sob crept from her mouth and Noon stood straight, staring ahead, the picture of strength amid grief. She held his arm and out they went, through the mocking golden hallway and out before the Grand Canal. Noon did not mind the game, because it had ended in the holding of his hand, this touch.

They were not alone before the casino and she released herself from Noon. She had been caught up within her role, but now managed a smile from under the tears, as if to say she had done what she wanted and was now returning to the person who had entered the casino.

'Such emotion,' she whispered.

'Is this how you entertain yourself?' said Noon.

'I have never done it before,' whispered Natalia, 'but there was some pity in there.'

'There was no pity,' said Noon. 'Most likely familiarity.'

A man exited the casino behind them and stepped in their direction. Natalia dipped her head and brought her hand to her face.

'Friends,' said the man. He was Venetian, dressed in a suit of yellows and reds, far too gaudy a choice for any aristocrat: a man of some wealth and no taste. Noon had lived long enough to know that strangers who greet you as friends are as unlikely to have your good intentions at heart, as friends who greet you rudely mean harm.

'I could not help but see,' said the man softly, 'distress occurring among such beauty. I have a question for you to consider.'

'What is it?' asked Noon.

'Where are you from?' asked the man, seeming to be wary of Noon's accented Italian.

'What does it matter?'

'Nothing, friend, nothing at all. Merely, that if your young sister is ruined,' said the man, 'then perhaps I might find a position for her. A temporary one. A position that might be favourable to all, for a week or two.'

Noon's Italian was fine enough for him to understand the carnal insinuations that were masked in the words. He could not prevent his face from filling with disgust, as if a paying member of the audience had now leapt upon their stage.

'I think,' said Noon, with strained diplomacy, 'that we shall follow other alternatives.'

143

'Friend,' said the man and placed his hand on Noon's arm. 'You will find no one in all of Venice who will pay you what I can pay for her.' He leaned towards Noon's ear. 'I know you now. I can find you at any time.'

Noon had been hesitant before and it was the most likely reason he did not try to check his anger. He swung his shoulder, driving up through his right arm and caught the man across the jaw with his fist. The stranger collapsed immediately, flopping to the ground near the wall of the casino amid the puddles of piss, and he rolled once and groaned, making no attempt to rise. Those who watched did not move.

'Leave him,' said Noon and, pulling Natalia by the arm, signalled for their linkboy to follow them.

'I am sorry,' she said as Noon hurried her along. 'That was not my intention.'

Noon was angry at her, at the man on the ground, even at himself.

They walked briskly back towards the house of Martin Silver. She could see his anger and stayed a pace from him. 'It was not my intention,' said Natalia. 'I was glad that you would play with me and not give me away. I thank you for that, but it was for me. You weren't supposed to be involved. I was to entertain you.'

'You did not think of the consequence?' asked Noon.

She shook her head and seemed young and eager to him. Noon's steadiness made her feel sudden and child-like. It was not something she had known before.

'I am sorry,' she said. 'You must believe me.'

'Of course,' said Noon as they reached her father's

house. He turned immediately and walked away, leaving her under the light of the linkboy's torch, glowing in her orange gown, utterly perplexed.

It was a grand exit, and would have been much grander had he known where he was going, but without a linkboy he found himself lost within three turns. It took him an hour to return to Pisani's house, but he benefited in midnight walking by considering his evening. If Venice were truly a city of eyes, ears and tongues then what if this man had already known who they were? 'I know you now,' he had said, but in retrospect it was a vaguer sentiment than Noon had thought. But what if he had struck, not some procurer of flesh, but an agent? He must hold his temper. He did not wish to be responsible for an elevation of violence. There might be a code he did not understand, where one blow was returned by two and a split lip required a broken bone. He may have submitted to his father's game, but he did not wish to drag Natalia in beside him. By the time he reached home he had begun to see that Natalia's surprise and regret were truthful compared to his own behaviour, and in their way all her actions had been enchanting. His only irritation had been in her casual disregard for money, months of wages slipping carelessly through her fingers. Noon caught himself, *That is who you were, not who you have become.*

CHAPTER TWELVE

'And how did you pass your night?' asked Noon the next morning.

'Most productively,' said Jelborne. 'While you were applauding some howling or screeching, Silver and I were at a game of *biribisso* that resulted in a large donation to our cause. They have this silk purse with three dozen numbers inside and you wager on the particular number emerging. I was lucky with sevens.'

Noon could not keep suspicion from his face.

'Don't look at me with those dog eyes,' said Jelborne after a moment. 'You were doing exactly what you wished. And if what you wish is to chase around after a merchant's daughter, then so be it. I'll not stand before you and wag fingers. And if you wish to listen to things that will change nations, it is just as easy for you.'

'I suppose I wish both.'

'A young man's wish and it presents no problem. Your

father knew full well that you and His Lordship would be lapdogs to one bosom or another. He did not expect you to take a full part in his business.'

'I want to take part,' said Noon. 'For his sake.'

'You already play your part to perfection,' said Jelborne. 'I dare say you are doing exactly as His Lordship would have done.'

'I wish to learn more,' said Noon.

'Very well,' answered Jelborne, 'so you shall have to divide your time. Leave a little less for the signorina and attend me further.'

'I saw the Chevalier last night.'

'Of course,' said Jelborne. 'What did he ask?'

'If you were still a drunk.'

Jelborne laughed. 'Is just as well. What did you reply?'

'That you thought sobriety the greatest of all sins.' Noon had thought hard on sin during the night. Abroad, it seemed more nebulous, but it had not escaped Noon that in England Jelborne's actions, his father's actions, his own actions, were treasonous. *You may play me lightly, Mr Jelborne*, thought Noon, *but I am not unaware. Grant me that*.

'Good boy,' congratulated Jelborne. 'Talk to him as much as you wish and tell him nothing at all. Tomorrow we shall purchase some *vedute*. Just you and me together.'

Noon looked puzzled.

'Views,' said Jelborne. 'Have you learned nothing from me? Paintings of views.'

'And these are messages for my father? As with Cragnotti in Genoa? When the paint was fresh?'

Jelborne nodded. 'We shall let him know how matters stand. They are as letters between two men who share a tongue.'

In Martin Silver's house Natalia spent her day interpreting Noon's silence as anger and was filled with regret for the course of their night together and wished deeply that it was a day she might live again. When lost in thought she had the peculiar habit of staring off to one side and flaring her nostrils as if she were preparing a rebuttal of some offensive remark. It gave her an impression of aggression that was not unwarranted, for Natalia had always lived in the odd position of caring neither for her mother nor her father. She longed, as most do, to find he whom she had been waiting for. She had no list of requirements, no need for the man to speak a dozen tongues or recite poetry or ride a twenty-hand horse, no demands of blood nor money, she only wished that she would recognise him when he came, whatever guise he wore.

Natalia had never dissuaded her father from his impression that he had bred something infinitely better than himself. Nor had she corrected her mother's belief that she was angry and awkward, indecipherable because of this mixed blood of England and Italy. Those who live apart are often misinterpreted as proud, or loveless, troubled or remote, but Natalia was mostly patient. Her greatest fear in the days that were to follow was that Noon may well have been the man that she had waited for. He had looked at her, looked within her, had played her games, and if it had not been for that presumptuous stranger then life would still have lain smooth before her. Instead, there had been a sudden acceleration, a burst of emotion that had frightened her, though she had caused it, and now this man had withdrawn.

The same day Noon had concluded that he was no less intrigued with her than he had been on their first meeting and would have visited again, perhaps even the following day, had it not been for his conversation with Jelborne. He had learned enough in the evening to know that he had been accepted by her for who he said he was. Noon knew that Natalia was in Venice, that she would be with them in Naples, and at least for the time being such were the ties between her father and his tutor that they could not drift too far from one another even had he wished it. He had made a decision to concentrate on the matters that Jelborne deemed important. The more Noon had thought about his father's decision to betray a king accepted by Parliament, the more he knew he must approach the matter with gravity.

Noon had mentioned consequence to Natalia the night before and had thought hard on the matter. He had been trusted most implicitly by Jelborne and would surely be judged by the marquis on his return. All the information on which his father would base his judgement would be provided by Lucius Jelborne. Perhaps, thought Noon, he had been too free in his thoughts. Perhaps true freedom was something he must work harder towards, for the reception that awaited him at Dengby was uncertain. He had reason to hope that his position would be elevated, his birth acknowledged and his behaviour commended, but these were not certainties. He could see that Jelborne had a liking for him but he could let himself forget that in the next months he was on a trial of some length and severity.

Jelborne was surprised at Noon's application, which began that morning with the insistence on visiting the painter of *vedute*. The tutor wondered what had passed between Noon and Silver's daughter the night before, and congratulated himself that Noon was a wiser man than he had hoped for and had understood immediately that some women were simply dangerous to men's hearts.

It was then in mutual confidence that the two men set out in search of Vittorio Longhi, who for a dozen years had dashed off full and celebrated scenes that the wealthier of Venice's visitors secured during the months of the carnival. Longhi was not a happy man. He had been born with a talent, had nurtured and prostituted it and while favoured by foreigners was disapproved of by the nobles of Venice. He was now near fifty and his income was healthy enough during the carnival months to ensure a meandering life for those days when Venice seemed empty, giving Longhi more than enough time to dwell on his dissatisfaction.

A portly soul, Longhi was neglectful of his dress, and in his studio greeted Jelborne, Noon and Cesare barefoot below dark breeches and wearing a loose white shirt well marked with rainbow smears of paint. To his delight, these *stranieri* did not wish to purchase a Doge's Palace, a

Campanile, or a rendering of the *Bucintoro*, but rather a duck hunt, a scene he had never painted before.

'Four boats,' ordered Jelborne. 'Four men to a boat, one archer in each. A dozen geese rising in an arrow to the west. A heron upon the post. Eight dead ducks lying in the bottom of the boat.'

'There does not seem to be much room for interpretation,' said Longhi with great diplomacy.

'None at all,' said Jelborne. Noon listened carefully while walking in circles around the well-lit room. Neither the fineness of this young lord's silk nor his formidable physique were lost on the barefooted painter.

'I am not sure I have ever painted to such strict demands,' said Longhi softly, as if he were speaking to himself. He shrugged to imply that he did not know if he were capable of such a definite request.

'Last year,' said Jelborne, 'you sold a friend of mine three paintings for five hundred zecchini.'

'Let me see,' said Longhi, and under Noon's watchful eyes he curled his thick yellow toenails upwards. 'That would have been another Englishman, no?'

'Yes,' said Jelborne, 'and you will be paid the same amount for merely this one painting.'

Longhi nodded in appreciation. 'Well,' he laughed, 'I must go and find my inspiration.'

'There is no need,' said Jelborne, 'for you may accompany myself and His Lordship out towards the Lido tomorrow.'

'You have the Doge's permission?' asked Longhi in surprise.

'We are the guests of Morosoni,' said Jelborne.

Longhi smiled at the name of this marchese from deep within the Golden Book and thought what strange wonders a single day might bring.

Leaving Longhi's studio, Jelborne had not been in so fine a mood since before the death of Stilwell. It was, he knew, Noon who caused his happiness, with his decision to apply himself to the peculiar teachings of his tutor. On their passage back to the Pisanis' house, hiding from the heat of the day in a covered gondola, Jelborne questioned Noon.

'Now learn, Thomas. The dead birds?'

'Those who deny us?'

'Those who support us. The heron?' asked Jelborne.

'The Doge, the Council of Ten?'

Jelborne laughed. 'That we are watched. He is the Chevalier.' He tried again. 'The four boats and the four men in each?'

'Families we approach?'

Jelborne nodded. 'Better, Thomas. And the geese?'

'The amount you believe you have raised in Venice.'

Jelborne nodded and was pleased. 'Exactly so. If our hunt tomorrow is entirely successful, we might turn that dozen and double it. Morosoni is our surest wager, but it is a question of his commitment. He might see us as a diversion, but we must convince him that this is an investment that he might reap for generations.'

CHAPTER THIRTEEN

Though seabirds were inclined to settle on the lagoon as much at one time of the day as another, disturbed only by the passing ships or tempted by the bloody wakes of fishermen gutting their catch, there was a camaraderie in the duck hunt that required men to rise before dawn so that they might come together before the sun could divide them.

Morosoni was a kind man. He was also verbose, but only in his duty as an ambassador to Venice who thought that every young man, whether or not accompanied by a tutor, might benefit from his own elaborations of her beauty. One of the most influential men in the republic, he sat on the Council of Ten. As an erstwhile investor in Martin Silver's fleet, Morosoni was favourably disposed to the visit of this young English lord.

'You see,' he said, addressing Noon, 'these were all that were here before us.' He pointed at the seabirds which bobbed happily inside the lagoon. 'Their nests were before ours. The ideas were theirs, we are just their humble adherents. Still we try to follow them. Even our lions have wings.'

Morosoni had rough hands. In a life of ease where each day of his fifty years had been open with choice, he had always opted for labour and routine outside of his current duties to the council. He was a hunter, but also, like Noon, a swimmer. And where other nobles would have been content simply to hunt for the kill, Morosoni enjoyed the entire process, the gutting, the plucking and the eating of the life he had taken. It emphasised not a cruelness but an efficiency, which was supported by a direct stare and a straight jaw balanced between humour and disdain.

'I keep five hundred songbirds,' said Morosoni. 'It drives my wife to walk about all day, but my children, they are young, they adore them as I do. It is like the orchestra, you either hear the melody or you do not.'

'Why an arrow when you might use a gun?' asked Noon, who had been gripping the unfamiliar longbow for over an hour. He had been thinking of questions, knowing that he would betray less of himself by keeping the marchese talking.

'One shot,' laughed Morosoni, 'and ten thousand birds would take to the air. Besides, the bow is more suited to Venice. It is sly, you do not hear it coming until you are already pierced.'

They glided gently across the lagoon, past a gathering of ships all resting in a row.

'It is odd,' said Morosoni, looking at the ships. 'We have

a *capitano del golfo*, a superintendent of galleys, an admiral and a *patrono* of ships, and yet we have a poor navy. We prefer to hide nowadays.'

The Englishmen had retired early the night before, and once more Noon had lain awake listening to the floorboards reveal the passages of the Pisani brothers as they patrolled their little kingdom. Men who can't sleep are as apt to look at their past as their future, and Noon lay thinking of his daughter, who had been lost to his mind in the upheaval of the past weeks. He thought of what Pisani had told him, of how Sarah waited for him above, his family advocate clearing and cleaning her father's place. But what if he were not bound for heights but doomed to depths, who then would greet him? Those he had been born among and now directed him, for of all things, a man had no control over the place of his birth. He was born of the marquis, in the marquis's land, and the thoughts of the father would most certainly affect the destination of his sons.

Morosoni was busy signalling their second boat, where Noon could see his tutor asleep in the stern. Cesare was with him, and now, well over a mile from the nearest island and subject to the heave of the sea, the servant seemed no less green than his livery, hands gripping the gunwales.

Their two boatmen were poling their way slowly towards a pair of ducks who rose and fell in the slight swell.

'What do you think,' asked the marchese softly, 'of your new king?'

Noon was not sure how much Morosoni presumed he knew, but felt the man would perceive anything but honesty. The very question was a confirmation of how deeply

Thomas Noon was hidden beneath Stilwell's cloak. Jelborne had tutored him well in case such questions should arise.

'There is little sense,' said Noon, 'in calling a country a country if it cannot provide its own king.'

'But your people fear papists,' said Morosoni.

'They fear more change,' said Noon, expounding Jelborne's arguments. 'It is not a crime to befriend a Catholic. A man may spend not one day in your country before he can confirm this.'

'There are many differences between our countries,' said Morosoni. 'England is a nation of thinkers, Venice of sensualists. The English are unmoved, they admire reason. For instance, in our churches, I have seen Protestants recoil at the sight of a man kissing the toe of Christ. For them, it is idolatry – for us, expression. We believe without seeing, they see without believing.'

'England may not be like all of Italy, but she *is* like Venice,' insisted Noon. 'We are both trading nations. When the English take land we build taverns, not churches. It is just that we wish a difference from our neighbours. It is my belief that we have more fear of the French than of Catholic religion. Were Paris Protestant we should rush to kiss the feet of a pope.'

Morosoni considered these words. 'So you do not think your king will return? They will not have him because he sits in Paris?'

'I did not say that,' said Noon, smiling. 'He is English. More English than England's king and if he may divorce himself from France and prove moderate in his Catholic taste, then I believe the people will welcome him.'

'You may be right,' said Morosoni. 'In Venice,' he asked, 'have you gambled yet?'

To admit so was to admit to illegality but it seemed a small offence compared to those they were so openly discussing.

'I have.'

'And were you lucky?'

'I believe I was,' smiled Noon.

Morosoni pointed down at Noon's knuckle that was still grasping the bow. It was grazed and discoloured from the punch he had thrown outside the casino.

'And was this a fight that you won?' asked Morosoni.

'It was,' said Noon.

'With a single blow?' Morosoni asked pointing at the unscathed left hand.

'With one blow,' said Noon.

'Then perhaps it shall be the same for your king.'

No more was said upon the subject. A third boat, containing another pair of boatmen and Longhi with his papers and charcoal, had finally gained ground on the first two. He waved cheerfully to Morosoni and Noon. Morosoni rose carefully within the boat and signalled that Noon should follow suit. One of his boatmen raised his hand and, as he lowered it, the archers loosed their bolts. Noon's went sailing up into the sky and plunged into the lagoon, but Morosoni had struck one of the birds in the breast and it lay floating, lifeless. Their boat poled close enough so that Morosoni could reach and pull the duck aboard by its neck. He pushed the arrow through and passed the duck to one of the gondoliers.

They continued their pursuit of wildfowl in a slow and most deliberate manner until the sun raised itself to its full height, when Morosoni called loudly that the hunt was over. Jelborne woke suddenly with his bow at his feet and not a single bird in his boat. Morosoni called across the water to tease him.

'I trust you were not dreaming of food, my tutor, for it looks as if your table will be bare tonight.'

Jelborne laughed. 'Forgive me, marchese, the motion of Venice's water has a most soothing effect on me.'

Noon had made one lucky shot, catching a small bird through its wing as it took off, sending it spinning once in the air before it was dragged by the weight of the arrow back into the water. The marchese had taken great pleasure in Noon's untidy kill and pulled a feather from the carcass, a pretty stalk of sea green, marked with dark spots. He told Noon to keep it and to carry it back to England to prove to his father that he was the better shot with a bow.

Disembarking on the Grand Canal, Noon laughed to see that both Longhi and Jelborne had been scorched by the late September sun. Jelborne's nose in particular was glowing like a firefly's tail.

'You have never looked so healthy,' said Noon, and taking Jelborne's arm, the two walked towards San Marco to take an ice together.

The next day Jelborne and Noon spent in the pursuit of nothing other than education or at least its guise. Noon was surprised at his tutor's knowledge, knowing now how full his head was with political machinations. Yet he had written his book on Italy the previous year, and though they now laughed at the exaggerations and embroidery of its author, Jelborne did know many of Venice's more beautiful offerings. He showed Noon a tiny church that the servant would have walked past and dismissed for its lack of splendour, and revealed inside three paintings that hung upon her walls. They were all dirtied by the smoke of a century's candles but each mesmerised Noon. They were by a man called Tiziano Vecellio. There was pain within the paint and an illumination Noon had not yet seen in any of Jelborne's church art. And better than all of this, these were not the dry figures of chiselled saints who had never known doubt or seen things that might turn a man from God. These were men with unwashed beards, captured in thought, betraying hesitation, and they seemed so much poorer than saints, poorer perhaps than any man Noon had known.

Jelborne asked, 'Do you like them?'

'Very much,' said Noon. 'They are true.'

'Unlike the both of us,' smirked his tutor.

Noon disagreed but eased a smile from himself. He felt more kinship with these doubters than those embalmed on high or tortured low in hell. Who, thought Noon, knows what he deserves? Certainly not the figures that were painted before him, nor Jelborne, who did not seem to consider the gravity of his actions. The paintings signalled only doubt and Noon was amazed that such incertitude could be found in church. Had they hung in a grand cathedral he guessed they would long since have been banished to the crypt.

It had been Noon's intention to call on Natalia the following day, but that night there arrived at the Pisanis' a letter addressed to both Jelborne and the Viscount Stilwell which delayed his plans. Morosoni had written to express the joy he had taken from their time on the lagoon and in a postscript had pledged two hundred thousand zecchini for Martin Silver. He ended his note by asking the tutor's permission if he might relieve him of his charge for a day of swimming beyond the lagoon. The invitation happened to fall upon a Sunday and, even if Jelborne had been inclined to refuse him, Noon would have found a way to join the marchese. Besides, the division of labour was perfect. Jelborne would visit Longhi at his studio and now demand that a second skein of geese be added rising to the west.

'Your father will be surprised,' laughed Jelborne. 'He will uncover this painting and find that he can barely see Venice's sky because the sun shall be blocked by goose feathers.'

Jelborne did not know exactly what Noon had said to Morosoni during the previous morning, or whether it was his kill that had impressed the marchese, but Noon had obviously comported himself well. Morosoni was an intelligent man, not one who might be talked into a position he did not wish to take, so he presumed Noon's approach had been soft.

Morosoni had arranged to meet Noon not a hundred yards from the casino where he had accompanied Natalia three nights before. Noon waited alone by the side of the Grand Canal. The smell of yesterday's fish market had not dissipated and it was easy for Noon to imagine the barrels of writhing eels or the axes thudding into the flanks of dead tuna. Even under his feet there were remnants, not just scales and dried blood, but tentacles and fish eggs and the odd pale prawn not yet spied by seagulls.

Across the Grand Canal, in a doorway steeped in shade, sat a figure. Noon could feel the man's eyes pass over him every minute or two. *Come shadows, get your fill of me*, thought Noon. *For unless you walk on water, you'll have few words to describe my day.* He was amused at the inefficiency of the system. What could they possibly be sure of, when they could see but not hear, guess but not know. Noon sat down and watched everything, other than the watcher.

There was a different pace to Sunday, even in this city that Jelborne said had always replaced God with goods. Noon watched the gondolas move from either end of his view, as these black slender motes made their way to the cathedral of Santa Maria della Salute. Noon noticed statues perched on the cathedral's cupola, winged angels poised to dive into the water a hundred feet above the canal. Out poured the faithful from their boats beneath, jostling up the steps as if it were a new night at some prized theatre.

He did not know how formal Morosoni might expect him to be for such a simple task as swimming. He had dressed in the second of his new suits, again in the

Venetian style. It was of a wide-cuffed lemon hue. On an Englishman it would normally have stressed his pallid skin and yellow teeth, but Noon had seen enough of the sun that his suit now complimented his good health.

Morosoni's gondola was easy to spot, for it was the only one that aimed itself at Noon during the fifteen minutes he had watched and been watched. The marchese seemed pleased to see him and kindly admired his suit, though he was dressed casually, in a cream silk shirt and maroon breeches, suited to the heat of the day.

'I had a grandfather,' said Morosoni, 'who wore only red. This colour becomes you.'

They headed north past the island of bones called Sant'Ariano so that Noon could no longer see the Campanile or any of Venice's buildings. Instead, the lagoon became as it always must have been: butterflies that skitted between marshy reeds, cries of birds seen and unseen and tiny brown crabs that gathered on any piling or rock face that poked from the water.

'This,' said Morosoni, 'is my lawn. In your cities, you have forgotten that they are built on land, but we never forget the water.'

Noon stared out across the expanse and admired the emptiness.

'I said yesterday that we were indebted to the birds,' said Morosoni, 'but in truth we are like fish. Not because we eat them, but when we pull them from the water, we feel as if we have created them. Water is sometimes a mirror, no?'

Noon laughed at his exaggeration and felt wonderfully

free. He had been apart from Jelborne so little, and then only for his strange night with Natalia. This was a friendship that he had not sought, but Morosoni of the Council of Ten had chosen him, affirming his belief in his own role. Noon was flattered and happy and felt at ease with his glorious host. Morosoni had brought a little dog with him. It chased back and forth along the gondola and put its front legs on the prow trying to peer out at wherever they were going. Both Noon and Morosoni would laugh and the marchese would call out to his gondolier, 'Wherever he wishes to go, signore, follow his bark.'

Their gondolier murmured his assent.

'We think more than the English of our animals,' said Morosoni. 'For years, we were always alone. Better to talk to your dog than to yourself.'

It was a lazy hour of little conversation but good humour and Noon was relieved that the matter of business was not raised at all. Finally, when they were out of sight of Venice and in the shallow waters by a tiny strip of land that was lost to the sea for hours of every day, Morosoni raised his hand and called for the gondola to stop. The marchese stood and began to strip. When he was nude, his tanned face and hands in contrast to his milky middle, he grinned at Noon and dived head first into the water. Noon peeled his clothes from his body and his stockings from his legs. The slight wind told him that it would be warmer in the shallow water than on the boat. He dived, straight-backed, rocking the gondola but barely moving their boatman who now sat down to savour his rest.

Noon took ten powerful strokes through the water towards the marchese, then paused five yards from his host to see if his feet could touch the bottom. They could but it was a cloying mud, and Noon, still relishing the freshness of his nudity, preferred to kick out in the water, letting his constant motion keep his head and shoulders above the gentle sea.

'You swim well,' said Morosoni, 'like a Venetian.'

'Do all Venetians swim?' asked Noon.

'The whores swim.'

Noon laughed.

'They think it does them good,' said the marchese. 'That it keeps them clean. Where did you learn to swim?'

'At Dengby,' said Noon, 'there was a pond and a river not so far.'

'You have never tasted salt water,' laughed Morosoni and splashed against the sea. 'What good is saltless water for men like us?'

The marchese ducked under the dark ocean and in a moment Noon felt his host glide between his legs. He could not have been more shocked, but Morosoni emerged the other side of Noon laughing aloud until he saw Noon's face.

'And would you always swim alone?' asked the marchese.

'I would,' said Noon firmly, and he looked over his shoulder at the boat but could only see the soles of the gondolier's feet as he rested, and the tail of the pacing dog.

'No one can see,' said the marchese and paddled closer. Noon felt a hand shoot up his leg and cup his prick. He pushed the hand away. Did Jelborne know, he asked himself. What does this man expect of me?

'I think you misread me,' said Noon calmly, though his fists were bunched tightly beneath the water.

'Come now, George,' smiled the marchese, 'you followed me into the water naked.'

'To swim,' said Noon.

'And we are swimming.'

'And that is all,' said Noon sharply.

'You are sure?' asked Morosoni. 'I might double my investment.'

Noon said nothing but continued to swim in place.

'I shall not ask again.'

'I am most sure,' confirmed Noon.

The marchese tilted his head in acceptance, smiling at Noon. The servant turned and swam hard away from the little island, aware that he was watched closely, but angry and uncertain of what he had done to provoke such thoughts. He swam far until the strip of land could not be seen and the gondola was as small as an upturned coffee spoon on the water. Then he turned and swam at his leisure back towards the boat. When he was within one hundred yards of the gondola, he could see that the marchese was already aboard, dried and dressed. He leaned over and offered Noon a hand, pulling him from the water.

'I am sorry to have upset you,' he said to Noon in English.

'Forgive me,' said Noon and was relieved to feel the anger drip from his body.

The marchese handed him his clothes and watched as Noon dressed.

'Do not worry,' said Morosoni. 'This affects no business between us. It was simply that your father had worried last year that he was not sure what kind of man you would make. I thought he might mean that you would make a man like me.'

'Now we all know,' said Noon simply.

'*Andiamo*,' said Morosoni to his boatman and they suffered a long and silent journey back to the Grand Canal, the marchese always wearing an amused smile at Noon's discomfort, while scratching the furry belly of his dog with one bare foot. At the canal, Noon stood and kissed Morosoni twice on either cheek as he had seen Venetians do. In return he was given an understanding squeeze of the hand.

'I hope to see you again before you depart,' said the marchese.

'No doubt,' said Noon and dipped his head in respect.

Noon's mind was so occupied with the afternoon's events that it took him a full five minutes of walking, and the sound of another's footsteps behind, for him to remember the shadow that had watched him that morning from across the Grand Canal. He turned one corner, then another, scanning the ground and increasing his pace until, outside a black door, he stooped and gathered a broken section of a gondolier's pole. Holding his breath, he waited until the quickened steps rounded the corner and greeted the man with one firm blow to the stomach. He did not wait, but left the man collapsed in the alley and moved quickly onwards towards the Pisanis'.

Oddly, Noon felt almost giddy with laughter. What if he were just a man upon a Sunday walk? It made Noon laugh harder. He hoped he had not broken his ribs. Outside the Pisanis' palazzo, his laughter stopped. *I am*, he realised, *nervous in this skin. What am I doing?* He knew that his mind was not the same as Jelborne's, or even Stilwell's, and was not comfortable in the uncertain world of agents, with the potential of being observed. It was damaging his understanding of the world as a place of rigid lines.

If the thought of spending the day in the water had helped to keep Natalia's image at bay, the marchese's actions and his brief burst of violence had pushed her to the forefront of Noon's imagination. He smiled at Jelborne on entering the Pisanis' house and stopped to enquire about his tutor's afternoon.

'And yours?' asked Jelborne.

'I was followed back,' said Noon.

'Of course you were followed.'

'I beat him.'

Jelborne looked up and pointed a finger at Noon. 'Do not do it again. Do not bring an escalation on us. Do not let them think us men with secrets.'

'I am sorry,' said Noon and bowed his head.

'If I should take a beating on your account,' said Jelborne, 'be sure that I should pass it on.' Noon bowed again in understanding.

Dismissive of his chastisement, Noon retired to their

room where he quickly penned a letter to Natalia, requesting her company for the following night. 'It does not matter,' he wrote, 'what production we shall witness on this occasion, for it is enough for me to know that it shall be seen together. There is no man who looks forward to your company as much as your friend, George.'

Noon walked down to the kitchens where he found Cesare and begged him to run the errand for him, giving him two zecchini for his troubles. Cesare waved his money away.

'You are like me,' said Cesare. 'I don't forget this. We are both poor men and now it is good, but again maybe one day it will be bad.' He took the letter from Noon. 'You should do as I do,' said Cesare, leaning towards Noon and lowering his voice. 'You see my suit?' It was a foolish question for all of Venice knew Cesare's green livery by now. 'Inside this suit,' whispered Cesare, 'I have sewn almost twenty zecchini. It may be heavy, but I am my own bank. I shall do it for you too.'

'Does that not worry you,' said Noon, 'when you are out upon the water?'

Cesare shook his head. 'I think this: if I survive, then this suit shall ensure my fortune, should I fall and sink in these waters, then the angels will take my silver and pass me through heaven's gates.'

'And if they do not take Venetian coins?' teased Noon.

'You think they will take English?' laughed Cesare. 'The angels do not even speak your tongue.'

Noon joined his laughter. 'So you will carry my letter?'

'You wish me to wait for her answer?'

'Please.'

'All we think about is women,' smiled Cesare. 'I do this for you, because I know that you would do this for me. The fat man would not, but then he is not faithful to one woman. We are the same.'

Noon was too anxious for Natalia's reply to stay within the walls. He walked to the north side of the Grand Canal to the Campo San Polo where half a dozen bulls were being baited by men, dogs and children. The morning's spice market had been cleared, and the thousand scents of dawn were replaced by sweat and dusty cobblestones. He stood to the side and bought a piece of sugared fruit and listened to the bellows and the screams of delighted children and the giddy whoops of young men in limited danger. Noon knew the same went on in England, the same beating and exhortation of those stronger and dumber, but it struck him as odd in Venice, as if it contradicted everything that Morosoni had wished him to believe. Venetians were not at one with their creatures, they were not like their birds, or their fish, they were not so lonely that they befriended curs. And bulls would always be dumb and strong and wish to stand and fight, and men would always be good and bad, their women would always encourage, their children always emulate. He handed his sliver of fruit to a silent young girl who stood behind him and wondered back to the Pisanis', trying to imagine the note he would receive. He did not care if he was followed. *I have nothing to hide*, he thought. *Read my heart, there is no shame in it.*

Cesare was waiting for him and Noon took the letter from his hand.

'Our second adventure shall lack the drama of the first, for which I must still apologise and will do so once more in person. I shall surprise you, if you are agreeable, and shall await your arrival tomorrow night. With wishes that your days have been well spent and that Venice has not been shy in revealing herself to you, I leave you as your some-time guide, Natalia D'Argento.'

With Cesare waiting, Natalia had started and scribbled and shredded four different versions of her brief note. There had been such anxiety during Noon's silence that at one stage she had almost broached the subject with her father. Now she was glad she had held firm and not revealed her hopes, for he might have laughed, or been angry at His Lordship, or even let it affect the business that passed between him and Jelborne. Ultimately, she had concluded that her note should read no differently than as if had he called upon her the next day, for she could not see the benefits of exhibiting her agitation.

Noon arrived in his lemon suit, his skin still brown but reddened and healthy from his two days on the water. His buckles were set with brilliants and drew the last of the light. He had a charming mixture to him, she thought as he bowed before her, as if he had the soul and the skin of a fisherman, but was caught in the body of an English lord. Tonight she had dressed in meadow green,

material her mother had chosen in France to match her
eyes precisely, and the woman had chosen well, for the
silk made her eyes frighteningly direct. Noon stared at
her as he rose from his bow and was silent. They walked
together and Natalia could feel his eyes about her, but
they were peculiar, not the familiar assault of masculine
challenge, that sexual questioning. These were inquisitive,
gentle, they were in no hurry and were appreciative and
flattering.

Noon walked beside her and was soon laughing because
it was obvious that none, not even Jelborne, could see
what he saw and he was grateful for their blindness. He
could not believe he had let three days stand between
their meetings and regretted every hour that he had followed in other pursuits. Noon thought her a woman
made of tiny miracles. He smiled to himself to think that
Natalia had also risen from such odd stock: the mercan-
tile Silver and his distant wife. How could they produce
this? What an unexpected recipe of blood, as strange as
his own.

She, slim and slight, green-eyed with rising nose, not a
painted beauty and not a form celebrated – but that was
only taste and chance and it was Noon's taste and his
luck that she was his perfect reflection. Her nails, he
noticed, watching the arc of her swinging hands, were
bitten. What were they but signs of a turning mind and
their roughness was countered by slim fingers and a wrist
that disappeared under lace. Noon watched this point of
friction, watched how the lace rode up the arm an inch,

then downwards. He found this shifting motion of revelation absorbing. Like fingers tracing paths up and down
her forearm. Women put scents on their wrists. Noon
wondered if the insects they passed could smell it.

'What are you thinking of?' she asked.

'Nothing,' lied Noon. He studied her rosy cheeks, and a
pair of dimples either side of her lips that came and went
with smiles.

'Do you always stare so intently?' she asked.

'When my thoughts wander,' said Noon.

'And where did they wander?'

'Nowhere.'

'A man whose thoughts of nothing wander to nowhere.
Who were you thinking of?'

'Nobody,' said Noon and they laughed together and it
was her, he was sure he had not instigated the motion but
it was her, Natalia, intended for Mr Lucius Jelborne, who
took the hand of Thomas Noon, or did she take Stilwell's
hand, but either way it was Noon who felt it. She had not
even glanced at him but kept walking as if nothing new
had happened. But Noon's galloping heart knew that the
world might change again.

She called for a gondola along the Grand Canal and
gave hurried directions that Noon could not follow. He
looked over his shoulder at the shadow of the city they
had left behind. *Follow me*, he thought. *Come shadows and
share my joy.* Out they headed among the islands, past
Murano and into the night, tippling with the wind.
Natalia was restless and moved about the gondola, like
Morosoni's anxious dog, until the worried gondolier

asked her to calm herself, lest she upset them. She grinned and Noon could see her teeth illuminated by the lantern on the prow of their boat. Half an hour later, they pulled up at a poor-looking strip of land, the dock a collection of sodden pilings, and Noon had no doubt that she determined once again to surprise him. Noon paid the gondolier double his charge to ensure patience for their return.

There was music coming from the other side of the island. They walked towards it. It was not the measured sound of an orchestra, but looser strings, accompanied by clapping and song, one voice rising then dipping and disappearing beneath a chorus. The closer they approached, the more Noon could see. Dozens about a great fire, some men bare-chested, some in suits as fine as his own. One woman had stripped to all but a loose silk gown that the flames dissolved. He could see her breasts rise and fall as she danced and he turned to watch Natalia observe the scene with similar intensity.

As they neared the circle, a man came towards them, carrying a bottle in his hand. He bowed, offered it to Natalia and as she took it, he turned and danced away back to the fire. Noon removed it from her hands and took a long pull. She followed suit.

'Where are we?' he asked.

'I've been told of this,' she said.

'And what friend would know of this?' asked Noon.

The same man came spinning out of the fire again, singing at the top of his voice. This time he bowed before Noon, then offered his hand to Natalia, who, smiling at

Noon, took it and was taken towards the flames. Noon stood and watched her dance. Swaying and looking at the steps of those about her, then imitating and finding her own rhythms, and singing and joining, trying to lose herself among strangers. Thomas Noon smiled in the spirals of light and swigged at the bottle until it was gone. Out from the circle came the lady in the loose gown, calling him in Venetian. He took her hand, and she twirled in front of him, then danced back towards the bonfire with Noon trailing doglike.

Noon could only smile, as he moved, at the chance of it all. Of Natalia, not knowing who he was, pushing him here and there, unaware of how he might react, but trusting it might be the same reaction as her own. He threw his arms in the air like those men about him, then held up the tails of his yellow suit and hopped towards and away from the lick of flames, and was joyed to see Natalia's gaze follow him.

It seemed like hours to Thomas Noon that he howled and span and sweated to this strange Italian dance, and had there been another Englishman about, he would have known at once that Noon had betrayed himself, betrayed his supposed station. Noon had not felt so free, not ever. Outside the ring of fire, Noon dragged a lady to her feet and span her but her feet would not coordinate with his own rapid impression. Natalia looked on, an amused expression on her face.

Noon cannot believe he is of this world, then knows for certain that he *is* of this world. He could shout, then he does shout, he shouts with joy and Natalia is there, inches from him, and she echoes his outburst with her own. Noon imagines he is sweating through his shirt, rejoices in the fact, aims to dance until he cannot support himself.

Noon is now perfect to himself only because she is perfect to him. She is too slight for true beauty, her nose too angled, the eyes too large, but she believes in her own perfection and he sees it too. What magic to him. It is so evident in those eyes. He knows now that everybody could see it who looked, but also knows that it is meant only for him. Above her dress her eyes shine a dark green, the glow is that of a second creature that lies inside her, she is another. Her brown hair is unpowdered. They twirl again like a pair who may see the world around them but know that they are suspended above it together.

'I think,' she is whispering into his ear, 'that I could fall in love with you.'

They had kissed but drink had made his memory duller than he wished. He knew that he would kiss her again, not in sight of wine, and that he would seize that memory and burn it within him to remember for ever. He had pawed at her, he remembered, and she had laughed and pushed him away before dawn, the night passing and spinning more quickly than Noon had ever known. She had pushed him back down the path, as he had continued his tuneless singing. Every grab he made was eluded and laughed at.

Returning in the gondola, she had put his head in her lap and stroked his face and the fire was leaving him

175

and Noon felt oddly sad, a momentary unhappiness that fell without reason, as if a peak had been climbed that would never be reached again. He had wept. She could not see him. He lay there in silence, taken by drunken thought to those who had passed from his life: Stilwell and his daughter. I have failed you both, but in love and in obedience I will atone. By following this woman and in duty to my father, I will atone. They were surrounded by water and there he was, a child himself inside Venice's belly, his head against Natalia's warm thigh, and he slept.

A note awaited him in the afternoon, when he rose with a head aching and ringing as if chattering insects had gnawed through his ears and beat their wings inside his skull. It was from Natalia, informing him that her father would depart the next morning for four or five days, to travel into Padua on business. She said she wept at the thought of not seeing him on this day, but promised that they might pass each of the next nights together. Even in his dark state, Noon smiled and made his way slowly down the stairs in search of Jelborne, to offer his limited services for the remainder of the day.

'Dear God,' said Jelborne. It was obvious to the tutor not just that Noon was fragile as an egg but also that he had slipped and broken into love.

'For what?' muttered Noon.

Jelborne shook his head. 'She has you.'

'I am not a fish to be reeled,' groaned Noon. He sat

down heavily opposite his tutor and rubbed his temples with both hands.

'You are already reeled. In one night, she's drawn you from the water.'

'We have drawn each other.'

Jelborne groaned. 'You said you would follow *me*,' he almost whined.

'May we speak more gently?' pleaded Noon. 'I did follow you, and suffered through Morosoni and made you your money.'

'Suffered?' said Jelborne. 'Since when was a day on the ocean suffering to you?'

'When it was shared with a sodomite.'

Jelborne was wide-eyed for a moment, then he began to laugh hard.

'I am sorry, Thomas, I had no idea.'

'I thought so.'

'You defended yourself?'

'No,' murmured Noon. 'I bent double and held my ankles while thinking of your king.'

Jelborne was still giggling. 'It does not affect . . .?'

'No,' said Noon, 'it does not affect his pledge, he assured me of that.'

'What a very strange man,' said Jelborne. 'Not something I had suspected. A well-kept secret, how rare for Venice. I suppose it explains why you would run so hard to Silver's house.'

'I had been thinking of her anyway,' protested Noon. 'I had said that I would divide my time and have been most true to my word.'

Jelborne relented. 'I suppose it is true. And this girl,' continued the tutor, 'what shall you do when she leaves Venice, should we not leave first?'

'I will wait for her in Naples.'

'And hold your heart until then?'

'Of course.'

'And will she?'

'I do not doubt it.'

'It is always sad,' said Jelborne, 'to see a good ship afire. I suppose there is nothing that I might do but let you burn and see what I might salvage.'

'I wish you were not against her so,' said Noon. 'She will be in Naples with us and then to England.'

Jelborne winced at the thought. 'Plagues spread the same way. They sneak shipboard and ravage whole countries.'

Noon waved his hand at the tutor's hyperbole. 'You sit and call me mad, but listen to yourself.'

Jelborne raised his palms towards Noon in surrender. 'I am fond of you, Thomas Noon, that is all.'

His tutor had resigned himself to Noon's behaviour. Jelborne had urged Silver to take his daughter with him to Padua, but Silver had insisted he had no need for her and trusted Jelborne to stand in his paternal stead. They both knew what it meant. Silver was leaving his daughter for His Lordship. If that was what Silver truly wished, thought Jelborne, then he brings it upon himself. He hoped that Noon would bump her and forget her. Within days, they would leave Venice. There was little left for them to do. Of all places, it was not one for more than the veneer of pretence and there were few churches or cathedrals that might justify more than a single visit. Silver would raise more information in Padua from friends and should Jelborne be sought, then plans would change accordingly. But even should he still move lightly in Italy, he was concerned for Noon.

They spent the day soothing Noon with generous doses of ices despite the cooling weather. Noon looked the perfect young Englishman abroad, a yawning, distracted accomplice to his own education who stank strongly of last night's wine and kept to the shadows to nurse his aching head. When Jelborne realised how little conversation Noon merited, they stepped aboard a gondola and Jelborne ordered their boatman out past the Lido, telling Noon that he must swim. Noon stripped, pushed himself off the boat and sank under the waters, slowly rising to the surface again and spitting water into the air.

'Is that not better than a church?' called Jelborne.

Noon nodded from the water. He did not possess the energy to swim or even float on his back to face the sun so he turned his eyes from the day and spent a few minutes kicking in place. He was thinking how love required the suspension of sense, the willingness to ignore, to invite ignorance back into his life. And surely he should deny it, surely he should concentrate on the misery he had suffered. The death of his daughter should haunt him, the death of Stilwell should eat him daily, for these had been his responsibilities. If he accepted this ridiculous notion, that a girl might love him, not just love him, but love him as another, then he was encouraging a stupidity that must be inside himself. *Shall I commit myself to folly*, he thought. *Shall I take my history and my reason and cast them on the waters?* Finally, he paddled slowly towards the gondola.

'What are you thinking of, Thomas?' asked his tutor.

Noon smiled.

'Her?'

Noon nodded.

'How is your head?'

'It will be clear once the sun goes down and I sleep. Thank you for this. Thank you kindly.'

Jelborne threw him his stockings and directed the boatman back to Venice.

Noon rested well that night, knowing that across the water he filled a woman's dreams. The following day was simply a sun that rose then set in expectation of night. He wandered with Jelborne and Cesare. They had ices with Morosoni and visited Longhi to collect their painting and Noon held his silence, allowing particles of politeness to be all that slipped his lips. Morosoni did not seem offended.

Once Thomas Noon had decided that love was possible, everything was knighted with a sensuality that he had not seen before. As they were poled back towards the Grand Canal, he could see now that all cities were, one way or another, a loud and uneasy celebration of the masses, those who came together, a great pressing of flesh that could only result in expansion. More people create more people. The young glowed and he was near enough one of them, he knew he glowed as they did, young girls with their growing shapes, young men with the strict curves of their naked chests, legs astride fishing smacks. Noon felt at home.

He met Natalia early in the evening and they huddled together under the cover of the gondola and with only their boatman's back facing them might have done what they wished. Instead, they were uncertain and propped themselves at either end of the same seat and smiled fully. Neither doubted that what had passed between them was real but it was also from yesterday and must be tempted forward to join them again. Noon had brought wine and they drank together and began to laugh at their unease. It was a cool enough night. October had now settled and evening heat had departed for the year, leaving only the breath of winds that grew colder hour by hour. Noon unrolled a blanket and spread it across both their legs. Under it, his hand sought hers and he stroked it quietly as they drank, just a soft caressing. Her palm was moist.

'Are you nervous?' she asked.

'A touch,' he said.

'I am,' she admitted and brought her hand up to her heart. 'Everything is good. My head is clear, I am happy, but this,' she patted her hand against her heart, 'this beats a hundred times as fast as a week ago.' She laughed at herself.

'Your father left?' asked Noon.

'Yes,' she said, 'for Padua.'

Noon nodded.

'What did you think of me when you first saw me?' asked Natalia.

Noon smiled and sipped at his wine. 'What did you think of me?'

'I thought you insignificant,' she said sweetly. 'I didn't notice you, not at first. Only after we spoke, and then suddenly I was sure. I knew this would happen.'

'What would?'

She laughed and pointed about her. 'All of this.'

'I thought you strong,' said Noon. 'Most obviously beautiful, but not too much so.'

'Do I not turn a roomful of eyes when I enter?' she asked.

'You might,' said Noon, 'but you pass beneath the line of sight of any standing man.'

She laughed. 'What did you truly think? Did you think of this?'

'No,' said Noon. 'Who could expect such happiness? Who would tease themselves with such a thing?'

'I would,' said Natalia. 'I did.'

'It was a risk.'

'I know. When you did not call on me for those days I was destroyed.' She looked him squarely in the eye. 'Destroyed. I did not know what to do with myself.'

Noon shrugged.

'You are very nonchalant,' she said.

'I apologise.'

'Never apologise to a woman. Besides, I liked it. It lent you mystery.'

'You mistake mystery for my great age.'

Natalia laughed. 'I had always thought that I would spend my life with an older man. Much older, and he would show me things, teach me.'

'Tutor you?' teased Noon.

'But now I don't see it,' said Natalia. 'We are both young, but I could learn from you. I think I could learn from you.'

She turned and kissed him on the cheek and let her lips pause against his skin. She breathed him in.

'I like the way you smell,' she whispered.

'And how is that?'

'A little damp.'

Noon broke away and laughed. 'I don't think I should approve of that.'

'It's good,' grinned Natalia. 'You smell just like a man.'

They arrived at the island of La Giudecca, where they had planned to dine in a grape arbour. In one corner of the island stood a small house, from which the restaurant was operated. It was hemmed by planted gardens bred from imported soil. Natalia and Noon walked hand-in-hand between trees. These were the first plants Noon had seen since arriving in Venice. He reached up and pulled a leaf from a branch, then let it float to his feet. At the far end of the garden, out of sight of the restaurant's few guests, for it was still too early for heavy company, they sat together on a white marble bench. They kissed and Noon ran his hand up her calf, following her silk stocking to the boundary of the garter that circled her thigh.

'Perhaps,' she said, 'we should retire for supper.'

They were shown to a white candle-lit room above the restaurant, where a table with eight dishes of game, sturgeon and oysters awaited them. Each was set on a silver box filled with hot water to keep the food warm. Three bottles of wine stood at the end of the table. Noon paid the landlady handsomely. Walking her to the door, he suffered her smile as he insisted he did not wish to be disturbed even once during the night.

'Even if the house is afire?' she had asked quietly.

'Even should we both perish,' said Noon and closed the door behind her. He walked back to Natalia and accepted the glass she proffered. They sipped quickly, neither looking at the bed that lurked in the corner of the room, behind the closed shutters.

There had been something tentative and unmatched about their first kiss the night before where lips had met and tongues tangled but did not dance as their hearts had intended. Now, he could feel her giving herself to him. He kept his eyes open to see if hers were closed and felt all of her being poured into him. He held her waist, held it tightly and pulled her towards him. It was such strangulation that she pushed him away and then resumed the kiss, more gently.

'We are not very good at this yet,' she said. 'Have you thought of it?'

'Of course.'

'How do you think we will be together?'

'We will improve each time.'

'I think so too.'

She pushed herself away again and began to remove

her clothes. Not slowly, or even seductively, but simply to undress. She untied the six wide ribbons that fastened her dress in front, stepped out of the yards of silk crumpled at her feet and stood there smiling before him. It was so different and why should it not be? Before clothes had been items to bargain off a woman with kisses and promises and it had always been an evening's work for a hint of bosom and now here was Natalia, naked before him.

Her breasts were small, the nipples dark and pointed. She was compact and she was perfect. Beneath, in the dark V between her legs, she had cropped her brown curls close between her thighs. Such richness against the smooth pallor of her stomach and her hair draping down across her neck, falling between her breasts. Her eyes watched him watch her, adoring the adoration.

'Am I beautiful to you?' she asked.

'You are beautiful enough for us both,' said Thomas Noon.

She stepped towards him and her hands began to rid him of his clothes, nimble fingers picking at buttons and buckles and pausing to brush across his chest. When she had stripped him he stood before her naked and erect and she reached and touched his prick, wrapping her hands around it.

'I knew you would be like this,' she said and stood on tiptoes for a kiss.

He leant down and thought, *I am so much taller than her, I am so much larger now that clothes are removed, all artifice is gone and we stand now as animals.*

185

'Do you think you might love me too?' she whispered. 'I won't believe you tonight. You can say it as much as you wish and I won't believe it.'

Noon did not want to speak. He had the odd feeling that with Natalia his disrobement might lead to his unveiling, that in his trust, in this revelation of bare skin and under her intense gaze, she would see everything, even Thomas Noon lurking. What could she see when she ran her hand over his chest and stared into his eyes and claimed now to be able to read them?

In the morning, Noon slipped from the bed and watched the form of her body under the sheet. The restaurant was quiet beneath. Nothing stirred. He opened the window a few inches and watched the gentle breeze lift strands of her hair. Natalia was lying face down. Noon walked over and slid the sheet down her body, kissing the base of her spine. He ran his fingers up her back, wanting to wake her, to kiss, to talk and to play.

She was already playing. He could see the faintest smile on her lips and he knew that the spell was still thick between them from the night before. He ran his hands down her leg, so softly that had she been sleeping she would not have woken. Stopping at her feet, he raised them and pushed his palms against them out towards the toes, pressing the night from her body. When he had finished he placed her feet side by side and left her body for a moment. She stirred, wondering where his lips would land. Along the side of her body, above her hips, he kissed upwards towards her shoulder. Where he kissed the wind cooled, so that the sensation lingered, as if she were being kissed by a dozen mouths. She was smiling now, her eyes still closed.

'Shhh,' Noon whispered into her ear. 'Keep your eyes closed. Turn over.'

He pressed his lips between her neck and her chin. It was where he knew they belonged and he pushed harder, making her head arch back. His touch disappeared, and Natalia wondered where he had gone, where he would return to. She turned back over and felt a breath across her nipples but no contact, warmth on her wrists but no touch, the slightest graze of his chin along her thigh.

Noon pushed both her legs upwards and slid his tongue inside her, just once, but as deep as he could before removing it. He surprised himself, how he loved her taste, surprised by the pleasure he received from it. Her hand came down to investigate, and he caught it with his own and made it follow, made her touch herself. He took her finger and traced her outline up and down, allowing her to tease but not to relieve herself. He followed her with his tongue, then stopped and drew her finger into his mouth, sucking it clean.

When he was ready, when she was waiting, her reddened chest beneath him, her eyes still closed, he knelt between her legs, and pressed himself up against her. Neither of them moved, they waited for the first sense of pleasure to end, so that it might be increased. The moment he was inside her she opened her eyes and looked into his. He pushed harder and she winced, then smiled as he broke through again. Noon gave her pain and pleasure, but every thrust increased her joy, and his movements were perfect to her. He took her hands and held them above her head, pinning them hard against the pillow. Her eyes looked lost to him.

She thought, *I am giving myself entirely to you and you do not know it, you have stolen me by force and you are meant to be mine, because look at you, look between us and see how we are joined.*

Natalia looked up at his mouth and wanted to feel her tongue against his lips. When she kissed him again, she felt as if every ounce of knowledge she possessed, every emotion, was transmitted to him. She wanted to crawl inside him, to be absorbed. His weight, that was what it was, this great weight that turned her about and pressed inside her again. Now his breath was against the nape of her neck. His skin was pressed against her back and grew warmer and more demanding. *How deep*, she thought, *can I be broken?* The pain dissolved again and his intensity extended through her. She turned her head and saw him looking down at her. *Does he notice*, she thought, *how I am overpowered?* She closed her eyes and concentrated. His body was soothing and so heavy to lie beneath, knees tucked under her body.

Noon was moving much faster now and she could feel the speed of his heart against her back. He was more urgent and she tried to move, but he would not let her, so heavy she could not fight his weight. Noon bent his head to her hair and she could hear his soft moans grow resonant. The weight was gone, for she knew it was Noon who was now helpless and it made her shudder. He convulsed and leaned against her, her pleasure sustained by his weight. She grinned beneath him from exhaustion. Natalia had never felt smaller under God's sky, and she floated in her mind, up through clouds above the break of day and back into the night, levelling every star that she touched.

CHAPTER FOURTEEN

Love, if that is what it is, has changed Thomas Noon. His view is altered. Before it was assessment, now it is judgement. He has the blood to match his intelligence and, for the moment at least, he also has the wealth, the dress and the demeanour. And with such elevation, what he plans to feel on his return is not even contempt but pity, because life should be simple. Life was simple, now that he had fallen in love.

Why not believe? Why not believe in this love, despite its absurdity, despite the impossible walls that separated them, their status, their countries, their wealth. What a foolish thing to abandon yourself to, what idiocy, what suicide, but what surer way to live? It was as if he knew a joke was to be played upon him, and yet he was willing to continue in expectation of ridicule just for the pride of involvement. The laughter of those who would observe, the Jelbornes of the world, was more the sound of spectacle than participation. Noon walked through San Moise and passed beneath the most beautiful whores of the city and they were no more to him than panels in a church.

He expected to be watched by agents, by all. He felt like fire was bursting from behind his own eyes. How could he not be noticed? *Write of me*, he thought. *Try to write of kings and agents when love is the unearthly glory. Do you believe that?* he asked himself. *How foolish can you become?*

And when the Chevalier greeted him from a coffee shop, Noon did not care how measured the coincidence was. He sat down on a wooden bench beside the Chevalier and agreed to take an ice with the Frenchman.

'You look most content,' commented the Chevalier.

'I am,' said Noon, and couldn't stop himself from laughing. 'I am sorry.'

'The young girl from the ridotto?'

Noon nodded. 'I must introduce you.'

'I know who she is,' smiled the Chevalier.

Noon looked at him steadily. 'You do?'

'It is odd,' said the Chevalier, 'that whenever we meet you have escaped the escort of your tutor.'

'Strange,' agreed Noon, 'considering how much time I spend in his company.'

'You have different priorities perhaps?'

'My priority is one that cannot be shared.'

'You are in love?'

'I think I am.'

'And that is all that is important to you?'

'All?' said Noon. 'How could one have room for more?'

'For some love is divided between family and God, or money. I suppose they are all loves of a kind.'

'No, they are not,' answered Noon. 'They are all compromises.'

The Chevalier laughed at Noon's youth and began to think of him as so intoxicated by the fumes of his heart that he could not be manipulated. 'And your tutor's priorities are different from your own?'

'He is a social creature,' said Noon. 'He observes to write.'

'Yes,' said the Chevalier. 'I have read his book.'

'You found it . . .?'

'Illuminating,' said the Chevalier, 'for those who have not travelled before. He has many friends?'

'Everywhere.'

'And does your education suffer?'

'Horribly,' laughed Noon.

'These tours are not for education, are they?'

'No,' agreed Noon warily. 'They are to make men of boys.'

'This you achieved last night?'

'Many times over.'

The Chevalier had been watching a figure walk down the street towards them. Finally, Noon followed his gaze and to his amazement and sudden perturbation found himself face to face with another Englishman. It was evident in everything about the man: the cut of his coat, the style of his peruke, his colouring and the identical recognition that seemed to be processed in his face as he stared at Noon.

'Welcome,' said the Chevalier.

'I am sorry if I am late,' said the man.

'Henry Hawthorn, may I introduce you to the Viscount Stilwell.'

Noon rose and they shook hands. *Late*, thought Noon, *then in some way this is intended. What does he want of me? How can he seek to disturb my day when I cannot be disturbed. Not truly*. Despite this self-assurance, Noon understood the precarious nature of his predicament. How could he tell who Hawthorn was, or even if Stilwell had met him before? The first thought that occurred to Noon was not that he might be discovered as an agent of treason, but that his greater sin was treachery against his station, and that he would be thrust backwards into servitude, falling away from Natalia, from wealth, from this unfamiliar freedom.

'Did we not meet at Oxford?' enquired Hawthorn, his tone friendly but the question too quick, surely predetermined and absent of the politesse that Stilwell's title deserved.

'No,' said Noon. Impoliteness, he reckoned, should be returned with impoliteness. He barely looked at the man as he spoke. 'I was educated at Dengby.'

'And now abroad,' said the Chevalier.

'It is,' smiled Noon, 'a process of endless drudgery.'

Hawthorn pulled a chair up to the table. 'I feel sure we have met before. You are a friend of Lord Anston's?'

Noon knew him. A pompous neighbour who lived just far enough from Dengby for Stilwell to have nothing to do with him.

'I have some knowledge of him,' said Noon coldly, 'but would not call him my friend.'

'He thinks highly of you,' said Hawthorn, a petite smile addressed at Noon.

'I am most sorry that I cannot return the compliment.'

The Chevalier laughed. 'You are hard to please.'

Noon shrugged. 'One's own company is preferable to poor company.'

'Do you always go about alone then?' asked Hawthorn. 'Without so much as a servant?'

'I find,' said Noon, 'that servants are useful as assistants to action, but superfluous for thought.'

'Where is Dengby?' asked Hawthorn.

'Not far from Ironbridge,' said Noon.

'I have a friend in Bridgnorth —'

'Then perhaps you will pass the night at Dengby on your next visit.' Noon rose and when the others attempted to stand he bid them keep their seats. 'Good day. I wish you a pleasant stay in Venice.'

'You leave so soon?' asked Hawthorn.

'South for Florence,' said Noon.

'I expect we shall see each other there,' said the Chevalier, smiling.

'It would not surprise me.'

The Chevalier nodded his head politely then turned to demand coffee.

Noon reported the incident to Jelborne, who grinned and told Noon that it was the sign of a desperate man who knew less than nothing.

194

'So what is Hawthorn?' asked Noon.

'If the Chevalier were one of the king's hounds then Hawthorn would be the runt of a lesser litter.' The Chevalier would move weeks behind them, Jelborne insisted. In turn, the tutor described a visit he had made that afternoon to Morosoni.

'He said,' started Jelborne, 'that he might have said something to upset you the afternoon when you had swum together, side by side in the water.'

'I see,' said Noon, 'and what did you tell him?'

'I told him that your behaviour was indeed changed but that he should have no worries of being to blame. I said that you had fallen in love. He asked if it was with the merchant's daughter.'

'There are a thousand merchants' daughters,' snorted Noon. 'What did you say?'

'I said that you were in love with Silver's daughter,' replied Jelborne. 'He sits on the Council of Ten, Thomas, he knows more of your days and your nights than I do. At least he knows he has been bettered by the fairer sex rather than betrayed in buggery.'

'And your request?' asked Noon.

'Most compliant and gentlemanly,' said Jelborne. 'He has a third carriage, somewhat grander than our caleche, that he was to place on sale. Instead, it is ours until the New Year.'

Noon nodded. 'Success,' he said.

'At least we know the seats will be soft.'

'Why is that?' asked Noon.

'For his aching arse,' laughed the tutor.

'Have you told anyone of his sodomy?' asked Noon.

'Before I leave Venice?' asked Jelborne. 'How unwise that would be. He made the vaguest of references to his persuasion and I offered him the blankest face of incomprehension. I am sure he has trusted you well with his secret.'

'Yes,' said Noon. 'I cannot imagine you passing that information onwards.'

'Or ever selling it,' said Jelborne.

Noon spent the following three nights back at the island of La Giudecca, alone with Natalia in their white room, arriving by gondola at dusk and leaving at dawn, uncaring of Jelborne's world of agents and eyes. It left the couple only nine hours in which to make heady promises and entwine their bodies, pressing them against one another to pretend two one. Their second night together they discussed their love, the next their marriage and finally their children, and named all four. On each night, Natalia would play a different role, an English gentlewoman, a Venetian courtesan, a Parisian bone-setter, and she would encourage Noon to play with her.

There was a bright intelligence in her, devoted to transforming exaggerations into fact. Noon thought this a fine feat of imagination, and it made his own secret seem dimmer. He could not be sure, but he suspected that perhaps in her fevered play she had even less idea of an idea of who she was than he did. In this way, he suspected that their love might be one more of her temporary creations. It worried him, but he drew comfort from the fact that all roles would end in love-making. Noon would stare into her eyes, lying by her side, and she would wave her hand across his face to disturb his intensity.

'Why do you look at me like that?'

'Because you have no measure of your own importance,' he would say, with the slightest smile so that she did not know for certain whether he was earnest or teasing.

She would laugh and absorb the compliment and press her hand against her breast and look away as if such flattery were too much for a simple Parisian bone-setter to bear. He held his secret until the last night before her father's return, when he confessed that he would be leaving Venice before her, two days from now for Florence. They could not look at one another.

'We knew it would happen,' said Noon softly.

'Not so soon,' she whispered. 'Why can we not have our own world? Why would you not stay for me? You are His Lordship, he is your servant.'

'My father instructs and I must obey,' said Noon. 'At Naples, we are as one.'

'How can I trust you?' asked Natalia.

'Because I am truth. My eyes will tell you.' Noon meant it, though he knew he was far from truth. Can a love like this last, he thought, when you do not know a thing about me? When you do not know of my daughter, my past, my name, the contours of my heart? He was sorely tempted to reveal all, but this spell of intimacy would be broken and could never be recreated. He would rather have a temporary love than none at all.

'Why would a man like you not presume on me? Why would he not play with me abroad and return to forget? You might have a dozen English wives and I'd be no wiser. And so I believe you: you think I shine in sun, but how would you treat me in English rain?'

Thomas Noon broke into an easy grin. 'I could touch your face in a lightless night and still know your beauty. All you throw at me is doubt, while all I show you is constancy.'

'It worries me my father likes you.'

'Because he is suddenly more fond of lords than tutors?'

'I have never met your father,' said Natalia, 'but know mine. He has ethics of a variable kind. He may love me deeply but he thinks all the world is rigging to be climbed. It is all gold to him, but he is what I am used to, who else would care for me?'

'I would.'

'This is one time, and next year will be another, but you have a father of your own, with his rules and obligations, and you are his – you are his only son. You are not only an heir but an instrument.'

'We shall see each other in Naples,' said Noon, 'you shall have to trust me.'

They slept in each other's arms, but when Noon woke he felt a moment of security in his own sure words from the previous night and then an unfamiliar yawning that gave way to a sharp twist of the gut at the prospect of weeks without her. Without her he knew there could be only doubt. Let us not pretend that there is no one outside our world, reasoned Noon to himself, I have done that once and seen it unravel. Let us not do that. We have come to each other naked, we have held each other and together we can achieve simplicity. And it cannot be more than this, we cannot attempt to elevate it, or pretend that it has not happened before. And not just before, but every day, in every city in this world. So let us be sharper than that, let us know that love is a passing fume. But let us also believe in it, while it should last.

'Shall we write?' he asked as they sipped at their coffee, deposited outside of the room with a signal knock at the door.

'How can we?' she said. 'I shall be in a dozen places.'

'But I shall be only in Florence and Rome.'

'And you think I must write to you and bare my heart and must survive on nothing but sea air? Where is the love in that?'

'Then we shall write letters,' decided Noon, 'that we shall not send, but keep until we meet again. I will write and hold them, and you may do what you may.'

It was the sweetness of this, the surety of the proposal that touched her and made her nod in agreement. 'I will do as you do.'

Noon tried to cool his head after their goodbye but was surprised at his reaction. Neither wept, for both were too angry at life. Thomas Noon felt agreeable enough for an hour, but then panic swept about him as he walked and he could not swallow it. He stopped sharply and felt a need to purge. He hurried towards a barber in San Moise and bled himself of two ounces, knowing it was the only way to lighten his soul.

He knew how poorly matched they were. How he wished to reinvent himself once, while she was at constant play. His role was entirely serious, enduring; hers were a series of ephemeral sketches displaying the willingness to experience and the need to withdraw. The clothes he wore were the clothes he had wished to wear, while she would always wish a wardrobe of disparate garments. Yet, for whatever reason, love had descended and it was the one role they both might share and revel in.

To think that it might be mutual, that happiness might be there before him and returned soundly, it defied all presumptions and multiplied his expectations. Jelborne might have his agenting, and priests might have their gods, and his father might assist kings, but the fact lay plain and simple before Noon: none of these mattered at all. All that was important in life was that which lay before him, that their love might stand a chance at lasting.

For Jelborne, Noon's distraction was a comforting blindness and he went about the business of their departure with great efficiency and speed. He was much admired for the structuring of his deals and his promises signed with a flourish and locked within vaults. Wealth would accumulate under the sovereignty of James, and a portion of Venice would flourish alongside. Venetians might not return to their former glories, but they might fund the postponement of their decline.

CHAPTER FIFTEEN

Cesare inhaled deeply, standing behind the horses as if he were tasting the finest of imported perfumes. He had not guessed that a man could miss an entire breed. He spent half an hour walking in circles around these ordinary post horses, brushing their black coats and chattering softly while rubbing their noses. It was odd, thought Noon, how he barely glanced at the carriage. Morosoni's temporary gift was bedizened with a bronze trim of waves that ran above the doors and purple plumage that sprung from the centre of the roof. It was not to Noon's taste. The velvet upholstery matched the feathers. Jelborne smiled at Noon's discomfort.

'The end of Venice,' said Jelborne, looking back towards the lagoon. 'A wonder for a week and then what? Nothing but dirty water.'

Since Venice was soon to lose possession of Natalia, Noon was almost inclined to agree.

'You will miss your swims, though,' added the tutor.

'I can wait as long as Naples.'

'There are always the fountains of Rome.'

They headed south in the carriage, passing along the paved road away from the ocean. Noon stared at the sea behind them with its wintry promises, rolling up and away from the shore. A misty rain came down and merged with the coastal fog. Sight was lost and the smell grew heavy. A musty odour, that of the sea drawing a veil to bury its dead, fish heads and entrails interred beneath the sands. The shoed horses rapped against the flagstones as they trotted past reed houses that rose from the countryside waiting quietly for spring.

Watching the wheels of a passing carriage, Noon thought of his daughter. He had filled the wheelbarrow with straw and laid her upon her stomach. She gripped the sides and peered over as Noon ran her up and down the path behind the gatehouse. Though he could not see her face, he knew she was wide-eyed from the joy of her laugh. Noon could not help where his mind wandered next, to the limp little body in his hands. It was a familiar cloud that broke inside him, that would pour and then pass him to Stilwell lying beneath the branches. The birds must have picked at him, insects devoured him.

And where have you gone, he thought, *and what now do you think of me? 'I think you look well on it, but who do you do this for?' I do it for us. 'For our father?' Yes, I do it for him. 'And what do you gain?' I gain nothing. 'Do you believe that?' No*, admitted Thomas Noon. *'And do you worry for your life? How can you not, when mine was taken by chance and you are shadowed and threatened? Attention, Thomas, should you not be paying more of it?'*

The travellers spent their first night in Rovigo and, while Jelborne slept fast, Noon sat composing a letter to Natalia by a tallow candle. He wrote a small, sad poem and dedicated it to her, then folded it carefully and allowed his mind to rest. The next day they made fair progress, passing over four rivers to the city of Ferrara standing proudly on the banks of the Po. Cesare intended to stop, but Jelborne insisted they might reach Bologna before dark. As the sun faded into greyness they passed by a lake. Jelborne motioned if Noon would like to stop to swim, and was answered with a shake of the head.

'No,' sighed Noon. 'I am in a hurry for Florence.'

'How sad,' said Jelborne, 'for we are not headed for Florence.'

Noon looked up. 'Then for where?'

'Rome.'

'We cannot miss Florence,' pleaded Noon. 'If not for my education, then for the pretence of my education. Surely there is money in the Tuscan states?'

'There are other matters,' said Jelborne. 'Mr Silver has let us know that word is through from England. They now know that a company of four is agitating for gold.'

'But we are three.'

'And it is our finest, our only secret. They also expect us to be in Florence within a month.'

'If we do not appear,' said Noon, 'then do we not confirm their suspicions?'

'If no one appears, then they would be right to suspect. I have written to my friend Benjamin Evelyn, who travels with the young Lord Braithwaite, and have issued them a grand invitation to Florence, extended from a friend of your father's. Evelyn is far too greedy to ignore it. They travel as four already and shall be watched from Florence back to England. They will be ignorant of the interest they cause and we shall suffer no harm in Rome.'

'And the Chevalier?'

'He is an estimator and an instrument. He will be told where to go. To Evelyn and to Florence.'

'We shall not be followed?'

'You wish it?' asked Jelborne.

'I presume on it,' shrugged Noon. 'It is only that Natalia might send her letters to Florence.'

'She has said she will write to you there?'

'No,' admitted Noon, 'but she might.'

'Allow your mind to rest, Thomas. She travels with her father, the most stubborn and wilful man on God's earth. Should he say he will be in Naples at the end of December, then so shall he be, even if he sells his soul for fair weather. And she shall be as he is. If she has promised herself to you, then so be it. If she had meant to write to Florence, I am sure that she would have told you so.'

'What if they are becalmed on their way south?'

'I suppose if she really is in love,' said Jelborne, 'then she would do the same as you would.'

'Write?' asked Noon.

'Swim,' said Jelborne.

Noon laughed. 'I told the Chevalier that we would be in Florence.'

'See,' said Jelborne, 'you were hard at the work of deception with the greatest of accidental ease. Perhaps he will be kind enough to wait for us there.'

'About Natalia,' said Noon. 'I shall talk no more of her.'

Jelborne clearly didn't believe it, though his smile said that he appreciated Noon would lie so to comfort him.

They stopped outside Bologna, failing to bribe the guards at the Galiera gate to let them pass. The three men settled within the carriage and spent a miserable night snatching at sleep, the tutor complaining about his aching limbs. In the morning the carriage was inspected by customs, the officials encouraged with scrapes of gold, and the weary travellers decided that, despite their eagerness to work in the king's employ, they would spend a day in Bologna and treat themselves well.

Several rivulets cut through the thin city walls, which perhaps helped to explain why Bologna resembled a ship, her two enormous towers cutting the sky as masts. It looked like a city that might move on a stormy day. The inhabitants, thought Noon, might close their shutters and sleep and wake up next to Venice. Once inside the walls, Bologna revealed itself as a city of porticoes, arcades that shielded her large population from summer sun and winter rains. Every building was made of stone or reddish brick, occasionally plastered, and interrupted by piazzas and fountains.

Noon would have spent the day moving in Jelborne's shadow had the sun been strong enough to cast one. Instead, the clouds spat a mild drizzle and they strolled under the arcades from church to cathedral. It seemed to be a city of walkers. Even the women, well-dressed though they were, did not seem to object as strongly as Venetians to putting one foot before another. Jelborne's attempts at enthusiasm were greeted with grim smiles from Noon. Inside the cathedral were frescos of heaven and hell, separated only by an angel. Hell had humans penned in cages, the devil feasting on flesh, demons stringing up men like slaughtered cattle above boiling pots. Heaven, on the other hand, looked peculiarly like the cathedral they stood in. *Is this*, puzzled Noon, *as much as we might wish for?*

'My feet hurt,' said Noon, leaving the building having bowed solemnly to three priests by the door.

'Cathedrals do that to feet.' Jelborne considered his own state of exhaustion for a moment. 'I suppose that before we leave we must trudge and see Cecilia.'

'Who is she?' asked Noon, following him out into the street.

'A saint.'

'A dead one?' asked Noon.

'Show me one that lives,' groaned Jelborne, yawning and stretching, and led the way.

The church of San Giovanni in Monte lay on top of a small hill that crested by the city walls. It was dark and unloved, blackened by centuries of smoke. Jelborne gave a small donation for the use of a lantern and the two men entered. They stood before Raphael's celebrated painting of St Cecilia and Jelborne opened the gates of the lantern to flood the canvas in flame. The martyred saint stared upwards at angels.

'Why was she sainted?' whispered Noon.

'For her purity,' said Jelborne softly. 'She would not lie with her husband and told him that she was surrounded by angels. Instead of sleeping with her husband, she converted him, poor fellow. The Romans buried her alive and cut off her head.'

Noon could not understand why purity involved denial of the flesh. He could think of no better or more worthy desire than that of his to take Natalia again. It was, he thought, a consecration, if thoughts were pure. He could not imagine a more foolish reason to martyr oneself, unless, he supposed, she was requested to do so by God. If he did things entirely on behalf of his father and brother, then perhaps it was also excusable to direct one's life for God. Cecilia, concluded Noon, had been, like him, both a traitor and yet true.

They tramped back through the rain to a comfortable apartment they had rented for the night. The weather brought a sombre mood down between them. Jelborne watched his distracted charge spoon and sip at his broth, leave his dried beef alone, barely raise his wine glass. He had always thought of Noon as so much older than Stilwell, but there were not two years between them and never had Noon seemed younger. Instead of his direct eyes, deliberately quiet when serving but so alive in the weeks since Genoa, now his face was shaded downwards. The balance of Noon's relationship with Natalia has always been in Noon's favour, but Jelborne wondered if absence were tipping the scales, or whether he were thinking of His Lordship, or even his daughter.

'Do you think of *him*?' asked Jelborne when they were undressing for bed.

'God?' asked Noon.

'Stilwell.'

'I do,' Noon confessed, 'but I do so less and less.'

'Only of Natalia?'

'Is it wrong?'

'Nothing that is human can be wrong,' said Jelborne. 'Sometimes I miss his company.'

'As do I,' said Noon. He stretched back upon his bed, pushing his shape into the hard mattress. 'If we are discovered, what will they do to us?'

'I do not know.'

'Might we be tried?'

'I doubt they would bother.'

'How do we protect ourselves?'

'Deny all,' said Jelborne, 'to others and to ourselves.'

'In Naples,' asked Noon, 'when we have the gold, will that not be true danger?'

'Life shall be at its most exciting.'

'They shall not want us to leave, shall they?'

'No,' said Jelborne, his voice strong and serious. 'They will not wish it.'

They were already undressed when the knock came

upon the door. Before them stood a rain-soaked priest, hands clasped in apology. He began speaking in a cascade of words that ran together so fast that Noon had to signal for calm and beg him to repeat himself.

'An accident,' said the priest, 'on the road from Rovigo. He still lives but we must take confession. He speaks only English. You will come with me, you will translate?'

Jelborne and Noon dressed hurriedly, sombre and important under the weight of their imposed duty. A stranger, a compatriot, most probably a young man, no different from Stilwell, little different from themselves.

They hurried under the arcades, past the towers and out towards the stables by the gates of the city. A group was gathered under bracketed torch-light, protected from the rain by the portico of a small stone church. Before them, on a seat hewn from the walls of the church, lay the prone figure of the Englishman. Noon could see another body, outside the circle of light, that had been draped in cloth. The edges of the material had been tucked under the form so that the wind would not be tempted to reveal the dead.

The dying man had been stripped of his shirt; his pale breeches were soaked with urine. Whatever panic and pain had descended on him had now passed. His torso and arms were marked with the thin scars of fencing swords, crescent smiles of dead flesh that awaited the rest of his body. His peruke was missing. Priests huddled around his head, clearing at the sound of Jelborne and Noon's arrival. And there before Noon was Hawthorn, the

Chevalier's English friend, so inquisitive and impolite. Whatever his sins, Noon forgave him, looking instead at the purple swollen blotches about his body where broken bones had not pierced the skin but been driven within. *You are bleeding inside*, thought Noon. *You are drowning without the slightest sign.*

'You wish to take confession?' asked Jelborne. 'What faith are you?'

Hawthorn stared up at the vague shape addressing him in English.

'I am English,' he breathed and grunted in pain.

'I know,' said Jelborne.

Hawthorn watched the second figure approach. Noon did not know if he was recognised.

'You are not English,' whispered Hawthorn.

Jelborne raised his eyes to Noon.

'Does he wish to confess?' asked the agitated priest.

'No, but pray for him,' said Jelborne in Italian.

Hawthorn lay his head back against the table and was dead before the priests had completed their prayers.

Jelborne and Noon were thanked profusely as they were escorted back to their apartment. 'It is so important,' said the priest wishing them goodnight, 'to have no reason to fear your death.'

Jelborne closed the door behind him. 'What did he mean, "You are not English"?'

'He was a friend of the Chevalier's,' said Noon. 'Henry Hawthorn. The one who threatened me with questions of Dengby.'

'And you doubt whose side God is on?'

'I doubt that this had anything to do with God.'

'Mr Noon,' smiled Jelborne, 'you are beginning to see calculation and judgement where there is none.'

'It is all too strong for chance,' said Noon, and wondered if Jelborne had not fully explained the danger they were in. It seemed to Noon that Hawthorn's death was a strange reflection of Stilwell's murder, another stirring jolt.

Chapter Sixteen

Noon would remember Bologna for Hawthorn and for the towers that pierced the sky, one of which seemed always to be bent towards him, an accusing finger which traced his path. There was also a statue of Neptune in the Piazza Maggiore and this he could have stared at for hours. At the corners of the statue, beneath Neptune himself, were four ladies, facing the piazza. Each held her breasts in her hands, squirting forth water. Beneath, their legs were spread in provocation, their centres covered by tiny scalloped shells. They looked at him, teased him and asked him if he remembered what it was like to take Natalia. Noon thought a moment and then confessed, *No, I can't remember. Of all that I can remember, I can't remember those evenings. I can think of them in words of wonder, but I cannot conjure them well enough to* feel. Natalia had suddenly seemed as distant as the stone and the erection that had begun to grow opposite these sirens died of its own accord.

There were still over two hundred miles to Rome. Even on fine days they were the victims of inconsistency, subjected to post houses with poor horses or no horses, to ill-tempered landlords and uncertain accommodation. It was a rare day that they made over thirty miles, even when the land was as barren as that which separated Bologna from Florence. They were the only travellers on the road insisting on taking their carriage. So often did they have to dismount while the horses were driven over cracked paving or holes in the road that Noon understood the local preference for travelling by litters. For every stretch of good road where they trotted past a sedan and waved, came two where they were passed by an ambling pedestrian, amused at their presumption.

'Was Hawthorn murdered?' asked Noon, wrapping his arms around him and pressing his cold hands beneath his armpits.

'By his horse,' said Jelborne. 'Any man rushing unknown roads at night is wagering his own bones.'

'I suppose,' muttered Noon.

'Now ask yourself why he was travelling at such speed and why to Bologna, and then perhaps it has to do with us and then perhaps not. I did not *know* the man, you did not *like* the man. Let us make no more of it than that.'

But Noon was affected, for what had seemed a game now had permanent repercussions, lives given directly, or indirectly, to abstract causes. Stilwell's death, Noon concluded, had been both accidental *and* murderous and Hawthorn's demise could only be guessed at, but Noon did not put Jelborne above retribution. He had no wish to become another coincidence of the road.

Outside of Bologna the little fertile hills had given way to the ridges of the Apennines. The only joy Noon could find in these mountains was that they afforded a view of the sea. They passed an eternal flame that rose from the ground outside the village of Pietra Mala, close to the borders of the Pope's domain and the lands of Tuscany. The night was spent at a public house at Rifreddo, the highest village in the Apennines, and Noon thought himself taken with fevers, so much did he shiver. In his sweat, he was reminded of Venetian warmth, the sheen of Natalia's body, and then came the ache that it would be weeks before he might see her again.

Snows threatened all about and came in flurries, but it was still too early in the season for them to stick. A wary Cesare seemed to keep one eye upon the road and the other upon the sky, and Jelborne, despite his assurances that they could not have been followed, was always staring back down the road. It seemed some of Noon's nervousness had been passed to the tutor. Once over the steepest of the inclines, the paving improved dramatically and the party was able to make good pace down towards Florence.

They could see Florence beneath them, a city of gardens, so that if it were not for the amounts of marble, Noon would have thought it a city dedicated to agriculture. It sat between three hills, like the floor of an amphitheatre, each slope flecked with houses and olive trees that led down to the central gates. Noon could see that the Arno bisected the city, hooped by four bridges. To the west, the valley had managed to retain a hint of greenness, as if even the seasons could not entirely extinguish the richness of Florentine soil. Jelborne bid them pause a moment, and while the horses nibbled the high grass by the roadside, the tutor appeared to wonder what might wait for him below, weighing the danger of descending against the profits they might reap.

The tutor ground his teeth, the horses chewed their grass and Noon sat thinking of Natalia. He could picture her only in fragments, the whole had been lost. He wondered if he would even recognise her. Jelborne interrupted his thoughts by ordering Cesare to take them south.

'We'll miss nothing,' said Jelborne. 'Besides, they herd their women in Florence, drive them about and keep them close. It's a city for the eyes and not the hands.'

They changed horses at a post house in San Casciano, some nine miles south of the city, then paused in Poggibonsi for Jelborne to buy a wad of tobacco. They spent one night within the walls of Siena and the next at an inn in Radicofani. Noon wrote and rewrote to Natalia, always rereading in the morning and trying to strike the perfect balance. Expressions that revealed weakness were dismissed. Phrases that gave too much of love were balanced by strength. Noon was almost amused by his growing level of obsession.

After a week of rattling inside the carriage, grateful for the cover against the rain, they ran their horses hard up to a posting station outside of Vico where, once again, Noon could see the sea. While the horses were changed, Noon and Cesare walked quietly between rows of sycamores and chestnut trees. They wandered down to the lakeside and both hunted for stones to throw at the water. After a few minutes they grew tired and sat on a rock shaded from the threat of rain by a giant chestnut tree.

'How long,' asked Cesare, guessing at his thoughts, 'can you think without thinking of her?'

Noon laughed. 'A minute, sometimes two.'

Their final night outside of Rome was spent in Prima Porta, and Thomas Noon, suddenly prone to distraction, was confused by the promise of the city. Rome, which he had read of, Pliny's Rome, Cicero's, Julius Caesar's, was now within reach. Even Jelborne was roused from his casual manner, and the two men sat at a table, wine between them, talking of the greatness of the past, of figures, born two thousand years before, as if they were recently deceased friends. Yet neither mentioned Stilwell, that late shade that knitted them together as slyly as attic cobwebs, and Noon rarely talked of his daughter.

'We think always of progress in England,' said Jelborne. 'Everything must always get better, busier and bigger, but tomorrow you shall look at Rome and learn. At her height,' continued the tutor, 'perhaps two million inhabitants, and now, not one tenth that number. She is no hive of industry. It is the Queen Bee of Catholicism, sitting here, filled with drones. They do not know how malnourished it has become.'

Rome had not been abandoned by men so much as

reclaimed by nature. As they rattled along the stone paths towards the gates of the city, Noon could see that everywhere vines covered fallen columns and cattle stood in their shade. It was a city built of marble, its monuments so closely packed and so distinctive that the least knowledgeable of travellers might find points of interest. Everywhere there were traces of magnificence and symbols of devastation. Much of what the barbarians had spared had been destroyed by the subsequent generations.

Engravings of Rome lined the walls of Dengby and from the carriage Noon could see familiar objects in this unknown world. They were stopped at the Porta del Popolo and purchased licences, under false names, for an extended stay. They trotted past the Pantheon and, while Jelborne restrained himself, Noon was agape, reacting as much to the ancient structure as to the nonchalance of those Romans who walked past without even granting it a glance. And churches. Why, with every turn they took they passed another, as common as English taverns. And between the churches, robed abbots moved in lines, like black beads threaded on a single string. The vast dome of St Peter's across the Tiber must have been a mile away, but Noon held his hand up to it and still could not block it from view.

Jelborne had opted to use the marquis's money to rent an apartment within a modest palazzo rather than intrude on one of their noble connections. It was his aim to draw as much money from Rome as possible and he did not wish to hinder its flow by turning one family against another through his selection of lodging.

'We wish,' explained Jelborne, 'to make as few ripples as we may. The slower the news of our arrival heads north the longer we may move in safety.'

'But they will have news of Hawthorn,' interrupted Noon.

'Unlikely,' said Jelborne. 'Before we left, I sent gold to the priest for a gravestone. I told him to bury the boy as Watkins.'

'Why,' asked Noon, as Cesare pulled to a halt outside their palazzo, 'do they have the word "*Rispetto*" painted against their house?'

'Prudes,' said Jelborne. 'It stops the priests from pissing against it.'

The building was a low, flat affair, half a mile from the Castel Sant'Angelo, and if the Tiber had moved with any energy at all, Noon might have heard it from his bed. The ground floor was inhabited by their landlady, a woman whose age was buried beneath powders and perfumes. Her breasts were squeezed and supported by an elaborate rigging that would have brought admiration from architects and sailors alike. Within an hour, she had already given evidence that she was willing to swoon under Jelborne's charms. At least, thought Noon, such passion might translate into a constant state of cleanliness and the willingness to launder and scrub.

Noon was excited and distracted the first two days. While Jelborne issued letters announcing their arrival,

Noon begged a day or two of rest before business might begin. Jelborne was temporarily returned to his masquerade of educator. He enjoyed watching Noon's reaction to the strange city that Rome had become. They walked about the Forum, now a cattle market, past the column of Marcus Aurelius where the coffee sellers gathered to roast their beans each morning. Jelborne guessed there was almost thirty foot of earth on the Rome they read about, turning great columns into boundary stones and high walls into convenient seats. At the Arch of Septimus Severus, the two men paused for a shave and the smooth-cheeked Noon reached up to touch the cornice. Trees grew in arches, jasmine and acanthus hung from the crevices of walls.

Noon could not understand if he should take pleasure or feel pain at Rome's state. She seemed stripped and skeletal. Everywhere Jelborne pointed out trattorias and houses, shops and palazzi that had stolen marble columns from the ruins and used them as the spines of their structure. The entire city reminded Noon of a Capuchin church near the Piazza Berberini where the chandeliers were made of human pelvises and the candle holders were cut from the top of skulls. It was a city that constantly devoured itself so that it might survive.

On their third day, after their first meeting with a velvet-robed noble by the name of Corsini, where Noon had sat and nodded and thought of nothing but Natalia, his behaviour began to change. Noon didn't mean anything by it. He helped a porter take a heavy sack from his stiff shoulders and rest it on a windowsill outside a building. The man's thanks, his surprise at being helped, were genuine and they warmed Noon. Despite being both constant quarry and absent lover he could still smile in helping another, but it was a brief warmth, like passing in front of a fire in a great and gloomy hall, and so Noon attempted to repeat the process as often as possible. It was always with simple small acts (a door held open, a man allowed to pass), none ever unbecoming to a gentleman, and he began to survive on the scraps of gratitude that were cast his way. Noon's amusement at his state of love had begun to fade.

Jelborne noted and understood. The servant was starved in his absence from Natalia and the tutor sympathised but did not address the subject. He had warned Noon against her and was not about to retract his low opinion of how women in love behave. He preferred the company of his landlady, experienced but free from disease, grateful, and understanding that beds were made to be rumpled, and that passion was a passing thing. The condition of Noon's heart in the end meant little. There were infinitely greater forces at work and Jelborne was simply the miller who drove his horses in circles, anxious for grist. He was nervous himself, could not always conjure an erection to accompany the romancing of his landlady. Everywhere he now saw shadows.

On one of his happier days, a new thought had occurred to Thomas Noon, one that harnessed the most important parts of his life and unified them. There were three things that had ever mattered to Noon, three people that had focused and shaped his life: Stilwell, his daughter and Natalia. Through the only survivor, he now thought the others might be reclaimed. If he were to marry Natalia, if he were to return to Dengby and be accepted as a son by the marquis, then he might begin a family of his own and break the chain of bastardy so prominent in his life. The key to all, he thought, was Natalia, she who might, as his wife, bring Sarah back into the world, and if not Sarah, then another life to love. It was an absurd future that Noon dreamed of, but oddly was within his reach.

Rome in early December had begun to grow cold. More so inside than out, where the rooms had no stoves or fire-places and were good for little more than sleep. In their apartment, the travellers relied only on *scaldini*, small china pots full of hot embers which they grasped to warm their hands. There was a bust of Jesus Christ that stood on a pedestal in the centre of the room. It was where Jelborne hung his wig in the evenings.

The miserable are fond of the miserable and Noon was spied and engaged at a *conversazione* by a young man, about his own age and of ancient family. The name was in fact all that was still great about the family. They were so steeped in debt that they lived on the borders of the Trastevere where they were neither accepted into the merchant class, nor could they afford to move among their fellows. The youth, Arrigo Caetani di Sermoneta, had an ivory face, cut in fine angles and framed by curled black locks. He moved with great deliberateness under his *abate*'s cloak. It helped to disguise the thinness of his suits. A pair of forceful eyes challenged all who stared into them, making his haunted look resemble a form of nobility.

Noon was a man in love with an absent woman, but Caetani was in love with the dead. It was his grandfather who had ruined his father, his father who had passed on the great stories of their family to the son. Caetani now sought favour in the church, like a thousand other young Romans, each with their thoughts of priestdom and popery. Names are known in Rome, and those who remembered his late grandfather were still in a position to keep the grandson down.

Jelborne looked upon this sudden friendship with a mixture of amusement and suspicion. He had never seen a pair of tortured souls befriend one another so quickly. What struck Jelborne as entertaining was that they were both responsible for their own pain. Their imaginations would not let them rest. In any other city, Jelborne would have considered Caetani's position foolish and he would have recommended that the young man apply himself to work to regain his family's lost fortune. But Romans did not move far from Rome. It was all they knew and their sphere of influence was limited by the papal borders. The only advancement possible for a young noble was through the church and there, the tutor acknowledged, he would find himself as frequently blocked as promoted. It was also possible that Caetani was an agent, an agent against his own faith, but Jelborne thought him too self-indulgent to act for another.

On the fourth day of their acquaintance, Caetani persuaded Noon to accompany him on a visit to the church of Santa Maria in Aracoeli. It was, he explained, a depositary for written wishes and so the two men spent the evening before scribbling letters, trusting to one another the dreams they wished to realise. A visit to this church was, explained Caetani, the surest way in Rome to transform hope into joy.

'A woman?' Caetani had said, examining Noon's request, and thought it a touch disappointing, almost banal.

'Your family?' Noon had questioned looking up from his friend's letter, understanding that Caetani could never have thought himself in love.

The following morning, the Church of Santa Maria in Aracoeli loomed above them, a red-brick altar to the heavens. One hundred and twenty-four steps separated the aspirants from the sacred image of the baby Jesus inside. It had, Caetani said, been carved from an olive tree at Gethsemane. The icon of the *bambino* had arrived that morning in a golden coach and been escorted up the steps by a pair of Franciscan monks to a chorus of pleas and exhortation. On each step now an applicant waited, climbing upwards on bended knee. The better dressed were attended by servants, who laid a pillow to protect their dresses and breeches from chafing. Caetani had brought no such protection.

It took an hour of climbing under a light rain before

they reached the entrance to the church. It was filled with candles and a shuffling sound as the line wound slowly towards the *bambino*. The pale stone floor was inlaid with the figures of those buried beneath and cut by coloured mosaics that scraped against raw knees. On either side of the church ran a row of columns, each one topped with a pastel portrait of a saint. They all seemed to be asking the same question. *'What are you doing, Thomas Noon, on your knees in front of a Catholic god?'* Praying for a Catholic girl, thought Noon. *Praying for safety in a Catholic country.* Finally in front of the *bambino*, Noon delivered his letter into a brimming basket and looked up into the figure's eyes for some sign of recognition. The wooden child was decorated with jewels, his painted cheeks insolent and playful. *Let me have what I wish for*, prayed Noon. *Let me have her as she was, and what I do for my father, I will do for your Father. Am I not following the path of love, am I not following the path of duty? Are these not the foundations of your church?*

Outside the church the two men rubbed their knees. Caetani had rolled his breeches up to save them, but Noon had bloodied and chafed his skin.

'That is good luck,' smiled Caetani, rubbing life back into his legs. 'To bleed for the *bambino*, it will have seized his attention.'

'And how will we know?' said Noon, surprised at his own earlier devotion, which had passed almost as soon as he stood.

'If his cheeks glowed,' whispered Caetani, 'he favours you. If they remained pale, your request is ill-advised.'

Noon had looked hard in those still eyes, but there was

not enough light to give any hint of what the infant Jesus thought of his selfish request.

'What happens to our letters?' asked Noon.

'They are all burned each evening,' explained Caetani.

'Now this,' said Noon, 'is a wonderful test for your god. Perhaps the *bambino* shall return my love, or perhaps all he will have taken is the skin from my knees.'

'Do not mock him,' said Caetani. 'He has performed greater miracles for lesser men.'

Alone at night, before he attempted sleep, Noon imagined other men's hands on Natalia, other loves stronger, even more sudden than their own, and his skin would begin to itch. He grew so uncomfortable that he knelt within his sheets on the bed and wrapped his arms about his knees and tried to breathe himself towards good thoughts. I do not love you, he thought, I have loved only Sarah. I do love, but only because I do not know you yet. I cannot love you because I am but a grand lie, compared to your thousand small inventions.

Noon relied upon Caetani for relief from himself. He followed the young Roman about the cobbled streets until after two weeks it seemed as if he had stood outside and inside each of Rome's three hundred churches. Fully a quarter of her men dressed in papal cloths and Noon guessed that he had tipped his hat at half of them. He had prayed beneath the open roof of the Pantheon day and night, in sun and in rain, had even begun to speak to God in his churches, on the vague premise that Rome might have some strange connection to the divine.

Papism, thought Noon, first allowed a Protestant to feel superior, so crammed was it with superstition and relics, votive candles and sore knees. It stank of paganism and, even worse, the irrational. England had been so, and had evolved, adjusted a religion to suit a temper, for the importations from Rome were not suited to such a steady man as Noon had been. Now he understood that supplication was not the same as belief, but a more needy, more human emotion.

One of Noon's preferred diversions was to accompany Caetani on evenings with the Accademia degli Arcadi, a group of young men dedicated to the purification of Italian poetry. It had also occurred to Noon that Caetani might be an agent. Otherwise, he reasoned, how had he not felt the familiar threat of shadows in Rome? Yet it did not matter to him, for if Caetani was an agent, Noon had told him nothing and, besides, had pulled him away from Jelborne, the true man of business.

The poets met near the Janiculum and after walking a mile or two down the Tiber would retire to a member's house to discuss Petrarch or Platonic idealism. Noon was welcomed, albeit as one from an inferior land who used an inferior language. His own grasp of Roman was grudgingly appreciated by these men Noon considered barely fit for work. Had they been born to servitude, they would have been abandoned on a hillside years ago: eaten, not reared, by wolves.

It was always Caetani who raised the most interesting of questions, insisting, for example, that true art was neither poetry nor painting, but a mixture of the two, and no man could be an artist without being a poet and vice versa. His colleagues would never let Caetani have the last word in any conversation, since there was a brutal hierarchy within the club where wealth and blood reigned over intelligence.

The Accademia's meeting on Noon's third Thursday in Rome was well attended. Noon sat in a courtyard and listened to some shoddy pastorals, rewarded with much applause, and barely thought to look up until a familiar face caught his eye. There, across from him, sat the Chevalier, who smiled in his direction as if it were merely another in a long line of pleasant coincidences. At the conclusion of the meeting, as they headed for the brisk air, Noon turned to greet the Chevalier. Noon's time of peace was over. *What*, he thought, *do you know now? That we are what we are? That there is no more doubt? That you suspect us for Hawthorn and now come for us?*

'Truly,' said the Frenchman, 'we seem to follow the same path.'

'It is a well-trodden one,' said Noon calmly. 'Permit me to introduce Don Arrigo Caetani.'

The two men bowed before one another, both intrigued as to each other's meaning in Noon's life.

The Chevalier looked down at Noon's legs. 'I have heard you have been seen on your knees in Roman churches. You are not about to suffer a conversion, I hope?'

'No,' said Noon, managing an accompanying laugh. 'My father should be most disappointed to see me return strung in rosaries and the bones of saints.'

Caetani gave a cough of objection.

'You were merely observing customs then?' asked the Chevalier.

'I think,' interrupted Caetani, 'that milord was conducting an experiment as to the effect of our religion. If his wishes are granted, then perhaps together we might convince him from Saul to Paul.'

'And what does the decision weigh on?' asked the Chevalier.

'A woman,' said Caetani, answering on Noon's behalf.

'Then your Protestant soul is safe,' smiled the Chevalier. He put the slightest of stresses on the word 'Protestant', thought Noon, as if the Chevalier was doubting his faith.

Caetani began to nod in agreement, but then shook his head when Noon did not commit to a reaction.

'How did you find Florence?' asked the Chevalier politely.

'I am afraid we were too anxious to reach Rome,' said Noon.

'Such a shame.'

'I trust,' said Noon, 'that you found time in your own itinerary for such a stop.'

'Yes,' said the Chevalier. 'You have not come across Henry Hawthorn on your travels? He has missed an appointment we had promised to keep.'

Noon avoided his gaze. 'I have been lucky enough to avoid all compatriots.'

The Chevalier said nothing.

'The less English I speak,' continued Noon to fill the silence, 'the more Italian I become.'

'And when do you head south?' asked the Chevalier.

'I do not know,' said Noon. 'I am my father's son. I believe he wished me to winter in Rome.'

'When Naples would provide such warmth? Perhaps then our paths shall have to diverge. Another month of damp and my bones will rot.'

'He cannot leave,' said Caetani, 'before I have shown him my seat at Ninfa.'

'Is that not south?' asked the Chevalier.

'A day or so,' said Caetani, 'depending on the weather. If it would interest you, you should join us.'

'I would like that very much,' said the Chevalier. 'Join me now,' he continued. 'I am off to the dealer Paggiani. Perhaps you might find something for your father.'

Caetani encouraged Noon. 'He is the best in Rome.'

'Very well,' said Noon, feeling odd regret at Hawthorn's death. He knew he must remain silent, but wished to explain how the Chevalier should not hold them account-able. How accidents happened, even to agents; how the Viscount Stilwell could attest to that.

They rode in a gold carriage that the Chevalier insisted had been lent to him by the French ambassador.

'Rome,' the Chevalier said on entering, 'can be inter-preted through her carriages. Red for the cardinals, black for the nobles. And this gold, this is a disguise.'

'And what does it disguise you as?' asked Caetani.

'Better blood than I have – an ambassador.'

'I will give you my blood,' said Caetani, 'in turn for your reputation.'

'Be careful,' chided the Chevalier, 'for no man knows his own reputation.'

The primness of their host and dealer Paggiani was in utter contrast to his collection. It was simply too large to bring order to. Paintings touched, frame to frame, on every wall from floor to ceiling. The small garden was choked with statues, nymphs' hands accidentally brushing against satyrs' bellies. The Chevalier told Paggiani that he was uninterested in painting, having already purchased a Tiepolo and Guercino in Venice. What he needed now, for Paris, was a fine sculpture.

Under a light rain, Paggiani led them out into the garden. They had to weave between the carved limbs until they reached a life-size horse made of white marble. On top sat a soldier. 'Guess which is real?' asked Paggiani.

'I don't understand,' said Noon.

'The Roman, the general. I had him built.'

'Why?' asked Noon.

'Because my expert assured me there was once a man atop the horse.'

'How do you know what kind of man sat atop him?' asked Noon.

'Only the generals rode,' said the Chevalier.

'Why would you not leave the horse alone?' said Noon.

'It would be incomplete.'

'Instead, it is uneven,' said Noon.

'He is right,' agreed the Chevalier. 'Show me more.'

Paggiani bowed to Noon's taste, swallowed a grimace and walked them to the largest sculpture in the garden, a copy of Hercules himself. He stood a dozen feet high holding an apple in his hand, a moment of relaxation after completing his first labour. Noon wondered which piece

of art reflected him best. Was he this Herculean imitation, or a mosaic made of a thousand pieces, deliberately
shattered and rejoined beneath their feet? Or like the cen-
turion upon a horse, was he a statue pieced together from
those that were broken about him? They were led from
one sculpture to another, until the Chevalier eventually
excused the little party, correctly believing that interest
was on the wane. He promised to return the next day to
conclude the purchase of Hercules.

'Has ever there been such creation again?' asked
Caetani as they climbed into the ambassador's golden carriage. He seemed to pause before entering, perhaps
hoping that some passer-by might see his ascent.

'Again?' exclaimed the Chevalier. 'You must consider
before. It is all Greek. The Romans thought nothing of
copying exactly.'

'They did it very well,' said Caetani.

'Hawthorn was a great judge of this,' said the Chevalier.
'He was a dealer of paintings.'

'Was?' asked Noon. 'And has he retired?'

The Chevalier stared at him and nodded as if had not
expected Noon to be so quick. 'We shall have to find him
to ask.'

The two young men were dropped off by the Chevalier
close to the Castel Sant'Angelo. They walked arm in arm
to Noon's apartment for a glass of wine.

'True charm,' said Caetani. 'The Chevalier is a very
well-mannered man.'

'A man,' replied Noon, 'who is made entirely of manners is not a man at all. He is a house without windows.'

231

Caetani seemed surprised by Noon's reaction, but knowing they had been in Venice together, presumed there was a touch of jealousy in their relationship and reasoned that perhaps the Chevalier had also competed for Natalia's hand.

CHAPTER SEVENTEEN

Jelborne went about his business at night to avoid the Chevalier, using carriages sent by the different families, sometimes dressing the larger servants in his clothes and sending them for rides. He continued to meet, in secret, with the families of Albani, Corsini and Cenci. Rome was fond of intrigue and though the Chevalier must have soon suspected that he was made sport of, he maintained his outward serenity. Jelborne supposed he had no choice so close to the Pope. During the days the tutor slept and kept the company of their landlady, a strategy that frustrated the Chevalier and amused the Romans greatly. Jelborne felt safer with the Chevalier about, a spy but not an assassin, a ranker of lower orders who was there to observe, evidence of doubt concerning their actions.

Jelborne always employed the same reference to ease any tension between his digger and Roman gold. The noble families would know of His long-faced Lordship

who occasionally accompanied Jelborne, and there was
not a man among them who did not recognise and sym-
pathise with Noon's condition of love. They hoped, as
much for Jelborne's sake as for Noon's, that the poor
Englishman would not torture himself throughout his
visit. They would think of ways to divert both tutor and
noble, but once Jelborne would reveal Noon's friendship
with Caetani, they would sigh and shrug, as if to say
melancholy had won and there is nothing they might do.
Soon, all the autumnal sun that had disguised Noon's
fatigue faded from his face. Smudges appeared beneath
his eyes. Jelborne was sure of it; they made their way
slowly south, dark clouds of exhaustion that were not har-
bingers of a storm but signs of a steady depression that
was looming over Noon.

Every day it seemed to Noon as if his tiredness burned in
him a little deeper. He was always tense, could feel an
eternal ache between his shoulders. He knew he was not
breathing in enough air, and would sit there and try to
steady his breath, but a sudden picture of Natalia or the
Chevalier would appear before him and his heart would
quicken and any sense of relaxation would be banished.
His eyes were the most tired of all, tired of the world that
he looked at, tired of all the faces, exhausted by everything but the chance of seeing Natalia again. His head
always ached now, though he could reach a sweet relief
with wine. Sleep was never measured in more than restless hours. Noon devoted too much time both to love and
doubting love. Such thoughts were eroding Noon. First

his mind and then his body, so that within the month, his suits hung a little off his shoulders. Only his collection of letters for Natalia grew.

Jelborne's continuing work had the tangential effect of leaving Thomas Noon almost entirely in the hands of Caetani. Noon avoided the high nobility as best he could. He had accepted their kind hospitality, but felt that he was treated as an average piece of exotica, an addition to *conversazione*, thin as paper. If he could not talk openly of Natalia or of Jelborne's work, then he did not see the reason to talk at all. Caetani suffered endless descriptions of love and doubt, but he bore it well, enjoying his discovery of a fellow spirit and wondering if finally he had found someone more beset by the world than himself.

'You're not plotting to kill yourself?' asked Caetani one day as they walked over the ruins of Nero's palace, stepping over artichokes that had been planted.

Noon knelt to fill his pockets with pieces of granite and porphyry which lay, numberless, on the ground. He looked up and laughed. 'In many ways I have never felt so free.'

'Good,' said Caetani. 'This is Rome. We are happy to kill others, but not ourselves. It would be impolite to make such a scene.'

On the contrary, Noon was slowly beginning to see that Rome was having a beneficial effect on him. If Natalia, or at least her absence, had revealed to Noon his own weakness, then he believed he might learn new strengths from the city. It wasn't the beauty, nor the odd feeling from having history rise before him, it was endurance. No matter that the city had emptied, it was merely a tidal push. She had had two empires, and perhaps a third lay before her. But she still stood, and in that simple recognition Noon felt an odd bond to Rome.

Noon had read so much about it and he wished his choice were more original, but standing in the shadows of the Colosseum, he understood the difference between admiration and awe. He returned at the end of each day. Often when Jelborne met with one family or another, Noon would walk with Cesare and wait for the light to fade, and no matter how well he thought he remembered it from the day before, the size of the Colosseum continued to shock him. Beggars lived in her vaults and when the sun set they lit fires, the smoke gathering over the vast ruin, the moon making it look like mist rising from a mountain lake.

Jelborne could not hide his distaste for Caetani, a man who chose to wallow rather than crawl forward, and while he was happy to see Noon, he did his best to avoid instances where the three might be together. Caetani seemed to have an equally low opinion of the tutor, believing he was filled only with surface knowledge and incapable of any depth of thought. The only time they submitted to each other's company was during a visit to the Sistine Chapel that Caetani had arranged. They tipped the custodian from the marquis's money and were allowed to enter with food and wine. The three men lay down on the floor and discussed the work above them. Caetani mooned over the transcendence of beauty, all the while debating whether their use of candles was ethical, smoking the ceiling but allowing them a momentary clarity. The tutor condemned himself for ever in the eyes of Caetani by falling asleep on the papal throne.

Jelborne spent the next weekend organising a collection of two hundred wax impressions of antique carved gems he had bought. He sat ordering them within their box, ascribing dates and explanations to the pieces. They were not selected for the charm of their motifs, but were set to a code established with the marquis dictating the response of the wealthiest Romans to their cause. Noon volunteered his pen and sat transcribing the tutor's dictations. When they were finished, he asked his tutor, 'How are we doing?'

'*We?*' asked Jelborne.

'I suppose I am still of some use, no?'

'Of course,' said Jelborne. 'Just a trifle distracted. Look at you, you barely sleep.'

'I am not sure I am quite that lost,' said Noon. 'My eyes are open.' He tapped his boots and laughed. 'My feet upon the ground.'

Jelborne smiled. 'And if she no longer wants you? What will you feel?'

'Anger,' said Noon. 'Is there anything else?' He stood and arched his back, stretching towards the ceiling. 'The Chevalier is accompanying us to Ninfa tomorrow,' he added.

Jelborne sat up straight. 'That is a long time to spend with him, Thomas. Do not err.'

Noon shrugged. 'You said he made no difference.'

237

'He should still be in Florence,' said Jelborne, 'observing our friends.' He thought for a moment. 'They suspect what we are doing. We can be sure of this, I think. Greater care must be taken. He may have a hare's brain, but he has the nose of a dog.'

'I am not so good at this. Between the Chevalier and Natalia, I am beginning to tire.'

'You are a wonder,' said Jelborne. 'Without you, I would have failed.'

Noon smiled softly. 'You are kind.'

CHAPTER EIGHTEEN

The small company leased horses at the southern gate of Rome, paid for from the marquis's funds. Noon was now well accustomed to money, and sums he had once considered great fell from his hands without thought. The Chevalier, Caetani and Noon galloped along the Via Appina, slowing some miles from the city when the traffic was light so that they might ride abreast of one another. The sun had emerged but the weather had an odd heaviness to it, as if summer were trying to poke through winter's cold crust. They removed their top coats and rode with the sun in their faces.

'Tell me,' asked Caetani, 'is it true that in England your priests allow you to take a pretty girl without marrying her?'

'If you asked they would tell you no,' said Noon, 'so nobody asks. We don't have confession, so nobody tells.'

Caetani nodded and digested this information. 'What freedom,' he murmured.

'I have heard,' said the Chevalier, 'that King George is a Catholic. They say that the Pope has given him a special dispensation and that he has his own secret chapel. It is why there is peace in Europe. He can't tell his people that he is a Catholic, for they'd not have it. Is it true?'

'If it is a secret,' said Noon, 'then how could I know?'

They could not reach Ninfa before sunset and since there were no inns in the vicinity they were forced to stop some miles away at a grubby institution, where the Caetani name brought a snort of recognition and a grudging acceptance. The young Roman insisted that Noon and the Chevalier take the best of the beds and he waited patiently to make sure they slept. He wished all to have fresh eyes for his family seat. In the morning, he rocked them awake gently and had their horses already watered and saddled. It was not two hours' ride from the inn.

'This,' said Caetani, reining in his horse along a skinny path, 'is Ninfa. My family, we were the finest in Rome until recently.'

'When?' asked the Chevalier, dismounting.

'One, two hundred years ago,' said the Roman, indicating where they should tether their mounts.

The undergrowth was thick at their feet. As they stepped away from the sound of the horses' breaths, they were encompassed by a cradle of greenery, its growth unchecked. It had the effect of amplifying the sounds of smaller creatures. The scuttling lizards and tiny birds that brushed against dried leaves sounded like a troop of horses cracking down city streets. The three men could not move thirty yards in any direction without running against a wall or broken shell of some building. Some were draped in greenery, home to vines and mosses, yet the taller walls were prouder, empty of infection.

'Do you not feel the sadness?' asked the Roman.

'I do,' said Noon.

'What will you do?' asked the Chevalier.

'Wander amid your family's history for the rest of your life?' asked Noon.

'The English,' replied Caetani, 'are young. Money is new to you. You think it can change everything.'

All that was left of his city of wealth were trees and the ruins of seven churches that stood in the soft land. The three men wandered among them, past faded frescos that had been bleached by sun and swept by rain for more than three hundred years. Noon thought the place dead until he heard the sound of running water. Caetani had yet to see Noon smile so broadly. A battered and moss-covered Roman bridge crossed a slim river before them, dressed on its bed with graceful weeds.

'I could swim,' said Noon, as much to himself as to his host. 'You have shade and water and stone,' continued Noon, removing his clothes. 'All that remains is labour and you might rebuild your town in a year.'

'And for labour, money, and for money favour. I have been born with a name still unpopular in Rome,' said the youth.

'Then there is only hope and patience,' said the Chevalier as Noon stepped down the bank and into the water. He waded into the middle of the river. The water barely came to his thighs.

Caetani spat between his feet.

'Be careful,' said Caetani, walking up to the bridge and sitting down, his legs dangling over the edge. 'It is filled with agues, you might catch yourself a fever.'

'I've had one for weeks,' Noon called back. 'Ever since I saw her in Venice.' He flopped on his belly in the shallow water and let it spin him gently downstream, then he stood up and spat a jet of water in the air up towards the two men.

'Does it not even make you happy, being here?' shouted Noon.

'We were rich because of this water,' said Caetani. 'It was a mill town, grains, tannery, leathers, we were wealthy. My cousins fought over this and destroyed it.'

'And these cousins of yours, what kind of men were they?' asked the Chevalier.

'Fools,' said Caetani. 'They threw three priests from a tower. And when they tried to rebuild, the plagues came and took all life. Even had I the money of an Englishman, I could not bring this back.'

'Perhaps English families will be like his,' called the Chevalier to Noon, 'gambling on power, risking families, villages, men and servants. They will all be cast down. Their children will be trampled, and those that survive, their only duty will be to mourn the mistakes that have been made.'

'It can happen,' agreed Caetani, 'and now all we have are ghosts who wander here at night.'

Noon paddled downstream, pushing his hands against the bed of the river, running his fingers through the weeds. The Chevalier's attempt to unnerve him slipped past in the water.

'Ghosts?' called Noon. 'Not here. It's not scarred, only sad.'

'You wish to spend the night?' challenged Caetani.

'We have no wood,' called Noon. 'We might turn to ice.'

'Come again,' said Caetani. 'Come back through Rome in the spring if she is not constant, come back and join me. If I do not see you by the summer I shall know of your happiness and it will bring me some joy.'

Noon nodded and stood up in the water and bowed towards Caetani. 'You can't see the beauty here, can you?'

Caetani shook his head. 'It's reserved for those I bring.'

Noon listened to the hum of insects, could even see red fish speed past him. Being in such melancholy company made Noon remember laughter and joy. Despite his losses, his worries of Natalia and the presence of the Chevalier, he felt that Caetani deserved laughter. He did not know how to provoke it.

On their return, with Caetani trotting alone and lost in thought, the Chevalier pulled his horse alongside Noon.

'I have enjoyed our day,' said the Chevalier.

Noon nodded in agreement.

'May I talk openly?'

'Of what?'

'Once you are in Naples,' said the Chevalier, 'you will realise that this is not a game that we have been playing. That your father and Mr Jelborne are placing you in a position that I believe you do not care for.'

Noon looked at the Chevalier. 'Am I supposed to know what you are talking about?'

'I am not asking to learn of your movements, I am simply informing you that up until now all is conversation, rumour. In Naples, there will be no protection. We know of Martin Silver. We know of his ships. Even should you manage to sail, you will not make England.'

'Directness does not become you,' smiled Noon. 'You are paid for your observations, so perhaps you should observe.'

The Chevalier laughed. 'I am paid for information, not observation.'

'Are you so poor an agent,' asked Noon, 'that you are often pressed to plead for your knowledge?' Noon rode on a little way. 'What I will share,' he said, 'is how little Jelborne tells me. So far, he seems to best you.'

'If you will continue with him,' said the Chevalier, 'you must be certain of what you do. In our friendship, I believe that it is clear you care not one way or the other which king sits upon a throne, which God is bowed to. You bow before neither, then you bow before both. You have not spent time in London, have you?'

'No.'

'It teems with life and money. Your country flourishes from trade. Where there is so much money there will be steadiness in government, steadiness in church. England will not revert to Catholicism. She is already too fat and comfortable in vicars and vestments.'

Noon smiled. 'I am most uneducated.'

'You are most level-headed,' said the Chevalier, 'but it shall not matter in Naples for you will be counted as he is. I beg you not to go. Stay in Rome. Return to England in a year.'

'I must go.'

'For love?'

Noon nodded.

'Send for her,' said the Chevalier. 'We are alike. Love overshadows everything. You know this. These games that we play at mean nothing against our love.'

Noon nodded again, but remained silent.

'For my own conscience,' said the Chevalier, 'admit that you have understood every word that I have spoken.'

'I can offer you that assurance,' said Noon, 'and I thank you for your concerns.'

Jelborne was in the apartment when Noon returned. He sat grasping a *scaldino* and had two blankets across his lap. His head was cocked back, and loud snores rolled around the room. Noon called for the landlady and ordered more embers for his pot. His tutor opened one eye, then the other, and coughed some sleepy phlegm from his mouth.

'I have been waiting for you,' said Jelborne. 'We have news from Silver.'

'She wrote to me?' asked Noon.

'*He* wrote to *me*,' said the tutor.

Noon tried to maintain an interest.

'Silver's grand web of spies have concluded that the Chevalier is a Protestant agent.'

Noon laughed. 'I hope he paid well for the information.'

'How was our French friend?'

'Well enough,' said Noon.

'What did he talk of?'

'He had little chance,' said Noon. 'Caetani was too excited to be at home again.'

'I wager he was.'

'He said that he knew us. He mentioned my father and Silver.'

'Conjecture,' said Jelborne. 'A low bluff. He worried you?'

'He spoke with gravity.'

'He looks for weakness. You're a strong boy,' said Jelborne rising.

'So Natalia did not write to me at all?' enquired Noon.

Jelborne smiled and pretended to look under his chair. 'Yes,' said the tutor, feigning distraction, 'the packet was so laden with letters of love and sat so low in the water that the customs men have impounded her words. They are censoring them for scandalous content and will return them to you with the most exquisite passages deleted.'

'Thank you,' said Noon.

'You have a pagan nature,' said Jelborne. 'Intelligent men seem more likely to doubt God than love. We cannot see either, so why believe in only one?'

Noon laughed. 'And you believe in kings' blood and bank notes.'

'Everybody believes in money,' said Jelborne. 'It is the only thing that can bring countries together.'

'As does love.'

'Drivel,' said Jelborne. 'You shall end your days a poet.'

'I am tired,' laughed Noon.

'Then sleep.'

Noon could not. The Chevalier's plea that he should stay in Rome was bothering Noon. He knew that the Frenchman should not be trusted, that he would, by nature, attempt to shake his faith, but it did make Noon question exactly what his faith was. God, no. Jelborne was a demifriend, not a faith, and with his father it was a question of filial duty. He believed only in Natalia, and yet he was frightened of this faith, for if it was not returned, then it was not true. Love was a private religion of their own making, and must be kept by both or none at all. To stay in Rome would be illogical. Natalia would arrive in Naples and Noon must be there, or be the first to betray his true faith.

He was forced to watch the days drip past. He had mustered feelings for and been awed by Rome, had made a friend in Caetani, had fenced well with the Chevalier and had ignored his role as money raiser, though Jelborne did not seem to mind. Noon knew himself to be more in love than he had ever been, and found it extraordinary how forgiving his daughter and the ghost of Stilwell had proved.

The next evening at dinner with Caetani and his fellow

poets in a restaurant not far from the Piazza Navona, Noon grew drunker and drunker, despite, or perhaps because of, the presence of the Chevalier. The two men did not speak, but their eyes clashed and the Chevalier's were filled with forbearance and expectation.

Noon did not want to lose control of his tongue, but wished to prove himself better than all these high-born strangers. He stood upon his chair and slurred praise on the beauty of Rome as he struggled to keep his balance. Caetani looked on in disappointment and excused himself. His disappearance only encouraged Noon to raise his voice with another toast. Half an hour later he wobbled down the steps and out of the palazzo, followed at first by the Chevalier, then the smattering of poets, who had never seen anything but grace and patience from the English lord. Noon ended his uncertain tour by stepping into the Trevi fountain. He cupped water over his head and splashed about despite the coolness of the season. The poets gathered and laughed at his antics and were split by those who viewed the display as embarrassing drunkenness and those who thought it evidence of Arcadian thought. Noon saw the Chevalier disappear into the darkness as he collapsed into the foot-deep water. Propelling himself about with the flats of his hands, he blew bubbles into the fountain.

Noon paddled in circles looking out for Caetani and the Chevalier and knowing how foreign they were, how odd and uncertain, and how English it made him feel. He knew that he did not belong in Rome, despite the occasional wish otherwise. Neither he nor Jelborne belonged.

They did not belong anywhere, not amid this laughter. He felt a weight on his back, heard laughter and then his face was thrust under the water. He pushed his hands against the bottom of the fountain and pushed his head up for air, gasping and spitting water.

'Arrigo?' he spluttered, catching a glimpse of a hand. Even in his drunkenness he knew it was not Caetani's. There were other sounds filtering about the piazza: voices, footsteps and still laughter. *Did they wish it?* Again his head was thrust down. Noon tried to turn under the water to see who did this, but the strong hands would not be shaken. They held him down then dragged him up for air. Noon began to retch, and the firm grip on his nape and back were abandoned.

'Stop,' he cried.

He was still on his knees, vomiting a concoction of wine and water into the fountain. He could not stop weeping. Again, he was thrust under the water, his head cracking against the bottom, the breath forced from his lungs, water sucked in through mouth and nose, desperate attempts at breath. *I am dead, among these men, they do not know, they cannot know. Another moment, and I am nothing.* The hands hauled him out.

'*Possiamo ucciderti questa notte,*' whispered an unknown voice in his ear. *We could kill you tonight.* Noon could only hear the laughter around him, vomit bursting from him. Once again he tried to turn his head to look, but could see only the hilt of the man's blade from his teary eyes. He held his breath, received the shock of the water as his face was driven back in, then twisted, reaching behind him to where he knew the sword would be. He pulled it free of its sheath in a sweep and suddenly he was alone. He heard the splash of feet fleeing the fountain, then stood with the blade in his hand, facing thirty men laughing at him as he wiped water from his eyes.

'You can't kill me,' screamed Noon to the poets. 'You can't kill me!' He coughed and spat water out of his mouth then brought the sword down so hard on the edge of the fountain that a brief blue spark bolted from the blade. '*Nessuno vuole ucciderti*,' shouted one man. *Nobody wants to kill you.*

Noon, still drunk, his eyes still filled with tears, tripped as he tried to step from the fountain. It caused more laughter. *Who are you all*, he thought. *Do you know what was happening? Do you think these were games?*

'Fools,' shouted Noon. 'You do not know what is among you.'

A couple of the bolder souls tried to talk Noon into calmness, but any who approached him were waved away by angry thrusts. 'You cannot have me,' shouted Noon. 'Get away!'

He chased a group from the piazza, screaming at the top of his lungs, waving the sword above his head. They scuttled laughing down an alley, running like children from the chosen friend. 'He is dead,' Noon called after them into the darkness. 'Stilwell is dead but you cannot have us *both*.' He turned and ran back into the piazza, the blade held over his head. To his great relief Caetani had reappeared and brought Jelborne with him. Noon lowered the sword and running to his tutor hugged him close. 'They are trying to *kill* me. They are all against us.'

'Calm yourself, child,' said Jelborne.

'They know me,' wept Noon. 'It is not safe.'

'Let us carry you home,' said Jelborne.

Jelborne was in a buoyant mood the next morning, barely considering Noon's state of fragility. Noon rolled over to find himself splashed with water. He shouted and woke, thinking he was still under the fall of the fountain.

'Good morning,' said Jelborne.

Noon calmed his breathing and sat on the edge of his bed, rubbing the water across his forehead. 'They wanted me dead.'

'Then you would be dead,' said Jelborne. 'You were very, very drunk last night. According to your friend Caetani, you drained a hogshead on your own. Had you not coughed most of it into the fountain, you would probably *be* dead. Perhaps they saved your life.'

'No,' said Noon. 'They told me they could kill me.'

'You were shouting last night,' said Jelborne. 'There are degrees of drunkenness, and some tend to loosen the tongue. Do not mention Stilwell's name again.'

'I do not remember that.'

'Of course you don't. Yet you remember someone was trying to kill you. Perhaps they were merely mocking a drunk,' said Jelborne, 'who happened to be you.'

'Was a warning to us.'

'Against strong wine.' Jelborne stood to leave the room. 'When you are able, we shall head south.'

'Now?' said Noon. 'I cannot stand another day of this.'

'Or another drink?'

'They do not want us south,' said Noon. 'They will kill us.'

'Not until Naples,' said Jelborne. 'Not until they are certain.'

Noon shook his head and lay back on his bed.

Jelborne woke him that evening with a dish of pickles, ham and goat's cheese. Noon had their landlady make a large pot of tea, drank four cups, then consumed the food in one sitting.

'Ask Caetani for a favour,' Jelborne said while his charge ate. 'Tell him to inform the Chevalier that we have gone to Ostia for three or four days, to visit the Bignardi.'

'Bignardi?' asked Noon.

'They are wealthy enough. He will believe and wait in Rome. It will give us a week to avoid him in Naples. Tell Caetani much to confuse him. Tell him we think of returning to Florence, that we only passed it by because we were avoiding an English friend. Tell him we plan either to sail from Naples, or perhaps to return to Genoa, and have even considered an Alpine crossing.'

'If the Chevalier appears in Naples?'

'Silver travels with our pledges. Everything that we have done will be gathered in Naples. We accompany gold, Thomas. We return with gold, for to draw on banks for such a size in London would have every Englishman scrambling to inform his king.'

'So whoever appears in Naples . . .'

'Disappears.'

'How?'

'In Naples,' said Jelborne, 'it is a surprisingly common fate.'

CHAPTER NINETEEN

Any sadness Noon might have felt in his goodbye to Caetani was overshadowed by the prospect of propelling himself towards Natalia, a happiness that lay outside of his fear of harm. Outside of the city lay the Pontine marshes, the excuse all Romans used to avoid the south, a belt of foul air, a dangerous, invisible miasma that forced all but the bravest north. The marshes sat in a wide valley that ran parallel to the coast, stretching either side of the Via Appia, bordered by a crumbling canal. The travellers had been advised not to sleep within the wet country and so demanded coffee at every post house between Rome and the town of Fondi. It exhausted Cesare, but drove them forward and kept them free of fever.

Their quarters between Rome and Naples were miserable without exception, but Roman rumour had prepared Noon for such disappointment. The further south they headed, the wider the wheat fields and more orderly the olive trees. Their silvery leaves rippled welcomes at the travellers, flashing in the winter sun. Even when the road passed the marshes and reached higher grounds, the rocky soil was still planted with olive groves and orange trees and there, far beneath them, was the rocky crop of Vesuvius. Noon wondered if Natalia had already arrived.

'What did he say at the fountain?' asked Jelborne.

'That he could kill me if he so wished.'

'Odd that they think your fate might alter my own determination. Why not threaten me instead?'

'Because *you* would not be affected.'

The crescent coast arched before them, islands beyond Naples, the cone of the volcano ceding to a new mountain chain. The weather did seem to change from day to day, warming as they trotted south. Laurels and boxwood began to flower, and all about was the faint taste of almonds. They would come across clusters of thick purple poles, Judas trees, whose flowers grew from their bark, so that it looked as if a thousand velvet butterflies had descended to rest their wings. At their bases, clusters of daisies gathered in obeisance. The road rose and dipped over volcanic hills under a sky that grew cloudless above them. Every poor house they passed, flat-roofed and ill-built, stood empty. In such a climate, no one wished to stay indoors. The peasants perched outside or walked about, but always stared at Morosoni's golden coach with distant wonder as it passed.

Five weeks without Natalia had done much to Noon's mind. He had despised her, elected never to see her again, wanted to rush across mountains on horseback and seize her and make peacock displays of his love. He was a man apart, a man in doubt, a man in love. His greatest desire was to tell her the truth of him, and the more he thought of it the greater he realised the impossibility. As Thomas Noon he could have offered only humiliation, the certainty of not only rumour trailing behind them, but laughter, which would have broken them immediately. Mixed parentage, however, might be acceptable to Natalia: she was not of lordly birth, she was stained by merchant blood. Noon comforted himself with the fact that she was not a woman of convention, but the very sight of Naples made him nervous.

Never had Noon seen so many people as on their entrance to Naples. Rome had lost her numbers and Venice hid them in her alleys, but Naples was teeming with life. The streets were broad, well-paved and cut with channels to carry away the dirt. They made their way past the great citadel by the sea to the Largo del Castello. Even though there was no great heat, at either end of the Largo men dragged rotating barrels to sprinkle the streets with water, keeping the dust down. Stalls sold fried dough, one man tending to the fires and the black oils, the second throwing and pulling twists from the pans. Noon could smell sugar on the cooling air.

Beggars leaned against one another, and a pack of strays galloped back and forth questing for scraps.

He did not know what language the people about him spoke. It was a tongue apart from Roman, guttural and dark, simian to Noon's ear, relying almost exclusively on the syllable *'mo'*. *I shall not try to learn this*, he thought. *I do not need it. Where is she?* At one corner of this open cobbled piazza, dominated by the yellowed crenellation of the castle, sat a large house in which Jelborne had decided to rent an apartment. It had a grand corner room which opened on to an iron balcony. The perch drew Noon immediately past the coffered ceilings and back into the open air, where he stood while Cesare unpacked.

Noon watched the passers-by until the sun dipped, hoping to catch some glimpse of Natalia. A blacksmith was working a cartwheel under their window. He lit shavings, heating the band until it was soft enough to fit. His assistant swept up the glowing ashes in the darkness and six little boys rushed to the spot where he had worked. They sat pressing their hands to the stone slab, letting the warmth run up into their bodies. *Do they pay you to watch us?* Noon threw them two silver pieces. They begged for more until he turned back into the corner room, where Jelborne sat close to a metal pan that brimmed with heated charcoal.

'Was it not cold out there?' asked Jelborne. 'Is cold in here.'

'What is that?' asked Noon pointing at a letter in his lap.

'There you are,' said Jelborne, handing him the letter, 'you accuse me of so much and here we are, only two days before Silver and your beloved.'

Noon could not hold his smile in. 'Two days?' he asked.

'They are off Sicily,' continued Jelborne.

Noon's eyes were barely capable of blinking. It was an extraordinary feeling, a sudden vitality, as if his blood had been restored and he was only now granted the memory of how she had once allowed him to feel.

'And how,' asked Jelborne, 'would you like to spend your final hours of peace? Vesuvius?'

'I should like to hold off a day or two. So that we might all go together.'

'Virgil's tomb, the Phlegraean Fields? The caves of the Sibyl?' asked Jelborne. 'You might ask her a question or two.'

'I promise,' said Jelborne standing outside the duomo the next morning, 'that I will not prod you inside another church in my life.'

'I thank you,' replied Noon, 'from the bottom of my feet.'

The cathedral was remarkably light, thought Noon stepping inside, mainly due to the absence of dark stones. An unusually light yellow marble was used, the panels were pale figures and the gold always afire. It was almost light-hearted compared to the gloom of the more sombre cathedrals. It looked more the shade of skin than stone, a physical connection to God. On the roof balanced angels, children's faces that had no bodies, only wings. How peculiar, thought Noon, to turn angels into bats.

'Let us test your education, Thomas Noon,' whispered Jelborne. 'Describe the cathedral.'

'Large,' said Noon.

Jelborne laughed. 'Excellent. You have survived Italy unchanged.'

'It is three churches,' said Noon, 'three churches within

one. There is the cathedral, the baptistery and a chapel up front. Whoever thought to have three churches each in contradictory styles? Every column is different.'

Jelborne shrugged. He knew no more than Noon.

They walked out, past the Molo, the busiest corner of Naples, where a small wooden stage had been built, now occupied by a girl involved in an intense debate with a monkey. Beside her was a man distributing nostrums, and in-between the press of Neapolitan flesh, darker than Noon's, so that he felt like a white fish against dark coral.

'What is south of Naples?' asked Noon.

'Nothing save Africa,' said Jelborne.

That afternoon, they took a boat along the coast and walked inland, up a steep path, about the strangest domain Noon had ever seen. Beneath them, the cool blue of the sea, aloft a burning sky, but underfoot the very land Virgil had called hell. Solid hills of ash spilled a dozen, perhaps a thousand, years ago, forbidding the growth of any life. There was a putrid smell of sulphur that Jelborne attempted to laugh off. 'Poor for the nose,' he said twice, 'but good for the liver.' Only where little pools of water had gathered did vegetation erupt from the earth, but even then it was bitter and resentful of its banishment, manifesting itself in thorns and bristling limbs, nettles and brambles.

The sweet sound of birds was accompanied by the percussion of lizards rattling over dead leaves close by the Sibyl's caves. Once they stepped into the caves all noise died, replaced by the disturbing sound of a thousand flies, their hum echoing perpetually against the stone. Noon thought there must be dead meat about to cause them such fever, but there was nothing, only enclosure and expectancy. The darkness intensified the heat. This, said Virgil, was the entrance to hell and Noon was inclined to agree.

'Do you know how the Sibyls kept their knowledge?' whispered Jelborne.

'Memory?' guessed Noon.

'On palm leaves. Unfortunately, highly susceptible to fires.'

Both men backed out of the cave, not from respect but from an unconscious fear, and only when the sun hit the napes of their necks did they turn their backs on the cave. Noon followed his tutor up the hill to look out over the sea beneath. A shattered temple lay on the peak, stubby battered pillars on a smooth stone floor scattered with pebbles and dried leaves.

'What did you ask your Sibyl?' enquired Jelborne.

'Whether we would leave this city alive.'

'And what did she whisper?'

'She has promised me so,' said Noon.

'Should the Chevalier arrive, you'll not let him near us?' asked Noon as they neared their boat.

Jelborne shook his head. 'Are you anxious? You seem most calm.'

'I am imitating tranquillity,' smiled Noon. 'I have learned that much from you.'

'The external,' agreed Jelborne, 'should never reflect the internal. And which side shall you present to Natalia?'

'I shall be like an orange, thin rind and ripe, but still I must be pulled from the tree if she wishes to taste.'

'God, man,' said Jelborne. 'You talk just like a woman.'

Noon laughed. He let his hand trail in the water all the way back to Naples, staring at their little wake as it cut the sea.

In the morning a letter awaited them, the footman expecting an immediate answer. It announced the arrival of Martin Silver and his daughter in the city of Naples.

'They ask us to climb Vesuvius with them tomorrow.'

Noon looked reproached.

'I doubt you are made of such patience,' said Jelborne. 'Send a letter ahead announcing your arrival, and add that you shall not wait for a response but shall arrive at such and such a time. It leaves no room for feminine manoeuvre.'

Noon nodded and went to his desk.

He walked faster than necessary through the permanent spring, Naples' poor imitation of winter. His mild sweat raised the musty odour of his silks. He slowed in an attempt to cool his body and ambled, with his bundle of letters pressed between his arm and body, feeling quite the gentleman. He might have been followed by a dozen men as many yards behind and would not have heard a footfall.

CHAPTER TWENTY

She was wearing a pale cream dress, embroidered in green silk. The green lit her eyes as the cream darkened her hair and Noon knew now why he had remained faithful to a memory. He could not help but smirk. She rose and kissed him shyly on either cheek. Both seemed uncomfortable, but it was not an unpleasant feeling. Noon felt as if they were standing on opposite sides of the same hill, and if they both chose to rush upwards, they might be together again, surveying all beneath them. He coughed to break the silence and held out his letters before him. Natalia put her hand to her heart, smiled and took them, then indicated that he should sit across the table from her.

Noon had taken the letters to a bookbinder and they made what looked like a considerable novel. He had wrapped the book in a bow the same colour as the one she wore on the day they had met. She untied it.

'Not for now,' he said, and put his hands over hers. 'Read them when we're apart.'

'I can't believe it,' she said, withdrawing her hands. 'I did not think I would see you until tomorrow.'

'Where are mine?' he asked quietly.

'Your?'

'Letters,' he said.

She paused and pulled her hands away from the table. 'There are none,' she said, 'I could not do it. I could not bear it.'

Noon looked down.

'I believed in you,' continued Natalia, 'but I didn't dare believe that you might share what I felt.' She was speaking very softly as if she did not wish to make the candle between them flicker with her breath. 'I did not know how long five weeks might be,' she said.

'I know,' he muttered in confusion.

'Tell me I have done nothing to us?' she whispered.

'You are here,' he said stiffly. 'It is enough.'

'We must meet again. I mean here, now, it is as if we must meet again. This is awkward, is it not?'

Noon was still breathless and unsure. He nodded.

'We shall move together. We shall go hand in hand slowly forward and we shall not be disturbed from our course. My father expects me now. We shall meet again tomorrow.'

Noon walked alone, dizzy at his dismissal. There were no letters to read and occupy the time between this moment and the next that he would see her. Instead of the passion

263

of arms wrapped about him and the heat of flesh and instead of the indignation of fury and betrayal all Noon received was a pair of slow and tender kisses on his cheeks. They had lingered just long enough to convince him that they were not ordinary.

Angry at himself for ever letting her from his sight, he could not believe that he had chanced their separation. How to cast the same spell twice? It still hexed him, but she had snapped it. How had she broken it, or was he imagining that? Was it still there and he could not see it? How strong was their love? Because their promises matched, had that made it stronger or did they mean nothing? Until he had given her his letters, everything had been mutual, but now she had an imprint of his love and desire. He had unbalanced them, but only because she had stepped away from the scales.

CHAPTER TWENTY-ONE

All trips up the volcano were conducted by litter-bearers, porters, and three men armed with lanterns in case they should choose to descend at night. Jelborne had selected a guide, a flat-faced man of sense who knew the difference between the excitement of spectacle and danger. His role was to give the travellers enough heat and noise to concoct an anecdote, but not to lose his clients or their limbs to flying rocks and lava flows. Noon was the only traveller who rode a donkey. The rest preferred the equally uneven jolt of the litter. Having spent so much of his life serving, Noon had decided it was better to exhaust animals rather than men.

He was straining to keep a distance from Natalia and sought to quiet his doubts through tricks of the mind. He imagined Stilwell beside him. How he might shake his head or offer the simple reassurance of a hand against his back. Or better, his daughter's small arms closing about his neck.

'Have there been eruptions this year?' asked Jelborne of their guide.

'Only one,' he said, 'a month ago. It lasted for a week.'

The path wound past vineyards and was covered in high thick grasses, the odd tree, barricades of brambles. With these familiar signs about them, the ground beneath began to transform, vegetation evaporating, giving way to a bold moss that clung to older rocks. At a small hut not a mile from the cone of the volcano, the travellers rose from their litters and Noon tethered his donkey to a hitching post. They continued on foot, the four travellers and the four porters, each now wearing a leather thong about their waist which their charges were instructed to hold on to, to assist their climbs.

The earth felt loose beneath Noon's feet, ash-like, as if he were walking through the remains of a dead fire. A boot would occasionally break through one layer of crust to meet newly formed rock. Wisps of smoke were blown over the cone and downwards, but the guide insisted on their safety. He walked them all to the rim. All four, encouraged by the guide, stared into the depths.

Jelborne thought of Pliny, taken by this volcano though he was miles away on board a ship.

Perhaps, thought Natalia, peering into the darkness beneath, *I am now as strong as it*. She had walked up to the edge and looked down and had dared it to erupt and it had not. *I dare you*, she challenged again, but the volcano did not answer.

❊

Noon had watched Natalia gaze for a while, wondering if she thought of him. In defiance, he made himself concentrate on the acute stench of sulphur that pervaded this land. Why did the natives not even climb the volcano's slopes? Why was it always the travellers? Because it was Neapolitan, theirs by right, and for a southerner to exercise such a right would be to betray a lack of confidence in their land? *Why has she not kissed me yet?*

The guide ordered them away, insinuating a sudden danger designed to quicken the pulse. Though Noon guessed it was a fabricated effect, having them hurry away as if they might be chased by streams of fire, he could not deny that his heart beat faster. It made Natalia skip down some stones towards him, wide-eyed and smiling, and for that he was grateful. He offered his hand to Natalia to help her down a steep incline. She took his arm and looked him in the eyes.

'Are you angry with me?' she asked. 'You shouldn't be angry. I was thinking of you.'

Noon made sure that she had regained her footing, but he did not answer.

'You don't understand,' said Natalia. 'I have told you nothing but truth.'

'I know,' said Noon, attempting to retain at least the veneer of strength. 'May I be honest?'

'Of course.'

They kept pausing, as Noon accompanied her rock by rock until they reached even ground where they were able to walk side by side.

'You wish to speak?' she said.

Noon smiled. 'I am thinking of how to say everything in as few words as possible.'

'I don't mind words,' smiled Natalia. 'You may throw as many at me as you wish.'

'I do not ever wish to be plagued by regret,' said Noon simply. 'I feel most strongly for you. I wish to spend my life with you.' He knew it was an absurdity, the very exaggeration that he had silently accused her of, but it was also an emotion and he could not think of a surer way to express it.

Natalia seemed taken aback. Her eyes could not meet his. 'No one has ever said that to me before.'

'Good,' said Noon smiling.

'I had not realised the depth of your intentions.'

Noon felt his stomach tighten into a white-knuckled fist.

'Do you know what the Pope says about marriage?' laughed Natalia. 'That all women should taste it so that they might one day know the blessings of widowhood.'

Noon managed a hollow laugh.

'Tomorrow,' said Natalia, 'join us for dinner.'

Noon did not sleep. He did not even close his eyes to tempt rest, for he knew it was far from him. *Who is she? Who was she before and who is she now? Who was he before and who is he now? Which is real, or are both real, and if the two selves are real then which to trust?*

Martin Silver was in the room when Noon arrived the following evening and made talk with him on the state of

268

their affairs, though Silver would have been able to tell from Noon's constant glances towards the door that the young man could not have been less interested in the business of the exiled king.

'Jelborne tells me you have worked well, milord. Your father will be most proud. Where is she? My girl, in this respect, is no different from all others,' he jested. 'A good girl though, good enough for any.'

Finally, Silver decided there was little point in talk and the two men sat in silence, interrupted once a minute by Noon's enquiries over whether Natalia was expecting him or not. Silver made a show of his exasperation and pressed his hands to his knees and hauled himself upright.

'I shall find her for you,' he said, 'even should I have to drag her down by her hair.'

Noon smiled but he did not find the joke amusing.

There was a book on the table that had separated father from suitor and poking from it was a folded letter. Noon could not be sure if it belonged to Silver or to Natalia. He ignored it for a minute. It sat there, innocent enough, peeking like a shy child behind a mother's skirts. He considered it. If it was Natalia's book, then it was her letter, and it was not from him. He wondered who might write a letter that she might carry with her, a letter that she had read and wished to reread. Her father, a friend? And if it were such a thing, then why should he not read it, and if it was a darker thing, why should he not know? Because he did not wish to. He sat and waited for her, even wondered if she had descended and was spying on him, testing him.

Standing, he walked about the room and out of the door until he knew himself to be alone. It still stared at him.

He slid it from beneath the book and allowed himself to read it.

I cannot believe the words that you have written to me. I have questions for you, carissima. What is your opinion of adultery? Does commitment to another have to fade when one finds oneself with love at hand? Shall I tell my wife? Better men than I know this, let us ask Señor Quixote.

> *'Tis said of love that it sometimes goes, sometimes flies;*
> *runs with one, walks gravely with another;*
> *turns a third into ice, and sets a fourth in a flame;*
> *it wounds one, another it kills:*
> *like lightning it begins and ends in the same moment:*
> *it makes that fort yield at night which it besieged but*
>   *in the morning:*
> *for there is no force able to resist it.'*

Perhaps when you return again we shall walk by San Marco. I wonder if I shall tell my wife of your arrival? Faith is a false illusion when compared to joy. Joy that might be taken from one, or from many. For now, you are my joy and I trust I bring as much to you. How shall we shape our worlds towards each other? I will do as you do, I will do more.

The letter was signed 'MGB'.

He did not think he would react physically, but he did, his eyes filled with tears, his throat closed and he sucked the flesh of his cheeks between his teeth and bit down. But the sharpest ache was inside him, what they called heart ache, but it wasn't the heart, it was nameless and affected his lungs as much as his heart and stopped him from breathing. *I should be glad to know*, he thought. *'What do you know?' I know that she is loved by another. 'But does she love him?' She has not told me about him. 'But she has left the letter where it might be read by you, showing trust.' I do not like it. I do not like it all. What can I do? 'Breathe. Take air in, release it.' What should I do about her? 'You can hide it. Watch how she behaves.' I must confront her. 'You have not been true with her, she owes you nothing.'*

Noon could not stand to be betrayed again. Before, he had been left Sarah. Now there would be nothing. He had hoped more of Natalia, wanted all of her, though he had never given all of himself. While he should have been grateful that he had protected the truth, instead he was angry that he had not trusted her. He could feel little other than the shame and anger of betrayal.

Men and women attempted to behave apart from nature, not to move with seasons, not to strive in autumn, to survive winters, smile at spring and live in summer, but it was so. As it was with plants that bloomed and died and water that froze and flowed, so it was with men and women, searching before winter, settling, rising again. He had conceived Sarah in April, watched her born in the New Year, and been left with her in spring. How could Natalia break this now, come January? Because it was the land itself, closer to the sun, where the order was disturbed and frost

271

was a foreign affair. Always summer meant always change, tempers only even in their inconsistency. Fool that you are, Thomas Noon, you are not a lord, you are no southern man, you tampered and you may be burned in this constant sun.

'I had not realised the depth of your intentions,' she had said. She had lied. Was it not she who had breathed the word love, she who had stood naked before him, given herself as wife to husband, who had talked of their children and named them, talked of their winters and of their ageing together. At what point, he questioned, was she unaware of the depth of his intention?

Outside of Silver's palazzo stood the Chevalier, chatting amicably with a pair clad in silk suits. His skin had grown dark under the Neapolitan sun as if he were a lizard that merged against his surroundings. He tipped his head in Noon's direction but did not even smile at this false coincidence. Noon had a momentary burst of panic that was immediately replaced by anger. He considered himself invulnerable, having no concern for his own fate. *Do you think*, thought Noon, *that you matter to me at all? That this is a surprise? I will not even stop to greet you. May the devil take you, there is nothing in this world that matters apart from the heart. Move towards me and I will beat you raw.*

Noon entered the apartment quietly and smiled at his tutor. He did not want to speak because he was afraid he would not be able to stop himself from spewing the banalities of the wronged man. What sympathy could he expect from a man who had warned him? For who could care about the end of love? How personal and how mundane.

'All is not good?' guessed the tutor.

Noon spoke despite himself. 'I fear she is not constant to me. A letter from another suitor. I read it.'

Jelborne observed that his charge was red-faced, very close to a burning anger. He poured Noon a large glass of wine and watched him drink it.

'Perhaps she is constant to you,' said Jelborne, 'and also to another.'

'That is not constancy,' spat Noon.

'To an Englishman no, to an Italian mistress perhaps. Besides, I would not worry myself if I were you, she is hardly the sort to open her quiver to any man's arrow.'

'To be unfaithful with the mind is as indefensible as by body. What did I expect? This *is* what I expected.'

'You are your own enemy, Thomas. Perhaps she is your love, perhaps not, but don't allow one letter to stand between you. A man can destroy his mind by knowing too little about himself or by knowing too much. You must choose which you'd prefer.' Jelborne paused for a moment, then added, 'It might be something else, Thomas.'

'What?'

'If novelty is the tyrant of her heart,' explained Jelborne, 'then you can do nothing. No man can make himself new to such a woman.'

Noon had always thought of love as a reflection, what you wish you were reflected in another's eyes. To last, it must be the perfect reflection. Love must be the mirror of love. And he knew he was not what she saw. He was not even the Viscount Stilwell, whom she *might* love. He was simply Thomas Noon.

'We were to have children,' laughed Noon, suddenly, in regret. 'A boy called Tobias.'

'She is like a die, Thomas. You might roll her but you cannot tell what face she'll show. All her faces are true. You and I have only two sides. Hers are all true and I am sure she never felt a lie spring from her lips, but now she has rolled again.'

They were interrupted by a red-faced footman, streaming sweat. He carried a letter from Natalia begging for Noon's company later that same evening in a walk.

'What should I do?' asked Noon.

'You will see her of course,' smiled Jelborne.

'What am I do?'

'React.'

So involved was Noon in his apparent betrayal that he had entirely forgotten to inform his tutor of his sighting of the Chevalier. He knew he would see Natalia, but for a moment he presumed on the strength to resist. At worst, he guessed, she will confuse me further. Perhaps, though, this will spur her to confess her love again.

He may as well have arrived without a strip of clothing on for all the defences he had prepared for his heart as they took their walk that evening through the Largo di Palazzo. It was a large open piazza, several hundred yards long and draped in evening shade cast by the immense palace.

'You do not think me foolish, do you?' asked Natalia as they walked, side by side, though not arm in arm, about the Largo.

'No,' said Noon coolly.

'If I had thought there was anything within the letter that would make you burn and turn you against me, then would I have left it before you where you might read it?'

'Perhaps you wished to make me burn,' said Noon.

'Michael was a man I met alongside my father. He is married, a fool. He took my smile and thought it love. What can I do? Men think this of me, they think a smile is an invitation. I cannot hide, but I can be true to you. He means nothing.'

'You wrote to him,' said Noon as lightly as possible.

'Once, five lines,' said Natalia, 'and received half a dozen letters in return. The unhappy do that, they pour themselves on the ground before you. You cannot stop them.'

'He is married,' said Noon.

'I did not know.' She looked down at her hands. 'You confuse me. This has all been very sudden. There is much to think of.'

'We cannot avoid each other,' whispered Noon. 'We travel together.'

'I know,' said Natalia.

'Why have you not yet kissed me?'

'Because you may think you love me,' said Natalia, 'but I am no longer sure that you like me.'

Noon nodded. She was correct.

Natalia thought she was confused, a better taste than the truth. And yet she suspected herself, knew that the whole world glittered to her, that her attention was pushed and pulled from one small drama to the next and that they were all there to be enjoyed. She did not mind tethering herself to a man, she believed that one day she would be capable of fidelity, but it was everything that sat beside the man, the weight of expectation, that she found so crushing. An English lord for instance, meant an English home, English custom, English servants and acquaintances and it seemed narrow and constrictive. It was her father's life that led to her freedom. As long as she remained within his shadow, there would always be change, a touch of mollycoddling, but always new cities and faces, admirers and wooers.

She looked about her at the grand Largo as the shadow crept towards them and thought for the first time of the pure beauty of winter light. More than anything, she was frightened of the ordinary. She needed to think her life worthwhile, but had not figured how this might be shaped out of convention. Stability was something to be feared. She would rather spin fast flowers of gold that would glint and die in the sun than lay the roots for a slow happiness.

Stilwell was a fine man and she believed in his love and part wished only to return it, but she knew her nature to be more consuming than his. And yet, beneath this sweetness, she was a little scared of him. There was an anger beneath, that eruptive flash she had seen outside the *ridotto* when he had struck the procurer. The occasion may have been her invention, but Stilwell reacted, revealing a brutish side that had, for a while, thoroughly appealed to Natalia.

They walked together outside of the Largo, back towards the castle. Their silence was both strained and unhappy. A passing funeral procession, headed by a brown-robed priest, interrupted their path. Neither reacted until the coffin appeared and then Natalia began to cry, for it belonged to a child. *If it was my child*, she thought, *how long would I cry for? What pain to bring a life into this world, to nurse it and be loved by it and for that love to pass from your life.* She wept freely and gripped Noon's arm as she shook.

There is real pain on God's earth, thought Noon, *and what are we?* Holding your lifeless child, now there is pain. Noon had a chance, at what he did not know. To be wound around, to be coiled and released by a capricious heart, now where is the lasting pain in that? And though Noon did not entirely believe himself, could not reduce Natalia to harmlessness, he pushed her a little further back and drew Sarah, his daughter, out from the darkness to join him. Noon pinched his nose to stop his own tears. They had a bitter tang, for his tears were for his daughter and not for Natalia, and they contained a happiness that held him upright.

Outside her house, they paused to say goodbye. She looked at Thomas Noon and thought he seemed very different from the man she had known in Venice. Thinner, more wary. *Perhaps*, she thought, *it is he who has changed and not me.*

'I do not know what to say,' she said. 'We should be better apart. Until we sail.'

'Of course,' he said quickly.

'We are too anxious,' she said. 'This distance has brought an agitation on us. Let us breathe apart for now. When we sail we shall have time for one another.'

'Until we sail,' said Noon with a smile, just short of a smirk, filled with odd confidence.

Noon turned and walked away, and thought of how he had turned his back on her their first night after the *ridotto*, of how close he had been to never seeing her again, and how he now felt. *I must create a distance for the growth of her desire*, he thought. *I might even have to mask love with apparent dislike.* He thought it might be surprisingly easy, so sudden and hot were the flushes of anger that burned him.

On his return, Noon found four chairmen waiting outside the door of the palazzo. He ran up the stairs, through the open door and saw Cesare waiting for him. The air smelled rank, all the windows were closed. The concentrated stench of shit and vomit filled the apartment.

'Mr Jelborne,' said Cesare.

Noon walked through to the bedroom, where a man was stooped over his tutor. At first, because the figure was cut in black cloth, Noon thought him a priest, but with relief he realised that man was a doctor. The smell was heaviest in the bedroom. Noon saw a damp pile of cloth beside the bed, soaked in excreta.

'*Che e accaduto?*' asked Noon. What has happened?

'Poison,' said the doctor.

'Will he live?'

'I have purged him,' the doctor said. 'It is all I may do for him. You wish me to stay?'

'What more can you do?'

'No more than you.'

Noon dismissed him, ordered Cesare to sit by the door with charged pistols and turned to examine his tutor. His skin was pallid and dank with sweat. A thick tongue forced his mouth open, like a bloated corpse. *Do not leave me*, thought Noon, *I am alone without you*. For the first time, Noon thought of the Chevalier and how he had let his tutor down. *My God*, he thought, *I have almost killed a man, not through anger, or betrayal, but mere inaction*. Throughout the night, Noon attended Jelborne, running wet cloths over his forehead and arms, imagining that he was sponging the poison from his tutor's body.

The next day Noon did not eat but kept his seat close to Jelborne, dipping his nose towards his tutor's mouth, finding the presence of the faint, fetid breath a comfort. *Why, how can she think herself apart? How has she separated herself from her own creation?* Noon knew that Natalia took so many joys from the looseness of her own position within the world, the daughter of a rich merchant but no one's wife, unaccountable and splendid, spoiled and self-ish, capable of happiness but not of causing it for more than a moment. And what to do with such a strange bird, but open your arms and let it fly?

The sweat had begun to dry on Jelborne's body, leaving white salt streaks on the darker clothes that Noon had applied to him. Noon continued to sponge his flesh, an automated ritual that cooled his mind. *Come back*, thought Noon, *so that I can hear my language spoken again. Come back, so that we might return to England, so that we might visit my father together. Do not join Stilwell, stay with me. We are all too alike*, he wept, *none truly dead and none alive, stranded as half-lives marked with the names of other men.*

Noon was asleep when Jelborne returned to the world. Weak as a new-born, Jelborne could not even prop himself up. He shifted his head to catch sight of Noon, and managed to drop a foot over the edge of the bed that caught his charge's boot. Noon woke and smiled to see Jelborne.

'How do you feel?'

'Alive,' croaked Jelborne. 'Hungry, thirsty.'

Noon called out for Cesare.

'I wish to leave this room,' said Jelborne.

'Tomorrow,' said Noon.

'You are not at a wake, Thomas,' said Jelborne, 'you may smile.'

'I am happy you live.'

'You did not wish to be alone?'

Noon looked up and conjured a smile. 'No,' he said. 'Not at all.'

'Tomorrow,' said Jelborne, 'if I have strength, we shall go to the docks.'

Noon looked up at his tutor. 'I saw the Chevalier. I should have warned you.'

Jelborne nodded. 'It would have made no difference. I did not think of it.'

'What shall you do?'

'It is in hand,' said Jelborne, closing his eyes.

CHAPTER TWENTY-TWO

Two days later, down by the docks, a rocky breakwater kept the winter waves from the shore. The largest of the merchantmen, including the *Henry*, were moored out in the bay, a constant stream of gigs and flat-bottomed boats ferrying goods and sailors back and forth. Those vessels with low hulls crept closer than the lighthouse, but Brigson, the *Henry*'s captain, had more than one reason to keep his ship far from shore. At sea, ships were fortified islands; docked, they were open to intruders and customs men, curiosity and fire.

At the entrance to the dock stood the customs house, two walls reinforced with confiscated barrels and crates. Her uniformed men gathered outside, soaking up the sun, and they waved the two Englishmen past without concern. A wagon bustled by. Jelborne pointed at its wheels.

'See the depth they cut,' he said pointing at the rut in the sandy soil.

'Yes.'

'And now look at the depth of the track a foot to the right.'

Noon observed that it was twice as deep.

'Our wagon, drawn of Roman bankers, laden so heavily. You should congratulate yourself.'

'If we are followed,' said Noon, 'do we not lead them to what they seek?'

'They know already,' said Jelborne, leaning on Noon's arm. 'All cards face up.'

They were rowed out to the merchantman in a freshly painted boat. Noon wanted to aid the sailors as they drove their oars through the water, wanted to feel the bite of resistance and the pleasure of momentum, but they were separated by silence. Noon did not wish to speak to them in English; he wanted to keep himself apart.

The *Henry* hardly looked like a ship capable of harnessing a revolution. She sat, fat-bottomed and ungainly, built for weight and not speed, but well cared for, an ageing mother manned by sailor sons. Noon counted over thirty crew on her deck. He wondered how many, if any, might know of their intent. He thought of their eyes, how they would follow Natalia about the deck from Naples to England, and how he must pretend an equal distance and an equal desire.

He guessed there would be no danger of recognition. In Genoa Brigson had looked through him and now he noted that the captain thought little more of a lord than of a servant. They were of the same kind to him: landsmen, far below the common deckhand. Jelborne, though, had some previous rapport and had his hand shaken furiously, one Englishman abroad to another.

There is the smell of the sea, and then the smell of a ship at sea. They were two very different things, thought Noon. The stretched planks, that thin layer that separated man from the depths, absorbed salt both from the water beneath and the crew above. It was this hybrid odour that smacked Noon, sea air and body must. It was foreign to him, and still reminded him of their journey from England rather than his return.

It did not seem enough to Noon to change a world, but Jelborne's eyes bulged in appreciation. The captain's cabin was temporary home to the riches that would be buried in their hold before their arrival on English soil. There were four chests present, each filled with gold coins of various denominations, Venetian zecchini, Roman scudi, Bolognese julios. This, thought Noon, is the end of Jelborne's intent. Gold has been gathered and all that distinguishes it is weight and glint. He smiled at the thought of the gold that lined his own hems, grinning at Cesare's foolish mistrust of wealth.

'What do you say, milord?' asked Jelborne.

'Is a fortune,' said Noon. Brigson seemed little interested in the reply.

'Is an army,' corrected Jelborne. 'What you see before you is nothing less than the grace of change. It shall be well concealed, captain?'

'They shall know nothing,' said Brigson.

'The Chevalier?' asked Noon.

'We meet with a friend this evening,' said Jelborne.

They waited until darkness to row back, the sound of the oars as they clipped the growing sea of comfort to both men. Jelborne watched the moon play on the water and knew that he was not the miser who counted out his pennies, nor the niggard who ran his hands through coins. He understood that gold, at a certain temperature, was liquid and in its liquid form, moulded by hot words, might make one man do as another wished. These were the pieces that would change a country. He felt pride, an endless justification in his decisions and behaviour, and knew that if individuals would not forgive him, then King James, God's man on earth, would.

In their absence from the apartment, a gentleman had been introduced. He sat on the edge of a chair and stood and bowed when Jelborne and Noon entered. Jelborne walked quickly forward and apologised in Italian for their slight delay.

'This is Alfredo,' said Jelborne, turning to his charge. 'For one day, he is our best friend.'

The figure nodded in Noon's direction. Alfredo was large for a Neapolitan, Noon's height, but broader in the shoulders and as wide at the chest and hips, a paragon of solidity. Some men are made of curves or of delicate angles, but Alfredo was constructed of blocks, his chin square, his nose broken and set straight. Even his ears were like eaves that guttered a stone block. It took Noon a moment to note that he was missing both his eyebrows, as if he were too smooth a surface for the growth of hair. *I would not like you against me*, thought Noon, *nor even beside me.*

Jelborne and Alfredo conversed in Italian. Noon followed, interpreting the Neapolitan's mumbles as a rough sign of efficiency.

'*Diciassette*,' confirmed Alfredo.

'Seventeen?' repeated Jelborne. 'That is all?'

Alfredo nodded. '*Abbiamo i nomi*,' he said. We have the names. '*So dove possiamo le trovarli*.' I know where I can find them.

'Does that include the Chevalier?' asked Jelborne.

Alfredo shook his head. '*Questo e mio*.' That one's mine.

Noon marvelled at man's ability to plot and to act against man. They were talking of murder as calmly as the marquis might have ordered his hounds ready for a ride. It did not upset Noon, as he thought it might do, for he could not care about another living soul. Men were made from paper, might be blown down with breath, while Natalia had been his chance of warmth and love incarnate, and the brighter she had shone, the more the rest of the world had receded, seeming distant and false in comparison.

Yet, after Alfredo's departure, Jelborne sat looking at Noon and seemed to feel the need to justify himself.

'Do not forget what we are, Thomas,' explained the tutor. 'There are three instincts to an animal: to feed, to procreate and to destroy what might destroy you.'

'Or to make others destroy for you.'

'That is progress,' smiled Jelborne.

CHAPTER TWENTY-THREE

The Chevalier might have had good reason to think seventeen would be enough to stop the departure of the *Henry*, to burn the ship to the bottom of the harbour, but Jelborne was well informed and had no single interest that ran outside his small circle of ambition. Alfredo had hired five men to apprehend each of the seventeen, a temporary army of eighty-five of the worst that Naples had to offer. The Chevalier's seventeen were all disposed of in the same evening, not necessarily in the same way. Some ended in the ocean, a pair were strangled in their beds, two brothers burned in their house a mile from the city, but most succumbed to the knife.

There was more than enough gold gathered in Naples for Jelborne to have bought ten thousand lives. Jelborne hated to waste an ounce of the metal but an imperceptible movement in history's wheel was already occurring that justified any expenditure. He felt sure the marquis would agree that the gold was well spent.

Noon woke at midday when Alfredo came knocking. The square-jawed Neapolitan collected the remains of the gold owed to him and brought with him a locket that he had torn from the Chevalier's neck to prove his capture. Jelborne received his parting bow and turned his attention to springing the mechanism. Noon sat directly in front of him.

'Why do you pay him now?'

'Because his business is done,' said Jelborne, and stood to bring the locket closer to the light from the windows. 'We may go and see the Chevalier when we are ready.'

The locket clicked open. Jelborne looked down and then up at Noon.

'What is it?' asked Noon.

The tutor considered the truth in his palm.

'You understand,' said Jelborne, 'that I have no taste for revenge. It is inappropriate in my endeavours, but in this case it is a matter of efficiency.'

'What do you wish?' asked Noon. 'You seek my approval?'

'He seems almost your friend.'

'Is true,' said Noon, 'almost.'

'Well,' said Jelborne, the locket dangling from his fingers, 'this might secure your vote.'

'Why did you get this?'

'It had interested me.'

'You thought it filled with secrets of state?' smiled Noon.

'And so it is,' said Jelborne, 'but not for me. For you.'

Noon caught the locket that Jelborne tossed to him. Staring up at him was a beautiful miniature of the Chevalier. Noon turned it over in his hand. On the other side was a matching portrait of Natalia.

'A woman,' said Jelborne, 'with not one, but many admirers.'

Noon clicked the locket closed, first Natalia's portrait, then the Chevalier's.

'Is a good likeness,' he said.

'Do you wish to come with me?' asked Jelborne.

At midnight, they hastened to where Alfredo waited with the Chevalier. A building, windows blackened, close to the docks where rats outnumbered men. Five sat outside, each tipping imaginary hats to Jelborne and Noon in recognition of their purpose as they passed. The men did not rise, but stayed seated with the confidence of those who had already successfully completed their tasks.

And what will Thomas Noon make of this? thinks Jelborne. *What will he make of this half-dressed man weeping in pain, eyes bleary and mouth open? A man with no pride, no confidence, only the understanding that he is powerless and moments from his death?* Alfredo's face is empty and his manner efficient. The Chevalier cannot defend himself, his arms are both broken. He cannot stand, because Alfredo has hamstrung him. He is flesh. *Now*, thinks Jelborne, *agenting is not a game, is it?*

❊

Noon had killed, but only in reaction, not this meditated destruction of the soul through the body. He is watching, but does not entirely believe what he is seeing. The Chevalier does not look like the Chevalier. He cannot cast his measured glances and infuse his voice with cadence. Noon feels all the steam of his anger evaporate, and pity, a useless emotion, wells within him. Alfredo turns the Chevalier so that his belly is against the stone floor and drags him across the room to where a single step leads to the door. He brings an iron bar down once across the Chevalier's jaw, breaking it. Then he sets the man's teeth against the right angles of the step, so that it looks as if the Chevalier is trying to bite the step. Alfredo slams his boot down upon the Chevalier's head. Noon turns away at the screech of teeth against stone. He can hear the broken teeth as they skitter across the floor.

As if they are attending a play and do not wish to offend the actors, Jelborne tips his head towards Noon and whispers, 'What do you wish him to do? Would you rather partake yourself? There is reason.'

Noon shakes his head, will not even look at Jelborne with his calm speech, his steady voice.

Jelborne has not said a word to the Chevalier since entering. He is about business and not prone to parting words or gloating. The Chevalier starts to convulse and Alfredo looks up at the two men. Should he clear the man's throat to prolong the suffering? Jelborne answers no. After a half minute of agony, the Chevalier lies still, corrupted, unrecognisable and lifeless.

Jelborne has avoided the blood on the floor. He lowers a candle to check if any splatters have caught his shoes or stockings and then leads Noon from the room without a word.

Noon never wants to act on another's behalf again. He runs his tongue over his own teeth. He does not want to give an order, does not want to take an order, does not want to depend on another, does not want to love another. Not when such things exist. In the name of kings, in the name of fathers, and, yes, his blood had boiled in the name of love. But none deserved this.

'Tomorrow,' said Jelborne as they climbed the steps to their apartment, 'we sail.' Noon was silent. 'There is no better man than Brigson,' continued Jelborne, 'and there are a thousand ports before England should there be winter winds. It is a sure enough wager even in hard seas.'

A day or two, thought Jelborne, *and you will forget enough. I should not have taken you. You surprise me. I'm not convinced you are in love. You have cured yourself, haven't you? Or did I cure you?*

Noon found sleep elusive, for he was not sure of his own emotions. He pulled the blankets above his head to block the moonlight that drenched their room. Natalia was a confusion, the Chevalier dead, Jelborne determined. The sands beneath his own feet were shifting. He could hear their grainy squeal. England was suddenly and uncomfortably close.

The next morning Noon woke to find that Jelborne had risen before him and had already explained their

hasty departure to Cesare. He had eased the sting of separation with one hundred zecchini. Cesare looked
unruffled, as if he would see them tomorrow, or perhaps
in a year, somehow ignoring that they might never meet
again. Jelborne's munificence was, however, to be earned.
Cesare revealed to Noon that he had been asked to drive
their golden coach north again to Rome, to reunite it with
Morosoni.

Cesare clasped Noon to his chest and kissed him on
either cheek. 'Come with me,' said Cesare. 'I shall be your
servant. Do not stay with the fat man.'

Noon shook his head.

'They are not the same as we are,' said Cesare. 'They
think nothing of you before, it will happen again. But you
do not go for him, you go for her.'

'I do not know why I go.'

'She does not deserve you, he does not deserve you. I, I
am the only one who deserves you and you cannot see it.'
He tugged at Noon's fine lapels. 'They are like mine, now,
with their gold. You will always have them.'

'It is all my father's money,' shrugged Noon.

'Now it is yours,' said Cesare. 'I have done the same for
myself in silver.'

'It will not last,' cautioned Noon.

'But while it does . . .' gestured the Genoan with open
palms of innocence.

They kissed again and parted.

Noon could trick his mind, but he could not fool his
appetite. He swallowed pieces of dried bread without
enthusiasm and drank heavily, but took no delight in any

of his senses. Oddly, smell and taste were the most repulsive to him, they the most luxurious of senses, those a man might almost do without. By the time he stepped aboard the ship, he had lost the better part of a stone in weight since he had arrived in Italy. Jelborne noticed, but said little.

The moon had conspired with the oceans to grant them a high tide and fair winds. Natalia, coming aboard at dusk, glowed quite differently from the sun-burned sailors. She remained in her cream dress and it absorbed the moon glow, as if she were some shard of light that had fallen from the night to the *Henry*'s deck. The crew might be working, they might be scuttling up the masts with hands and feet and singing rough shanties to set sails, but their eyes followed Natalia beneath. *Will it be better or worse by day*, wondered Noon coldly, *when they can see the green of her eyes and the close cut of the dress that she allows to kiss her body? Can I go a month without speaking to her? How can I talk when I know what I know about her, about the Chevalier, about myself? The lies and dirt are heaped knee-deep around us, and worse, they are our own excreta.*

The winds were strong but moody their first day at sea, blowing for them then turning in sudden gusts of betrayal that had the steersman fearing that they might be taken aback. Progress was made, the coast of Italy abandoned, dawn revealing a grey and brutish sea. It was winter and the oceans no longer cared whether light danced to parade their colours. Now the waters were aggressive, for it was their time for reclamation, where rocks might be ground into sand and coastlines battered and reshaped. The *Henry* bowed to the troughs of the waves and broke their peaks, too large, too heavy to sweep and duck like a cedar sloop. Determined and faithful, the ship was plagued by a rolling motion, common to the great merchantmen, which lent their advance a queasy lassitude.

For his first two days of sailing aboard the *Henry*, Noon ailed and kept to his cabin. Despite the odd motion of the ship, it was not simply seasickness, the same as had racked Stilwell on their outward voyage. Nobody but Jelborne knew Noon was invulnerable to that common complaint. It was Noon's mind, not his stomach, that was disconcerted. Noon knew that he had been manipulated. That Jelborne had chosen to show him the locket to encourage him to participate in murder, at least as a witness. Noon felt a stirring of revulsion towards Jelborne, much as he had towards the Chevalier. He tried to control his feelings towards the tutor, only because he now regretted his sudden resentment of the Chevalier. In truth, he wanted little to do with anything else. He wanted to be away from Jelborne, away from his role of Stilwell, perhaps even away from Natalia.

Jelborne, who shared Noon's cramped cabin, had been silent their first days at sea. Not since Stilwell's death had Noon seen him so pensive.

'There is something,' he said, sitting on the edge of Noon's bed and tapping him gently on his leg, 'that we must discuss together. On your return,' he continued, 'perhaps I can speak for you.'

'It would be kind,' said Noon, propping himself on his elbows.

'I may tell the marquis of your service.'

Noon nodded. 'My father will understand how I have changed.' The kindness of the marquis was all Noon might rely on. Noon had never seen someone so uncomfortable: slouching, slumping, crossing legs, uncrossing, pinching his knees, knitting his fingers together. 'You are nervous?' he asked.

'Yes,' said Jelborne.

'Of the sea, or of telling the marquis of his son?'

'Everything,' confessed Jelborne. 'The gold, the responsibility. I have worked hard.'

'He will be pleased with you.'

'The king?'

'My father.'

'I must admit something,' said Jelborne. 'Perhaps it is better now. I shall speak for you, of course, to the marquis, that is.'

'You have already said.'

Jelborne sat upright. 'He is not your father, Thomas. He is not your father.'

Noon smiled and laughed. 'Of course he is,' said Noon. 'You said so yourself. I am different, have always been different.'

'You are not his son,' said Jelborne, 'at least not to my knowledge. I will speak for you, I am certain you will run his estate. Perhaps a more serious reward for your efforts on his behalf, a financial behest. I am sure I might arrange it.'

Noon pinched his nose between thumb and forefinger, then did it again, as if to wake himself. 'Then why would you have said so?'

'You were not with me, Thomas, do you not remember? You said you'd not do it for God.'

'Nor would I have,' said Noon. 'I would do it for my father.'

'Your master,' said Jelborne, 'not your father. And you are invaluable.'

'Natalia,' said Noon, as much to himself as to Jelborne. 'What will she make of this?'

Jelborne grimaced. 'It does not matter, for Silver will not favour the match.'

Noon swung his legs over the bunk and stood softly. 'What makes you think you might play us so?'

'We are not important,' said Jelborne and opened his palms in innocence. 'None of us are. The gold influences the return of England. It is all that counts.' Noon sat down beside his tutor. He felt worryingly sick, a wave of nausea breaking over him. Dreams were cracking inside his head, left and right, like icicles snapped from wintered eaves. The ship rolled heavily beneath them.

'She'll not take Thomas Noon,' breathed Noon. 'Not ever, she'll not have him.'

'If it were love she would have,' said Jelborne, 'but she does not love, not that one. You are too good a man for her, Thomas. You do not love her.'

Noon stood again and swung once and hard at the tutor. Jelborne turned his face in fear and the blow caught him across the shoulder and sent him spinning onto the floor. Noon walked over his body and closed the door behind him. Jelborne sat on the floor and raised a hand in supplication to the door, a gesture of forgiveness that was entirely lost to Noon in his departure.

The tutor emerged onto deck a few minutes later. Noon had not dressed for the cold wind that shuddered the sails above, slapping the canvas with their gusts. In the grey light, Noon did not shiver, but let the wind send billows and tremors through his silk shirt. Jelborne watched Noon staring at Natalia. *The presumption*, thought Jelborne, *that hearts and mind move in pace with one another, that one thinks as another, that is where all our misery is founded.*

The tutor was sorry in his deception, but unrepentant. It was a necessary thing. He walked over to where the servant stood and put a hand on his back. He could feel the muscles beneath tense up. Noon stood and went below. Jelborne followed him to their cabin.

'I am sorry, Thomas.'

Noon looked up.

'You are what you are,' said Noon calmly, 'and nothing to be proud of.'

'I know.'

'Six months,' said Noon, 'and neither one of us has changed.' Noon said so, but he did not believe it. Everything had changed, it had changed once and now once again. It was all that kept him sane, to think that it might change one more time.

'You have talked to her?' asked Jelborne.

'Tell her nothing,' said Noon.

Jelborne sat heavily beside Noon and Noon immediately stood.

'We are both good men,' said Jelborne, 'let us not sink so low. I am a friend to you, Thomas, whether as lord or servant, these things make no difference to me. I shall speak for you. If you wish nothing more of Dengby, then come into service with me. It will be a change, but I don't see why you might not work beside me.'

Noon laughed. 'So great is the trust between us.'

CHAPTER TWENTY-FOUR

Three days of poor weather were lengthened by the silence Noon employed against Jelborne. The tutor sat there sadly at night, resigned to and understanding of Noon's anger, feeling as if he had martyred their friendship to history. He almost rued the decision.

Noon's continued absence from the captain's table had also caused complaint between father and daughter. Silver wished Natalia to at least enquire after Noon's health, but she would not. After four days, she found that she missed him, but did not think it was the return of love and thought it would be unfair to instigate the contact he seemed to be pining for. They might, her father said, have another week aboard, but the quarters were too close for her to decide about her love one way or the other. There were the eyes of forty men upon her, of some appeal, but not a time for so delicate a choice. Let her see land again, let her see His

Lordship at home. Then he would have the strength of England and she would have a fresh freedom of thought.

The more resistance she saw in Stilwell, the more her thoughts had turned to other admirers. The Venetian sugar merchant and his endless quotes, the Chevalier and his genteel courting and fidelity. They were, in the end, all flames that sprang from the same hearth to warm and illuminate her, to glorify and celebrate her. Why rely on the love of one man, when three had already volunteered their hearts?

The weather had grown rough enough to worry Brigson, though the crew did not seem concerned by the rising waves, even though the wind caught their tails and whipped them to whiteness. Noon had never seen seas half as high and despite his wish on their outward journey to witness the power of an ocean, he now wished that it would submit and allow them passage.

Brigson's choice was a simple one. Either ride the growing storm at sea, or if he deemed it sensible, make for a safe harbour. In such poor weather, there was little hope for the accuracy of a dead reckoning, and the driving rain merged with the fast spit of the sea to blur the coast. Brigson knew he was about the French coast, close to the town of Le Havre, but in such weather it would be a hard risk to come close to land without certainty.

The *Henry*'s weight worried her captain. The gold was inconsequential, but the manifest revealed a ton of marble and hogsheads of varied wines, as well as Genoese velvet and Neapolitan soaps and silks. She had sailed angrier seas, been used in the triangle between England, the Indies and Newfoundland, but now had retired to a simpler Mediterranean route. When waves sought to roll her, she would dip her bow and test her strength by plunging through the ocean, raising a deck full of water that would come hissing back towards the steersman. It was her habit, just a form of behaviour like any other animal, but it was a worrying one in heavy weather, even to a captain as experienced as Brigson. It led directly to his decision to make for a safe harbour.

His relief at spotting the lighthouse at Le Havre was considerable. Though he could not see it he knew Le Havre to have a wide harbour with only one reef to avoid, which even in such a blow was a simple enough manoeuvre. He ordered the mainsail trimmed and watched his first mate and four deckhands scale the mainmast and secure a reef. The light flickered, through the driven wind and rain, drawing the *Henry* on.

Close to the light, when the open bay of Le Havre should have calmed the waves and settled the captain's stomach, the *Henry* was brought to a grinding shudder. It threw both captain and steersman against the wheel, knocking them flat to the deck then allowing the oncoming ocean to wash them against the bulwarks. Brigson dragged the man to his feet and they staggered up the tilted deck to the wheel. The *Henry* backed off and was driven again onto rocks that should not have existed.

'There is no reef here,' said Brigson in disbelief.

The *Henry* groaned and shifted on the reef, pressing her hull against the spine of rock. There was another, more

familiar sound, that of breaking waves. In the cast of the
fire on shore, Brigson could make out a beach, not two
hundred yards from their jagged position. There were figures on the shore, gesturing at the ship. He sent below for
the passengers, though needn't have, for they were fighting their unsteady way to the deck.

Brigson ordered chain shot to be loaded in the bow
chaser and linked it to the longest line the *Henry* contained, a strong thin rope. The explosion sounded above
the storm and the captain's eyes traced the arc of the precious strand as it shot towards shore. It landed in the
violent surf. *Come now*, he thought, *be brave there and take
hold of us.* A pair ventured into the surf and, to his delight,
he watched them emerge with the line. They secured it to
an outcrop of rock and Brigson knew that at least his
crew might be saved.

Noon broke onto deck before the others, slid and was
hauled to his feet by the bosun. He was wide-eyed.
Jelborne appeared moments afterwards, hands grasping
for support, holding fast.

'Do not worry, Mr Jelborne,' shouted Brigson above
the wind. 'We are a short row from shore. All may be sal-
vaged.'

Jelborne nodded.

Silver emerged with Natalia, her little figure wrapped
beneath his cloak, the green eyes peeking in sublime
horror at the situation, but Noon could read them
nonetheless. There was no worry of death in them, just a
purified excitement and expectation of arousal.

The crew was busy lowering the rowing boat from the larboard side. Luck had left them leeward, allowing the boat to descend smoothly, hidden from the wind. As soon as they untied the ropes, she would be driven away from the rocks towards the shore.

Natalia looked for Noon, looked at him. *Will he come with me?* she thought. *Will he protect me, or must he stay behind?*

'You shall be first,' said Brigson to his passengers.

Jelborne shook his head. 'One chest first, captain. Then we shall have reason to follow.'

Brigson shrugged and ordered four men to the hold. They emerged three long minutes later struggling with the weight of the smallest of the chests.

It was lowered into the bottom of the rowing boat. Noon looked down and saw Silver, still with his arms around Natalia. He did not know what to shout. *Look up,* he thought, *look up at me and meet my eyes.* A slap of spray stung the back of his head and, as it splashed down to the small boat, Natalia did glance up, screaming words, but Noon could not hear. He strained his ears as the boat pushed off and she was calling out for him but still he could not hear.

They watched the boat ride the shorebound breakers and one glance at Brigson to see the intensity of his gaze would have confirmed the peril of it, racing across the whiteness, dipping in and out of sight. Noon waited as it rode the breakers to shore, until he could see Natalia, her dress whisked by the wind around her, carried up the beach away from him.

The rope that stretched between the shore and their ship was tauter than a tendon. A hard wave ground the ship against the reef and the mast which the rope was tied to snapped and crashed into the sea. The sailors on shore fighting to push the small boat back into the ocean were turned by the first wave and spat into the ocean. They were so close, not two hundred yards separated them from the beach but it may as well have been a thousand miles.

'We have seen worse, haven't we, Thomas?' shouted Jelborne above the wind.

Noon despised the voice, recognised the panic of the cry. Sensible words betrayed by inflection. He thought them both dead. They watched the rowing boat attempt to crest another wave. This time it was flipped upside down. The figures ran about the shore, dragging the sailors away from the ocean. One was heaved motionless from the sea and most gathered around him while the rest stared at those remaining on the ship.

Jelborne skittered across the wet deck so that he was pressed against Noon. 'We must hope she doesn't founder,' cried Jelborne, pointing at the men at the beach. 'They will come for us.' There was no reason for optimism. Only two had gone chasing after the upturned boat, carried back and forth along the beach by the rolling waves, its black hull marked against the white froth of the water.

Five were thrown together. The ship screeched against the rock, then buckled and the angles were altered. A large wave that might have broken against the hull was suddenly given leave to crash across the deck. All saw it breaking. Jelborne froze, Noon turned from him to reach and hold to a line, but the power was too great, tearing his hands from his hold and sweeping all five before them in milky foam, over the safety of the deck.

Only now does Noon remember the gold-lined coat. He is tumbled and crashed under the waves as they roll towards the cliff. He bursts from the water to watch the sea heave itself against the rocks and spray a hundred feet into the air. He knows now the truth, all that is true, that he cares only for himself. He can see no one. He does not look again. Love is gone. He wants to live but he cannot fight this ocean, he can feel it pulling him downwards, but he turns and jerks his coat from him and is buoyant for a moment, his eyes closed against the water whipped into his face. Ahead the cliffs are now so close he can see a tree that clings to its side, unlikely survivor. And a small gap before him, invisible until now, a hundred yards ahead, a hole in the rock.

He does not know what it might be, but it is small hope and he strikes against the water so that the waves will throw him there. As he is pushed towards the cliff his shoulder strikes something beneath the water and white foam surrounds him and he cannot see but is whirled under and forced upwards until finally he breaks the surface again. He is in total darkness and the water draws him down, sucking him back under towards the night. The sound is extraordinary around him, he is inside the cliff, he is dragged against rocks, tearing at his hands. The next wave that crashes inside carries him up once again and he reaches and holds, is thrown and holds a side of rock in this darkness. Just the ocean's angry roar about him, and the stinging warmth of what must be blood within his eyes. His feet find purchase and he resists the booming crash of the next wave.

Noon reaches and drags himself a pace up. The salt is stinging the cuts on his hands and he is in darkness and can see nothing, but he climbs again and there is a fold in the rock, a crease which he rolls himself into. He lies crying, deafened by the thunder of every wave that reaches up for him, spitting spray down upon him again and again and Noon is weeping, thinking this was the true hell. Not cauldrons attended by devils, but cold crashing water that would not leave him be. He holds his bloodied hands against his ears and prays for salvation.

He did not know time. An hour, a day, it made no difference, but the ocean was easing and a second sound came to him in the darkness, that strange sound he had heard before, of rock upon flesh when he had beaten that man upon the road. Noon opened his eyes. Now that the waters were calmer, as the waves retreated from his chamber, they allowed a veiled light inside. He could see the ceiling of his tomb gleam, little pieces of metal within the rock that winked at him below. He peered over the side of his outcrop and saw a body, carried gently up and down in the swell, well pulped throughout the night, but the shape and black clothing were unmistakable. Lucius Jelborne was carried up by the tide, then down again. The redoubtable agent brought up towards him, then away. There were splinters of wood about him and, as the light came and went, Noon saw one more familiar sight. His own coat, pressed against the rock beneath him, torn in the middle of the back where it had been impaled on a sharp rock.

Noon could not bear his prison, nor the sight of the tutor. In the dim light he attended to his injuries. The skin of his shoulder was as dark as the chamber about him, all blue and black. It was stiff, but it moved and was not broken. His hands were bloody messes. Skin hung from his knees and shins where he had dragged himself upwards. He ran his hands across his forehead and felt the clotted blood above his right eye. Not so deep, he thought, if the salt water has already stopped the flow.

Where is she? he thought. *Weeping?* For him, or both of them, dead to her. He knew that she wept and he knew what he was to her. A moment, a piece of history that was now all hers, the toll of grief that she would make resound throughout her days, those lost days, when she had given her heart to a man who had been taken by the sea. It was to be loved, squeezed hard and discarded, to have had all of a woman and then to be cast away. It was not a question of love, but of knowledge, and he knew more now than before.

Noon reached over and brought his coat up to join him, crying out as his hands came into contact with the smooth fabric. He wrapped it about his head so that he seemed like a Turkish vizier and then stood on the end of his ledge. Five feet beneath him, Jelborne rose to meet him, then receded four yards towards the opening of the chamber. Noon timed his plunge, cut the water and howled under it, so that his own cry was muted by the ocean. He followed the light of day and swam, not even five yards, out into the sea.

It was a much calmer day than he had thought. There were no crashing waves to contend with, though the slight current kept him towards the rocks. Even then, it encouraged him eastwards, away from the upturned hulk of their ship, which sat broken on the shore. Noon could see men atop her, scavengers armed with axes, running across the shattered decks, throwing barrels and trunks to those who waited in boats patiently beneath. The current carried Noon about the face of the cliffs, and within an hour's swimming he spied a cove and pulled towards it. A dull rain had started and Noon's teeth chattered within his skull as he pulled himself from the water, stumbling up the rocky shore. A rowing boat had been dragged from the tides and was tethered about a natural column that leaned away from the cliffs.

Set a hundred feet above the cove, facing away from the sea, was a small hut, draped in fisherman's nets, smoke rising from its little chimney. A man stood outside it, in great leather boots that rose to his knees. He watched the appalling figure of Noon climbing, rock by rock, up the gradient of the rough trail that led from the sea. He cocked his head to one side as if he did not know what to make of him, then seemed to decide that man helped man and walked down to meet the stranger, taking him gently by the arm and helping him towards the hut.

The fisherman looked at the stranger's blue lips, his shivers and torn hands and wondered how on earth he might have swum in such a sea as last night. There was something frightening about this man, who had even held on to his coat, and though he was not religious he presumed that he was escorting a miracle of sorts. He made sure Noon lowered his head as they entered the hut. Noon sat himself cross-legged before the fire and gestured if his host would spare another log to increase the heat. The fisherman gave him strips of clean cloth to bind his palms, then draped a woollen blanket over him. He motioned that Noon should strip off his wet clothes. They hung them either side of the flames, Noon holding his coat before him.

Noon could not guess what rough dialect this man might speak, did not even know exactly where they were. He attempted French, English, Sienese, Roman and finally his sailor's Genoese. The fisherman laughed out loud.

'Where do you come from?' asked his host.

Noon winked and pointed upwards, making the fisherman laugh again.

'There are many from last night,' said the man. 'They stay at the inn. You wish to join them?'

'No,' said Noon.

'Why?' asked the man.

Noon had taken one of his coins from his coat. He did not let the man see where it had come from, but presented the gold to him as if by magic, for sitting naked there was no pocket for it to be drawn from.

'Does it matter?' asked Noon.

'No,' said the fisherman and kept laughing to himself. 'You may spend the night.'

Noon's clothes were dry by nightfall. He did not particularly trust this man, but at least it was merely one man, rather than a half dozen who might search his clothes for gold. Noon trusted instead in God above and fell into sleep. When he woke, the man had not moved, though many hours must have passed. Everything smelled of fish.

'Where are you from?' asked the man again.

'I am from Paris,' said Noon.

'And is that where you're going?' asked the man.

'Of course,' said Noon.

'How will you get there?'

'There is no coach?'

'Yes,' said the man. 'Tomorrow there is a coach. How will you pay?'

'You have already seen,' said Noon, 'that God favours me. When I need, he provides.'

The man smiled, as if he neither believed nor disbelieved his strange guest. 'What's your name?' he asked Noon.

The *Evening News*, 12 February 1715

It is reported that Lucius Jelborne, the celebrated writer of *Impressions of Italy* and friend to the greatest of England's families, has been lost at sea off the coast of southern France, along with his charge, the Viscount Stilwell, the son of the Marquis of W, a young man of twenty years. We hear that the storm was so terrible that it has not offered the bodies back from the sea, though the inhabitants of the town of Gavroche have stripped the vessel of her worth, including, this author supposes, the works of great antiquity that such a voyage of money and mind must surely have gathered in Italy.

Though this tragedy occurred less than a month ago, the goodly people of this poor port have found it in their hearts, and indeed their pockets, to raise a cross of bronze in His Lordship's memory. A crueller penman than this might doubt what good such a cross will do in domains of Catholic disposition, or indeed why a cross should be raised at all. We are told, by a trusted source, that it has been a habit of this town, during such weather, to light fires to draw ships to their rocks, not for murder, but for gain. On the oceans they call this habit that of Moon Cursing, and if it was true on this occasion, then we must conclude that it was not only the moon that should be cursed, but all of France as well.

Copies of Mr Jelborne's works are available at Golden Square.

The *Evening News* arrived in France a week after its printing. The article drew a particular smile from one broad-shouldered young man at a posting station on the outskirts of Paris. He seemed well dressed from afar, though those standing close in sunlight might have spotted skilled stitching that ran down the back of his coat. He was not far from the English Court in exile, but did not seek it out. He was not far from churches, but sought to pray alone. The call for his stage came. He raised his own chest and heaved it on the back of the carriage. Taking his seat inside, he stretched his legs and nodded to his new travelling companions.

Acknowledgements

Many thanks to Schuyler and Catia Chapin and to Lauro Marchetti for showing me the beauty of Ninfa. To Maddalena Paggi and Patrizzia Bigotti for corrections, conversations and kindness. To Bill and Jacqueline Govett, Amos and Serena Courage, and to my parents for their generosity in my travels. And to Chas Price, and especially Drusiana Sforza Cesarini for her invaluable encouragement and computer expertise.